CHESSBOARD PLANET

Also by Henry Kuttner
in Hamlyn Paperbacks

FURY
THE PROUD ROBOT

CHESSBOARD PLANET

and other stories

Henry Kuttner
with C.L. Moore

Hamlyn Paperbacks

A Hamlyn Book

Published by Arrow Books Limited
17-21 Conway Street, London W1P 6JD

A division of the Hutchinson Publishing Group

London Melbourne Sydney Auckland
Johannesburg and agencies throughout
the world

This collection first published in Great Britain 1983 by Hamlyn Paperbacks.
CHESSBOARD PLANET originally appeared as 'The Fairy Chessmen' in *Astounding Science Fiction*, January & February 1946; first book publication in *Tomorrow and Tomorrow & The Fairy Chessmen* (Gnome 1951); first publication as *Chessboard Planet* (Galaxy 1956); and first UK paperback publication as *The Far Reality* (Consul 1963).
CAMOUFLAGE first appeared in *Astounding Science Fiction*, September 1945.
ANDROID first appeared in *The Magazine of Fantasy and Science Fiction*, June 1951.
OR ELSE! First appeared in *Amazing Stories*, September 1953.

Printed and bound in Great Britain by
Anchor Brendon Ltd, Tiptree, Essex

ISBN 0 09 933270 1

INTRODUCTION

In 1940 two fine science fiction writers married. Not only did Catherine ('C.L.') Moore and Henry Kuttner marry their lives, but they also married their writing careers. From two good writers were born whole companies of pseudonymous great writers (Lewis Padgett, and Lawrence O'Donnell, to name the two most prominent). The number of pen-names used by the prolific partners together and apart at one time threatened to swamp the universe of quality science fiction – indeed, so great was their contribution that when Jack Vance started his illustrious career, a rumour quickly spread that this was yet another reflection of the versatile Kuttner-Moore genius! (A rumour, I hasten to add, that had and has no truth in it whatsoever.)

In 1958 this fruitful collaboration came to an untimely end. Henry Kuttner died at the age of forty-four, and science fiction was sadly diminished. C.L. Moore completed their first television script and continued to work in that field until after her second marriage six years later. She has written no science fiction since the late 1950s.

Hamlyn Paperbacks has already published *Mutant*, *Fury*, *The Proud Robot* and the collection, *Clash By Night*. I am confident that Kuttner (and Kuttner-and-Moore)'s work will remain available from now until entertaining and highly polished story-telling goes out of fashion.

So spread the word. Kuttner is back in print. It is now up to you to ensure that future generations of fans are not denied the opportunity to sit amused, baffled, delighted, bewildered, tickled, frightened, amazed, entertained and enthralled by the genius of the Kuttners, Henry Kuttner and C.L. Moore.

PETER PINTO, 1983.

Note on 'Fairy Chess'

The games of Go and Chess have evolved from a common ancestor, taking over a thousand years to reach their current, very different, forms. The process of evolution continues as players experiment with new pieces and new rules – if you were taught chess by someone who 'spotted' you his Queen, you have already played one possible variation. New pieces such as the Grasshopper and the Nightrider have distinct moves which generate new tactics and strategies, new boards extend the game in still further ways and there are games which allow each player to spend an initial allocation of points on the selection of his pieces – six Knights, two Bishops, six Pawns and a King, for example (totalling $6 \times 3½ - 2 \times 3½ + 6 \times 1 + 0 = 34$pts), while his opponent might have preferred five Rooks plus nine Pawns and his King ($5 \times 5 - 9 \times 1 - 0 = 34$pts). Or how about a game in which each player has two Kings, both of which must be checkmated to finish the game – which raises the possibility of 'rescuing' a checkmated King so long as the second King remains free?

If you are interested in further details of non-standard (or 'Fairy') Chess, Anthony Dickins, an International Judge of the World Chess Federation, has written *A Guide To Fairy Chess*, which is a Dover large-format paperback distributed by Constable and Co. Ltd.

Or, of course, you may simply experiment for yourself – as players have done throughout the ages.

Peter Pinto 1983.

Chessboard Planet

The doorknob opened a blue eye and looked at him. Cameron stopped moving. He didn't touch the knob. He pulled back his hand and stood motionless, watching.

Then, when nothing happened, he stepped to one side. The black pupil of the eye swivelled in that direction. It watched him.

Deliberately he turned his back and walked slowly towards a window valve. The circular pane lightened to transparency as he approached. In a moment he stood before it, two fingers checking his pulse beat, while he automatically counted his respiration.

The window showed a green, rolling countryside, checkered with the shadows of drifting clouds. Golden sunlight brightened the spring flowers on the slopes. A helicopter moved silently across the blue sky.

The big, grey-haired man finished checking his pulse and waited, not wanting to turn around just yet. He stared at the peaceful landscape. Then, with a faint sound of impatience, he touched a stud. The pane swung aside into the wall.

Beyond the gap was red darkness, and the sound of thunder.

Shapes swam out of the gloom of the underground city, immense, blocky colossi of stone and metal. Somewhere a deep, rhythmic breathing made a distant roar; a mechanical rales rasped in the titan pump's beat. Static lightnings flickered occasionally, their duration too brief to show much of Low Chicago.

Cameron leaned forward, tilting his head back. Far above he could see only a deepening of the shadow, except when the necklaces of pallid lightning raced across the stone sky. And below was nothing but a bit of blackness.

Still, this was reality. The solid, sensible machines in the cavern made a sound foundation to logic, the logic on which the world was built today. A little heartened, Cameron drew back and closed the pane. Again blue skies and green hills were apparently outside the window.

He turned. The doorknob was a doorknob, nothing more. It was plain, solid metal.

He rounded the desk and walked quickly forward. His hand reached out and closed firmly on the metal.

His fingers sank into it. It was half-solid jelly.

Robert Cameron, Civilian Director of Psychometrics, went back to his desk and sat down. He pulled a bottle from his desk and poured himself a shot. His gaze wasn't steady. It kept shifting around the desk, never settling steadily on any one object. Presently he pushed a button.

Ben DuBrose, Cameron's confidential secretary, came in, a short, heavy-set man of thirty, with pugnacious blue eyes and untidy taffy-coloured hair. He seemed to have no trouble with the doorknob. Cameron didn't meet the gaze of those blue eyes.

He said sharply, 'I just noticed my televisor's off. Did you do that?'

DuBrose grinned. 'Why, chief – it doesn't matter, does it? All the incoming calls come through my board anyway.'

'Not all of them,' cameron said. 'Not the ones from GHQ. You're getting too smart. Where's Seth?'

'I don't know,' DeBrose said, frowning faintly. 'Wish I did. He – '

'Shut up.' Cameron had turned the visor to Receive. A hysterical buzzing sounded. The director looked up accusingly. DuBrose noticed the lines of tension about the older man's eyes, and cold, frantic panic struck into his stomach. He wondered if he could smash the visor – but that wouldn't help now. *Where was Seth*?

'Scrambler,' a voice said.

'Scrambler on,' Cameron grunted. His strong, big-knuckled hands moved lightly over switches. A face checkered in on the screen.

The Secretary of War said, 'Cameron? What's wrong with that office of yours? I've been trying to locate you – '

'Well, now you've got me. Since you're using this call number, it must be important. What's up?'

'I can't tell you over the visor. Not even through the scrambler. Perhaps I made a mistake in explaining as much as I did to your man – DuBrose. Is he trustworthy?'

Cameron met DuBrose's blank stare. 'Yes,' he said, slowly. 'Yes, DuBrose is all right. Well?'

'I'll have a man pick you up in half an hour. There's something I want you to see. Usual precautions. This is priority emergency. All right?'

'I'll be ready, Kalender,' the director said, and broke the contact. He laid his hands flat on the desk and watched them.

'All right, have me court-martialed,' DuBrose said.

'When did Kalender drop in?'

'This morning. Look, chief – I've got a reason. A good one. I tried to explain it to Kalendar, but he's a brass hat. I didn't have enough stars on my shoulder to impress him.'

'What did he tell you?'

'Something I don't think you should know yet. Seth would back me up on that, too. You'd trust him. And – look, I passed my psych tests with honours or I wouldn't be here with you. There's a psychological problem here and the factors indicate that you shouldn't know the set-up until – '

'Until what?'

DuBrose bit a thumbnail. 'Anyway till I check with Seth. It's important that you shouldn't get mixed up in this affair right now. The whole thing's paradoxical. I may be all wrong, but if I'm right – you don't know how right that is!'

Cameron said, 'So you think Kalendar's making a mistake in approaching me directly. Why?'

'That's exactly what I don't want to tell you. Because if I did, it would – screw things up.'

Cameron sighed and rubbed his forehead. 'Forget it,' he said, his voice tired. 'I'm the guy in charge of this department, Ben. It's my responsibility.' He stopped and looked sharply at DuBrose. 'That word must have a plenty high emotional index to you.'

'What word?' DuBrose said flatly.

'*Responsibility*. You reacted plenty.'

'A flea bit me.'

'So. Well, it's the truth. If there's a priority emergency in psych, it's my business to know about it. The war won't stop while I take a recess.'

DuBrose picked up the bottle and shook it.

'Buy yourself one,' Cameron said, shoving the cup forward. The secretary poured out amber fluid. He managed to drop the pill into the whisky without attracting Cameron's attention.

But he didn't drink. He lifted the cup, sniffed, and set it down again. 'Too early for me, I guess. I do my best drinking at night. Do you know where I can reach Seth?'

'Oh, shut up,' Cameron said. He sat staring at the cup without seeing it. DuBrose went to the window and looked at the projected landscape there.

'Look's like rain.'

'Not under *here*,' Cameron said. 'Nohow.'

'On the surface, however . . . look. Let me go along, anyhow.'

'No.'

'Why not?'

'Because you make me sick,' Cameron said tersely. DuBrose shrugged and went out. As he reached for the doorknob he felt the director's eyes upon him, but he didn't turn.

He went quickly to the communications board, ignoring the receptive smile of the girl who sat before the flickering panel.

'Get hold of Seth Pell,' DuBrose said, curiously conscious of the tone of flat hopelessness in his voice. 'Try everywhere. Keep trying.'

'Important?'

'Yeah . . . plenty!'

'General broadcast?'

'I . . . no,' DuBrose said. He ruffled his yellow hair distractedly. 'I can't. No authorization. You'd think those pot-heads in charge would allow for – '

'The chief would O.K. it.'

'That's what you think. No dice, Sally. Just try your best, that's all. I may be going out, but I'll call back. Find out where I can reach Seth, anyhow.'

'Something must be up,' Sally hinted. DuBrose gave her a thin, crooked smile and turned away. Praying silently, he went back to Cameron's office.

The director had the window open and was staring out at the red-lit darkness. DuBrose slanted a quick glance at the desk. The cup was empty of whisky, and an uncontrollable tremor of relief shook him. Though even now –

Cameron didn't turn. He said, 'Who is it?' A layman would not have noticed a difference in the director's voice, but DuBrose was no layman. He could tell that the alkaloid had already reached Cameron's brain, via the bloodstream.

'It's Ben.'

'Oh.'

DuBrose watched the slight swaying of the big figure at the window. That should wear off soon, though. The disorientation period was very brief. He blessed the lucky chance that he had had a package of Pix in his pocket. Not that it was a coincidence; most warmen carried them. When you work on desperately overtime schedules, the slow process of getting drunk is a nuisance and hangovers are an occupational risk. Some bright chemist had taken time off to fool around with alkaloids and create Pix, tiny, tasteless pills that had all the impact of 100 proof Scotch. They created and maintained that roseate glow of synthetic euphoria which has been popular since man first noticed grapes fermenting. It was one of the reasons why war workers were willing to plug away at their interminable jobs indefinitely, in the long deadlock that had existed since both nations decentralized and dug in. The population in general, oddly enough, seemed to live a more secure and contented life than before the war; the actual job of battle planning and operation was limited to GHQ and its subsidiaries. In extremely specialized warfare, there is room only for specialists, especially since neither country used troops any more. Even PFCs were made of metal.

The set-up would have been impossible without the booster charge of World War II. As the first World War had stimulated the use of air power in the second inter-global conflict, so the war of the nineteen-forties had stimulated the techniques of electronics – among other things. And when the first blasting attack of the Falangists, on the other side of the planet, had come, the western hemisphere was not only prepared, but could work its war machine with slightly miraculous speed and precision.

War needs no motive. But probably imperialism, as much as anything, was the motive behind the Falangists' attack. They were a hybrid race, as Americans had once been; a new nation that had arisen after World War II. The social, political and economic tangle of Europe had ended in a free state, a completely new country. The blood of a dozen races, Croats, Germans, Spanish, Russian, French, English, mingled in the Falangists. For the Falangists were *émigrés* from all Europe into a new free state with arbitrary and well-guarded borders. It was a new melting-pot of races.

And, in the end, the Falangists unified, drawing their name from Spain, their technology from Germany, and their philosophy from Japan. They were a mélange as no other nation had ever been: black, yellow and white stirred up together in a cauldron under which a fire had been kindled. They spoke of a new racial unity; their enemy called them mongrels, and it was impossible to decide. Once American colonizers had pioneered westward. But there were no new lands for the Falangists.

So the last two great nations of the world had been locked for decades in a see-saw war, each with a knife against the other's armoured throat. The social economy of both countries had gradually adjusted to war conditions – which led to such developments as Pix!

Morale Service, backed by Psych, had sponsored Pix. And there were plenty of other quick-action surrogates that kept the war workers happy. Like the Creeps, as someone had irreverently dubbed the subjective movies, with their trigger-action emotional shocks. And Deep Sleep, and the Fairylands that could partially compensate for the lack of children or pets – or could even act as a psychological curative. Few men could keep an inferiority complex when he could be Jehovah to a fantastically convincing illusion of a little world of his own, peopled with critters he could design and create himself. They weren't alive; they were simply gadgets; but so intricately constructed that many a man, watching a Fairyland come alive under his guiding hands on the controls, had found it difficult to come back to the real world. As an escape mechanism, the devices were plenty useful.

DuBrose watched Cameron. He wanted to make his point before the disorientation wore off.

'We'd better get ready.'

'We?'

DuBrose put surprise in his voice. 'Changed your mind? Don't you want me to go along, then?'

'Oh. Did I . . . I thought – '

'Better not keep the window open. We might get some fumes in while we're gone.'

'No dangerous gases in Low Chicago,' Cameron said, taking it for granted that DuBrose was to accompany him. 'Not even in the Spaces.'

'Well, there are some mighty strong stinks,' DuBrose said.

'An underground city – '

'I know. No matter how high-grade the technics are worked out, it's still underground. But you're the man who made the plans for the scanner windows in the first place. Why not use 'em?'

Cameron swung the pane back into place and stared at the green hillside, shadowed now under thickening rainclouds. 'Claustrophobia isn't my weakness,' he said. 'I can spend months underground without getting bothered.'

'That's more than I can do.' DuBrose noticed that Cameron held his ersatz liquor well. That was fine; he hadn't hoped that the director would pass out. His plan was set for a longer range. Probably the emissary from the Secretary of War wouldn't even notice

Cameron's euphoria. He reminded himself to feed the chief a breath-purifier before –

He managed it just in time. A thin, sour-looking man with two weapons strapped to his waist was ushered in, after the precautionary identifications.

'Name's Locke,' he said. 'Ready, Mr Cameron?'

'Yes.' The director was reoriented again. 'Where are we going?'

'Sanatorium.'

'Surface?'

'Surface.'

Cameron nodded and started towards the door. Then he paused, frowning a little.

'Well?' he said.

'Sorry.' Locke opened the door and let Cameron precede him. When DuBrose followed, the government man barred his path.

'You're not – '

'It's all right.'

Locke shook his head. 'Mr Cameron. Is this man to come along?'

The director glanced back, his face puzzled. 'He . . . what? Oh, yes. He's to come with us.'

'If you say so.' Locke looked sourer than ever, but fell in behind DuBrose.

They went past Communications, and the secretary raised his eyebrows at Sally. She made a hopeless gesture. DuBrose took a long breath. It was up to him now. And he was very much afraid of what they might see in that sanatorium.

The dropper took them to a lower level, and now Locke took the lead, herding the others towards an express crosstown way. DuBrose settled back on the seat and tried to relax. He watched the ivory-pale, luminous ceiling of the tube slide past overhead, but that smooth synthetic substance made no barrier to his thoughts. They probed beyond, into the roaring clamour of the Spaces where the machines thundered in the heartbeat of the city, peopling those abysses with a clamorous life of their own. No men worked there. The men who ran the machines sat comfortably in the air-conditioned, soundproofed buildings, with the scanning windows giving them the illusion of a life that wasn't underground. Unless you opened one of the valves, you could spend your life in Low Chicago and never realize that it was more than a mile beneath the earth's surface.

Claustrophobia had been one of the first problems. And plenty of neuroses had ripened into full psychoses before certain necessities had been met and certain problems solved. Neuroses that only the warmen had, because the majority of the civilian population didn't have to live underground. Decentralization had saved them from being bomb targets.

'This station,' Locke said over his shoulder. DuBrose touched a button under the chair's arm. The three seats slid off the fast belt into a spur track, slowed down and stopped. Locke silently led the way into a pneumocar that stood waiting. He closed the door and reached for the controls. DuBrose grabbed a strap just as a lean finger stabbed at top acceleration.

His stomach massaged his spine. By the time his sight came back, after the momentary blackout, he was automatically playing the old game every warman played – the hopeless task of trying to orient himself and guess the direction in which the car was plunging. It wasn't possible, of course. Only twenty men really knew where Low Chicago was located – top-rankers at GHQ. The labyrinth of tunnels that branched from the cavern ended in as many different spots, some miles away, some five hundred miles. And, because of the winding course, all the cars took exactly fifteen minutes to reach their destinations.

Low Chicago might be under the cornfields of Indiana, under Lake Huron, or under the ruins of old Chicago, for all the war workers knew. They simply went to one of the Gates known to them, were identified, and got into a pneumocar. Then, a quarter of an hour later, they were in Low Chicago. As simple as that. Every underground city had the same system, a preventative measure against drill-bombs. There were other precautions, too, but DuBrose wasn't a technician. He had been told it was impossible to get a triangulated radio fix on any war city – and accepted the fact. War, these days, was more of a chess game than a series of battles.

The car stopped; they walked through a short tube into the cabin of a helicopter. The vanes shrieked. The plane rose and manoeuvred jerkily in a quarter turn. Through a window DuBrose could see the feathery branches of trees slipping downward. Then, as they rose higher, an arid stretch of hills was visible. DuBrose wondered what state they were in. Illinois? Indiana? Ohio?

He leaned forward anxiously. There was something –

'Eh?' Cameron glanced at him.

DuBrose spun a dial on the window frame; a circle in the plastic thickened to a lens, bringing the distant scene closer. He looked once and relaxed.

'Dud,' Locke said. DuBrose had not thought the pilot had noticed his movement.

'One of the domes, that's all,' Cameron said, settling back. But DuBrose didn't stop staring at the silvery, tattered thing on the hillside.

It was a hemisphere, a hundred feet in diameter, and there were seventy-four of them scattered over America, all exactly alike. DuBrose could not remember when they had been perfectly opaque, mirror-silvery shells; he had been eight years old when they had appeared out of nowhere, all at once, cryptic with their secret that had never been solved. No one had been able to get into them, and nothing tangible had ever come out. Seventy-four shining hemispheres had come from somewhere, causing a near-panic. Another secret weapon of the enemy.

An area thirty miles around each shell had been cleared of civilians, while experts tried to solve the problem, expecting at any moment that the things would blow up. A year later they were still working.

Five years later they continued their tests – more sporadically.

Then the unbroken smoothness of the domes began to be marred. Striae made networks across the polished substance that wasn't matter. And the webs broadened, as though quicksilver were flaking from the back of a mirror, until the shells were tattered and split. It was possible to see inside then, but there was nothing inside – simply bare ground.

Nevertheless no one had been able to get into a dome. The force, whatever it was, remained constant; something like solid energy, made an impassable barrier to solids.

Long since the public, continuing to think the enigmas a secret weapon that had failed, had named them Duds. The title stuck.

'Dud,' Locke said, and turned on the auxiliary rockets. The landscape vanished in a blur.

DuBrose glanced at Cameron, wondering how soon the alkaloid surrogate would wear off. Pix weren't infallible. Sometimes –

But sight of the director's calm, relaxed face reassured him. It would be all right. It had to be.

Cameron was looking at the altitude gauge on the instrument panel. It was smiling at him.

2

Dr Lomar Brann, the neuropsychiatrist in charge of the sanitorium, was a compact, dapper, alert man with a waxed moustache and sleek black hair. He had a way of clipping his words that made him seem brusquer than he was. Now his eyes narrowed a little at sight of Cameron, but if he noticed the director's euphoria, he didn't show it.

'Hello, Cameron,' he said, tossing charts on his desk. 'I've been expecting to see you. How are you, DuBrose?'

Cameron smiled. 'I'm under sealed orders, Brann. I don't know what I'm here for.'

'Well . . . *I* know. I've had my own orders. You're to examine Case M-204.'

The director jerked his thumb towards a visor screen on the wall. It showed a patient fidgeting nervously in his chair, while the oval inset screen just above held a close-up of a man's face. The audio was saying softly:

'They were always after me and the birds whose ferds couldn't stop and the noises trees freeze sees words always go like words – '

Brann turned the visor off. The wire-tape spool stopped unreeling; the recording faded and died into silence. 'That's not the one,' Brann said. 'He's – '

'Dementia praecox, eh?'

'Yes, d.p. Disoriented, rhymes words – usual case history. I'll have no trouble curing him, though. Two months and he'll be on a farm topside.'

That was the usual procedure after psycho-patients had undergone treatment in the underground hospital-city. They were put into the care of specially selected sponsors, where the cure could progress under more normal conditions. DuBrose had made a survey of the system as part of his psych field work.

Brann looked slightly puzzled. He had noticed the euphoria, then – but he wouldn't comment on it while DuBrose anad Locke were there. He said, 'I suppose we may as well look at M-204.'

Cameron said, 'His identity is secret?'

'Not my field. The Secretary of War will tell you later, don't worry about that. I'm just supposed to show you the patient. Mr Locke, if you'll wait here – '

The guide nodded and settled himself more comfortably into a chair. Brann ushered Cameron and DuBrose through a door into a cool, softly lighted corridor. 'He's my own private case. Nobody else sees him, except the two nurses. Constant attendance, of course.'

'Violent?'

'No,' Brann said. 'It – isn't my field, really. The man – ' He unlocked a door. 'Through here. The man has hallucinations. A perfectly ordinary case, except for one thing.'

Cameron grunted. 'What's the diagnosis?'

'Well, tentatively – paranoia. He's assumed another identity. A rather . . . ah . . . exalted one.'

'Christ?'

'No. We've plenty of patients who've taken on *that* identity, Cameron. M-204 believes he's Mohammed.'

'Symptoms?'

'Passive. We force-feed him. You see, he's Mohammed after Mohammed's death.'

'Old stuff,' Cameron said. 'Retreat to the womb – escape mechanism?'

'What's the position?' DuBrose asked, and Brann nodded approvingly.

'Good point. Not the foetal posture at all. He stays on his back, legs extended, hands crossed on his chest. He doesn't talk. He keeps his eyes shut.' The neuropsychiatrist unlocked another door. 'He's in this private suite. Nurse!'

A husky red-headed male nurse appeared as they stepped into a well-furnished, comfortable hospital room. A serving table stood in one corner; equipment for force-feeding was in its glass case, and there was a transparent-panelled plastic door in the further wall. The nurse nodded towards that door.

'The patient's being examined, sir.'

Brann said, 'A technician of some sort, Cameron. Not medical. I think his field's physics.'

DuBrose was staring at a six-foot stepladder which seemed incongruously out of place in the neat, sterile chamber. The plastic door opened. A worried-looking man popped out, blinked at them through thick-lensed spectacles, and said, 'I'll need this.' He seized the ladder and disappeared.

'All right,' Brann said. 'Let's take a look.'

The adjoining room was a solitary, but comfortable enough. A bed had been pushed out from the wall. A few pieces of technical equipment were on the floor, and the physicist was pushing the stepladder towards the bed.

M-204 lay flat on his back, hands folded on his chest, his eyes closed and his lined face perfectly blank and expressionless. But he wasn't lying on the bed. He was floating in the air five feet above it.

Automatically DuBrose looked for wires, though he knew there was no reason for hocus-pocus here. There were no wires. Nor was M-204 supported by glass or transparent plastic. He – floated.

'Well'?' Brann said.

Cameron said, 'Mohammed's coffin . . . suspended halfway between heaven and earth. How's it done, Brann?'

The doctor touched his moustache. 'That's out of my field. We've taken the usual tests. C.B.C., urinalysis, cardiograms, basal – and we had a time doing it,' he added, grimacing. 'We had to strap the patient down to run our X-rays. He – floats!'

The physicist, perched precariously on the stepladder, was doing cryptic things with wires and gauges. He made a low, baffled noise. DuBrose watched the technician move a gadget slowly back and forth.

'This is crazy,' he said.

'He's been here since yesterday morning,' Brann said. 'M-204 was found in his laboratory suspended in midair. He was irrational then, but he could talk. He explained he was Mohammed. After half an hour, he became completely passive.'

'How did you get him here?' DuBrose asked.

The doctor fingered his moustache. 'The same way we'd get a balloon here. We can manoeuvre him around. When we let go, he bobs up again. That's all.'

Cameron stared at M-204. 'Man of about forty . . . notice his fingernails?'

'I did,' Brann said grimly. 'Up to a week ago, they were well-kept.'

'What was he doing this last week?'

'Working on something I'm not allowed to know about. Secret military information.'

'So . . . he discovered a means of neutralizing gravity . . . and the shock of it . . . no. Because he'd be expecting just such results. If he'd been working on – say – a bombsight, and suddenly found himself floating up off the floor – ' Cameron scowled. 'But how can a man – '

'He can't,' the physicist said from the stepladder. 'He just can't do it. Even theoretical antigravity requires machines. My instrument must be bollixed up.'

Cameron said, 'How?'

The technician held up a gauge. 'It's registering – see the needle? Now watch.' He touched a metal-tipped wire to M-204's temple. The needle flipped back to Zero. Then it shot wildly to the limit, wavered there, and subsided back to the zero mark again.

The technician descended. 'Fine. My instruments don't work when I use them on that guy. They work all right elsewhere. But – I don't know. Maybe he's suffered some chemical or physical change. Though even then I should be able to make a qualitative analysis. It's crazy.' Muttering, he repacked his equipment.

Cameron said, 'It's theoretically possible for an object to float in air, though, isn't it?'

'You mean an object heavier than air. Sure. Helium will inflate a dirigible. Magnetism will hold up a chunk of iron. Theoretically it's quite possible for this man to float. That isn't the problem at all. Theoretically practically anything's possible. But there's got to be a logical reason. How can I find a reason when my instruments don't work?'

He made a despairing gesture, his wrinkled, gnomish face twisted in angry lines. 'They want me to work blind, anyway. I've got to find out what this man was working on. That's where I'll find the explanation. Not here!'

Brann looked at Cameron. 'Any questions?'

'No. Not yet , anyhow.'

'Then let's go back to my office.'

Locke was still waiting when they came in. He stood up impatiently.

'Ready, Mr Cameron?'

'What's next?'

'The Secretary of War.'

DuBrose groaned inaudibly.

3

Within the next four hours –

A rocket engineer traced a circuit for the ninety-fourth time, sat back, and started to laugh. His laughter changed to a shrill, incessant screaming. The infirmary doctor finally shot apomorphine into the man's arm, before painting the raw throat. But when the engineer woke up he instantly began screaming again. As long as he made noises he was safe.

The circuit the engineer had been tracing was part of a gadget the enemy had dropped in quantity. Four of these gadgets exploded, killing seven technicians and wrecking valuable equipment. The ones that exploded were the Duds.

A physicist rose from the papers on his desk, went quietly to his workroom, and rigged up an effective high-voltage circuit. Then he electrocuted himself.

Robert Cameron, a portfolio under his arm, returned to Low Chicago and hurried to his office. The doorknob felt normal as he touched it. He went to his desk and opened the portfolio, spreading out the photostats and charts. He looked at the clock and saw the hands standing at one minute to seven. He compared it with his wrist watch.

Cameron waited for the seven musical strokes. They did not come. Again he glanced up at the white, numbered dial.

A mouth had opened there. It said, 'Seven o'clock.'

Seth Pell was Cameron's aide and alter ego. He was thirty-four, had white hair, and a round, fresh face that might have belonged to a teenager. Next to the director, Pell was probably the most competent man in the psychometric field – probably better in neuropathology, though without Cameron's broader knowledge of technology.

He walked into his office with a reassuring smile for DuBrose. 'What'll you have?' he asked. 'A sedative or a stiff drink?'

DuBrose couldn't match that airy lightness. There was a dull pounding behind his eyes.

'Seth. If you hadn't shown up – '

'I know. The world would have come to an end.'

'Did the chief tell you what happened?'

'I didn't let him,' Pell said. 'I persuaded him to take a dose of Deep Sleep and he settled for ten minutes' worth. Then I got psychonamical. He's thoroughly hypnotized by now.'

DuBrose breathed deeply. Pell perched on the edge of his desk and began paring his fingernails.

'O.K.,' he said. 'I've taken your word that it's necessary to get the chief under hypnosis fast. You're the only guy I'd trust enough to do that blind. I don't usually buy a pig in a poke. So?'

DuBrose felt weak. If he couldn't convince Seth now – but he was certain he could. The danger was too real, too evident for misunderstandings.

He said, 'The Secretary of War – Kalender, you know – came this morning. The chief was busy, so I asked Kalender if I could do anything. He was plenty upset or he wouldn't have talked to me, even though he knows I've got the chief's confidence. He talked a little – not much, but enough for me to smell trouble. There's a problem. But – here's the catch. Everyone who's tried to solve it has gone insane.'

'Yeah,' Pell said without looking up.

'I don't want the chief to go insane,' DuBrose said flatly. 'I managed to slip a Pix pill into his whisky before Kalender got hold of him. It was all I could do. But it'll help if you think artificial amnesia is necessary.'

'Mnemonic work is up my alley,' Pell said. 'However – let's go see.' He slid off the desk.

DuBrose followed him. 'Kalender wouldn't let me in when he talked to the chief a while ago. So I don't know what they discussed.'

'We'll find out. Come on.'

Cameron lay relaxed on the couch in his office, the Deep Sleep plate still pulled out from the wall. His breathing was slow and regular. Pell picked up the unconscious man's wrist, while DuBrose brought chairs.

'All right. Now for the mumbo-jumbo. Cameron – can you hear me?'

It didn't take long. Pell was an expert psychonamics man, and he had Cameron's complete confidence, which helped. Soon Pell leaned back, crossing his legs.

'What's all this about Secretary Kalender, Bob?'

'He – '

'You know who I am?'

'Seth. Yes. He . . . told me – '

'What?'

Cameron didn't open his eyes. 'You have to walk in the other direction to meet the Red Queen,' he said. 'The White Knight is sliding down the poker'

Pell was startled. DuBrose whispered, 'He balances very badly.'

That drew a response. Cameron murmured, 'Something on that order. Is that you, Seth?'

'Sure,' Pell said. 'What about Kalender?'

'It's big trouble. We've got hold of a formula that doesn't seem to mean anything. It means a lot to the enemy, though. I still don't know how we got the equation. Espionage, probably. But it's important, and it's got to be solved, and it doesn't make sense.'

'What does it deal with?'

'There are general and specific applications. Like the law of gravitation. There are constants involved, but . . . the sum of the parts doesn't seem to equal the whole. The equation *in toto* doesn't make sense. *In partis* it does. You can suspend the law of logic, apparently. And the enemy is doing just that. They've dropped some bombs that can pierce force-shells. Which is impossible. When the bombs were examined, they didn't make sense either. But they tied up with that equation. The technicians are trying to solve that equation. But – they go crazy.'

'Why?'

Cameron didn't answer directly. 'M-204 was one of the first to work on the thing. He didn't solve it. He learned how to neutralize gravity, and went insane. Or the other way around. We've got to find a solution, Seth. I've been glancing over the equation . . . it's on my desk – '

Pell jerked his thumb; DuBrose rose and collected the papers, shuffling them into a compact stack. He gave them to Pell, who didn't look at them.

'We've got to find the answer,' Cameron said. 'Or else. The enemy will have unlimited power – '

'Have they solved the equation?'

'I doubt it. Partially, that's all. But they'll do it, unless we forestall them.'

Pell was grinning, but DuBrose noticed diamonds of perspiration on he man's forehead below the silvery hair.

'We've got to solve it,' Cameron said.

Pell stood up and beckoned DuBrose into his office. 'Nice going,' he said. 'You did the smart thing.'

'That takes a load off my mind. I wasn't sure – '

Pell said, 'If a man's wife breaks her leg, he's half nuts till the doctor arrives. Then it's all right – he can shift the responsibility to more competent hands and relax. It isn't his job any more. But the doctor is equipped to handle a broken leg. The responsibility won't bother him.'

'And in this case – we're not equipped?'

'I haven't looked at the equation,' Pell said, tossing the sheets on his desk, 'and I'm not sure I'm going to. I can just imagine what that fool Kalender told the chief. Fate of the nation rests in your hands. You're responsible for finding somebody to solve the problem. If you don't, you'll have lost the war for us. So. That shovels the responsibility right into the chief's lap – and he's got to solve the equation or go nuts. That the way you figured it?'

'More or less.' DuBrose chewed his lip. 'That case – M-204 – he learned how important the thing was; and took refuge in insanity. Paranoia in his case, you said. He must have solved part of it, and it couldn't have made much sense. The equation *is* the weapon, not its by-products.'

'If nobody worked on it, the enemy might solve it first. Even as it is, they can penetrate force-fields. What they might do if they got all the answers . . . ! No, we've got to keep working, but not the way Kalender has in mind. That idiot thinks you can cure leprosy with an order of the day.'

DuBrose said slowly, 'I figured we could erase the chief's memories of what's happened today. Implant pseudo-memories, harmless ones. And then present the problem to him after we've yanked out the poison fangs.'

'Smart boy,' Pell nodded. 'The trick will be to keep the chief from realizing his responsibility. That'll be our job. I'm not sure just yet – ' He glanced at his watch. 'The first thing is to treat the chief. Wait for me.'

He went out. DuBrose moved to the desk and shuffled the photostats and papers. Some of the symbols made sense; others didn't. Still, he noticed that pi had been assigned an arbitrary and erroneous value. Was that a basic?

Better not look. He tried one of the windows, but the landscape blurred before his eyes. Could an equation cause insanity?

Of course. The equation was simply the concrete symbol of the abstract problem. The old test of the white rat and the anxiety neurosis. Slam the doors shut when the rat doesn't expect it, so he can't get at the food. After a while the rat simply huddles down and shivers. Nervous breakdown.

To have this interminable, unending war over might be a blessing. But to lose it – !

Not to the enemy. Generations of indoctrination had made that unthinkable. Men were conditioned to war now. They didn't even hate the enemy. But they knew, very thoroughly, that they must not lose.

Bombs dropped on both sides. The robots waged their pitched battles. But the real warriors were the technicians who moved the chessmen and created new gambits. There were no more diplomats; there was no need for them. There was no communication with the enemy, except the sudden messages that roared out of the sky.

Messages were received – and sent. But they were not convincing enough. Aerial torpedoes could not harm the protected nerve-centres of either country.

The annunciator said, 'Mr Pell. A courier from the Secretary of War.'

'Mr Pell's busy,' DuBrose said. 'Have him wait.'

'He says it's an emergency.'

'Have him wait!'

There was a brief silence. Then –

'Dr DuBrose, he won't. He wanted to see the director, but Mr Pell ordered all messages relayed through his office, so – '

'Send him in here,' DuBrose said, and turned to the door as it opened.

The courier's brown-and-black uniform meant something; he was Secret Service. Men who wore the arrow insignia on their lapels were rare – and got their authority directly from GHQ. This man –

He was sturdily built, neckless, and with cropped bronze hair that glistened metallically in the cool light. But it was his eyes that held DuBrose. They held an odd look of restrained excitement, of joyous, wild exultation held rigidly in leash. The thin mouth was well under control. Only the black eyes were betraying.

He held out his disc. 'Daniel Ridgeley,' DuBrose read, and automatically compared the portrait with the man's face. That was scarcely necessary; when an identification badge was removed from the wrist of its owner, it went blank permanently.

'Mr Ridgeley,' DuBrose said. 'Mr Pell will be free in a few minutes.'

Ridgeley's deep, slow voice held impatience. 'Priority. Where is he?'

'I told you – '

The courier glanced at the door and took a step towards it. DuBrose barred his way. The strange, febrile excitement flamed behind the jet eyes.

'You can't go in there.'

'Get out of my way. I have my orders.'

DuBrose didn't move. The courier made a quick, apparently casual motion, and the secretary went staggering across the room. He didn't try to intercept Ridgeley; instead, he plunged towards Pell's desk and jerked open a drawer. A vibropistol was there, a lovely, intricate mechanism of sturdy crystal and shining metal.

DuBrose's hands felt clumsy, like mush-filled cloves, as he fumbled with the weapon. He felt ridiculously melodramatic; odd that in this war of attrition men had so little experience with physical combat. As far as he knew, this vibro-pistol had never been used.

He leveled it at the courier and said, 'Take it easy!'

Ridgeley was facing him, the heavy shoulders bent, the stocky body crouched a little. That inexplicable devil of half-mocking delight burned behind the man's eyes, and with it was something like fast, icy calculation.

Then Ridgeley walked towards DuBrose.

He shifted catlike on his feet as he moved, and four feet from the secretary he stopped, quite motionless, his expression blank and intent. DuBrose felt sweat trickle coldly down his ribs.

Ridgeley said, 'I've my orders.'

'You can wait.'

'No,' the courier said. 'I can't.' And his whole body seemed to draw inward, like a huge cat gathering itself together. Though he was holding no weapon, he seemed more formidable than the armed DuBrose.

A lock clicked. The door to Pell's consultation room opened. On the threshold stood a young man of about twenty, thin, pale and stooped in his wrinkled tunic and shorts. His eyes were closed. He was making a hacking, unpleasant noise in his throat, moving his lips jerkily as the sound rose and fell without cessation.

'*K-k-k-k-k-kuk*!'

He came forward. Thre was a chair in his way. He walked around it and avoided the desk, though his eyes were still tightly shut.

'*K-k-k-k-uk! Kuk-kkkkk*!'

DuBrose moved too late. The vibropistol was deftly jerked from his grip. Ridgeley stepped back, his gaze flashing from DuBrose to the young man.

'Who's that?' he asked.

DuBrose said, 'I don't know. I didn't know Pell had a patient – he must be a patient. But – '

'*K-k-k-k-kuk*!'

The boy's excitement was rising. He stopped, his whole body beginning to shake uncontrollably. That unpleasant sound rose to a harsh thick croaking.

'*Kuk-k-k-k-k-kuk*!'

'Well,' Ridgeley said, 'I've got to see the director. Is he in there?'

'He's busy,' Seth Pell said. 'You can talk to me. I'm second in charge.'

The aide was standing by Cameron's door, smiling casually, ignoring the vibropistol in Ridgeley's hand. 'Ben,' he said, 'will you take that patient back in his room? Give him a light shot if necessary. But a sedative should be enough.'

DuBrose gulped, nodded, and took the boy's arm.

'*K-k-k-kkkk*!'

He led the jerking, shaking figure back into the examination office and swiftly got him on the table. A heated blanket, a pink pill, and the boy lay quiet, his shivering subsiding. DuBrose adjusted an alarm to ring if the patient got off the table and hurriedly returned to Pell's office.

The vibropistol lay on the desk. Ridgeley was arguing quietly. Pell hadn't moved.

' – my orders. I'm to deliver this case to the director. The Secretary of War told me that himself.'

Pell said, 'Ben, get Kalender on my visor, will you?' He nodded at Ridgeley, turned, and disappeared through the door behind him. By the time he came back, Kalender's heavy, hard face was on the screen.

The courier took a cylindrical metal case from his pocket. Robert Cameron, behind Pell, ignored it. The director went straight to the televisor and faced Kalender.

'Oh – Cameron,' the Secretary of War said. 'Did you get that – '

Cameron said, 'Listen. All messages and contacts are to be filtered through my aide, Seth Pell, until further notice. I want nothing delivered directly to me. Hereafter all calls to me must reach Pell first. Including GHQ and priority calls.'

'What?' Kalender was taken aback. His strong jaw thrust forward. 'Yes, yes,' he said impatiently. 'But I want to talk to you. My courier – '

'I haven't talked to him. He must deal with Pell.'

Kalender snapped; 'This is official business, Cameron – and priority! I don't want this handled by subordinates! I want – '

'Mr Secretary,' Cameron said quietly. 'Listen to me. I'm not under GHQ. I'm running the Department of Psychometics my way, and I don't permit my authority here to be questioned. If I wish to use Seth Pell as a filter, that is my affair. Until the government gives you more authority than you've got now, you'll allow me to handle my own business in my own way. That's all!'

He snapped the switch on the apoplectic Secretary of War and turned to his office. The courier stepped forward.

'Mr Cameron – '

Cameron gave him a cold stare. 'Did you hear what I told Mr Kalender?'

Ridgeley said, 'I've got my orders.' He held out the metal case.

The director hesitated. Then he took it. 'All right,' he said.

'You've done your job.'

He handed the case to Pell and walked back into his office. The door closed soflty.

Pell tapped the metal cylinder against his knuckles. He waited, watching Ridgeley.

'Well,' the courier said, 'I gave it to the director, anyhow.' His eyes met DuBrose's briefly; then he saluted casually and went out.

Pell tossed the cylinder on the desk. 'Nice going,' he said. 'Lucky the chief backed me up.'

DuBrose touched the vibropistol with an exploratory finger. 'I . . . did the chief – '

'Its all right,' Pell smiled. 'We've time to work on the problem now. I gave our director the works – a complete quick mnemonic treatment. He doesn't remember anything that's happened today. I gave him some phony memories instead. Now we can let him have the problem without the responsibility – if we can figure out how to do that.'

'You didn't rouse his suspicions?'

'The chief trusts me. Completely. I told him I wanted to be a filter for a while, and not to ask me why. He'll wonder, of course, but he can't guess the right answer. I've wiped out the dangerous memories.'

'Completely?'

'Completely.'

Cameron opened the window and watched the red darkness pulse and shift. A vague memory troubled him, but not too much. It was simply part of this thing that had come on him – the thing he had to fight out by himself. There must be a reason. There had to be. If he submitted himself to psychiatric examination, he'd . . . no. That wasn't the way. Visual and auditory – and tactile – hallucinations . . .

That dim memory came back. It was impossible to place its sequence in the day's events – a fairly dull and ordinary day. He hadn't budged from the office, there had been few callers – but this memory, like the doorknob and the clock and the smiling altitude gauge, probed with soft insistence into his mind.

A man floating in midair.

Hallucination.

4

'The chief's gone home,' DuBrose said.

'Fair enough.' Pell spread papers on his desk.

'Shouldn't one of us – '

The aide glanced sharply at DuBrose. 'Relax, Ben,' he said lightly. 'Hypertension's setting in. The chief won't receive any calls. He'll have 'em routed to me. Mm-m– ' He hesitated. 'Look. Take these cards and alphabetize 'em while we talk. Or else have some Deep Sleep.'

DuBrose accepted the cards, shuffling them automatically into sequence. 'Sorry,' he said, 'this thing's got me a bit, I guess.'

Pell's white hair glistened as he bent forward over charts. 'Why should it?'

'I don't know. Empathy– '

'Orbs,' Pell said. 'I could be as jittery as you if I wanted to. But I've studied history and literature. And architecture, and a lot of things. Just to balance this psycho work. There's a lot more perfection in a Doric column than in you.'

'Yeah. But I can build a Doric column.'

'You can also build a backhouse. That's the trouble. You're as likely to do one as the other.' He chuckled. ' "I do not like the human race . . . I do not like its silly face." '

'What's that?'

'A guy named Nash. You never heard of him. The thing is, I'm part misogynist, Ben. If somebody wants me to like him, he's got to prove he's worth liking. Few people do.'

'Oh, philosophy,' DuBrose growled, dropping a card. 'What's this? Palate deformation developing at twenty with – '

'Group of cases I've been investigating,' Pell said. 'Academic value only, I'm afraid. No, it isn't philosophy; I just can't get excited over anything that threatens people in the aggregate. Humans aren't selective. They lost selectivity when they gave up instinct for intelligence. And so far they haven't learned to discipline their creative powers. A bird will build a nest that's a beautiful piece of engineering.'

'Dead end.'

'I'm not infatuated with birds either,' Pell remarked. 'They're too reptilian for my taste. But people – in fifty thousand years or three times that time, they may have learned the art of selectivity. They'll be worth knowing – all of them. At present genus homo is struggling up through the mire, and I'm fastidious.'

'Proving what?' DuBrose asked, irritated.

'Proving my egotism,' Pell laughed. 'And explaining why I'm not hot and bothered over this particular danger.' But, DuBrose thought, it didn't explain why Pell seemed so unconcerned about the danger threatening the director. Cameron was Pell's closest friend; there was a warm affection between the two men. It was something else in the aide's mind, a latent strength, a steel discipline, that enabled him to keep his balance.

DuBrose didn't know Pell. He admired and trusted him, but had never tried to encroach on a certain deep restraint that Pell kept buried, under his casual flippancy. Often he wondered. There were rumours, scandalous even in these amoral days, about Seth Pell's private life –

'Uh-huh,' the aide said. 'Quite a problem. Everybody who's

worked on this equation is either showing signs of strain or going nuts. *Unless* – here's a factor – unless they could delegate the responsibility. The enemy's been dropping bombs that penetrate force-fields. A few have exploded. Most haven't. Apparently the hookup's impossible. There's one gadget that can't possibly work on the same circuit with another gadget. Twelve men in various fields have already gone insane. Two with suicidal tendencies have committed suicide. Somebody named Pastor – physicist – says he'll have the equation solved within a few days. No way of checking that at the moment. And so on, and so on. We'll have to make some personal interviews. Our job is to gather the data and correlate it. Including the fact that part of the equation can nullify gravity.'

DuBrose had alphabetized the cards. He flipped them idly.

'How can we present the problem to the chief?'

'Well – he mustn't realize its importance. I think the best way is to bury it. Handle the whole affair casually. But *not* give him the equation. He's too good a general scientist to be trusted with *that*. If he tried to solve it himself . . . and it seems to have some sort of fascination. No, we've got to gather all the information that's pertinent, make sure it's innocuous, and hand it over to the chief. That means leg work.'

'Can we handle it that way? Isn't there a danger of emasculating the vital factors so much that – '

Pell said, 'We've got to find out exactly why technicians go crazy when they try to solve the equation. And the chief has to think of somebody who *can* solve it.'

He stood up. 'That's enough for now. Let's wind up the day.' He tossed the papers into a drawer and made adjustments. A dome of icy white light sprang into existence around the desk.

DuBrose said, 'Force-fields may not be so safe any more, if the enemy can drop bombs through them.'

'I set the incendiary, too,' Pell said. 'But who'd want to steal that equation? The enemy's got it already.' He went into the examination room. DuBrose following. The boy still lay asleep on the padded table, his eyes closed, his breathing even.

'Who is he?' DuBrose asked.

'Name's Billy Van Ness. Typical case – one of that group on the cards you were juggling. Delayed puberty, age twenty-two now, sudden physical and mental changes started two months ago. Only constant is the fact that all the cases were born within a radius of two miles from a Dud.'

‘Radiation affecting the genes of the parents?’ DuBrose was picturing the silvery, tattered dome on the arid hillside.

‘Could be.’

‘Enemy?’

‘A weapon that didn’t work, then. Only about forty cases in all. It’s odd; they were all perfectly normal up to two months ago – except for delayed maturation. Then they matured and some curious physiological changes set in. Deformation of the palate . . . but it’s the mental metamorphoses which are more intereting. They never opened their eyes – a familiar enough symptom. Recognize it?’

‘Naturally.’

‘But – ’

‘Wait a minute,’ DuBrose said. ‘That boy could see. He walked around a chair that was in his way.’

‘A little trick they have,’ Pell smiled. ‘ESP for all I know. They never bump into anything when they walk about – which is seldom – but they never go in a straight line. A twisting, erratic pattern always, as though they’re walking around things that aren’t there as well as things that are.’

‘Balance distortion?’

‘No, they’re steady. They just walk as though they’re threading a path through a roomful of eggs. What excited this boy?’

DuBrose made a few guesses.

‘It’s unusual,’ Pell said. ‘They seldom rouse from their passivity unless they’re near a Dud. That seems to excite them. They make that funny noise. Unpleasant, isn’t it?’

‘Any prognosis yet, Seth?’

Pell shook his head. ‘I’m going to try mnemonic probing. If nothing else works. I may be able to throw this boy’s mind back to his more normal past. Well, let’s have those cards.’ He tossed them on a table and rang for an attendant. ‘Billy can stay in the infirmary tonight – private room. Get your cloak, Ben. We’re going out.’

DuBrose said, ‘Any equipment – ’

Pell chuckled. ‘Not for this therapeutic work, brother. We’re going to extrovert for a few hours – but good. You’ve got a bad case of hypertension. Deep Sleep won’t cure it. If I told you to go out and eat Pix, you’d do it, but you’d still feel subconscious anxiety. This way you’ll be able to relax, because I’m your superior, and the responsibility’s mine.’

‘But . . . look, Seth – ’

‘You’re going through the mill tonight,’ Pell said. ‘Tomorrow we’ll go crazy together.’

Only a helicopter could have landed on this outcrop of the Rockies. A drill-press had run wild across the sky; the rarefied atmosphere made even low-magnitude stars brilliant. The path of the Milky Way splashed its cataract towards the Wyoming horizon eastward, and the frigid wind made DuBrose's jaw muscles tighten. Then the force-field lifted again, blotting out the sky in the curdled dome of silently crackling light.

The house under the field looked like a chalet, but those steeply sloping roofs were functional in a region where the snowfall was measured in yards. It wasn't snowing now; bare, brittle ground crunched under DuBrose's feet. He went on with Pell towards the porch and presently was standing in a huge room that might have been furnished by a colour-blind man. A dozen periods of furniture were represented; a Louis XIV sofa sat under a Gobelin tapestry, and the tapering sleekness of Brancusi's 'Bird in Space' perched incongruously on a Victorian marble-topped pedestal. Oriental rugs clashed violently with bearskins on the floor and trophy heads on the wall. One whole side of the room was a segmented projection screen. Beneath it was a Fairyland box and control panel, one of the most complicated DuBrose had ever seen.

'Wonder if Pastor furnished this place himself?' DuBrose muttered.

'Sure,' a voice behind him said. 'Just the way I wanted it. It scares people sometimes. Make your landing all right? The thermals are tricky around here.'

'We managed,' Pell said. DuBrose was staring at the gnomish little man, with his wrinkled nutcracker face. And Dr Emil Pastor stared back, blinking through heavy lenses.

'Oh, it's you,' he said. 'I never did catch your name.'

'DuBrose. Ben DuBrose. Dr Pastor and I met at the sanatorium, Seth – he was examining that patient, M-204. The one who floated.'

'Floated,' Pastor said, blowing out his cheeks expressively. 'You don't know half of it. I found out what part of the equation he was working on. Lovely stuff, pure symbolic logic, except for one thing. Two things, rather. If you neutralize gravity completely, centrifugal force will shoot you out in space at a tangent. Right? But M-204 just floated. According to his figures – based on that equation – the trick's theoretically possible. All you have to do is utilize the arbitrary values the equation assigns to two symbols – orbital velocity of the earth and the power necessary to lift a body out of the earth's gravitational influence.'

'*Arbitrary* values?' DuBrose asked.

'Sure. They're really constants. 66,600 m.p.h. for the first, 6,000,000 kilogram-meters for the second. The equation says it only takes 10 kilometres to get away from gravity, and the first constant can be ignored. It's zero. The earth doesn't revolve at all.'

'What?' Pell said.

Pastor made a significant gesture. 'I know. M-204 is insane. But his insanity is based on something peculiar. He thinks he can float because the earth doesn't revolve. And – he floats. Nevertheless it moves!'

The aide said, 'What about those 10 kilometres? Energy – '

Pastor nodded. 'That, too. Energy has to be expended constantly to maintain a balance like that – antigravity. Unless you have enough orbital velocity to keep moving, like the moon. But M-204 doesn't expend energy, does he? Or does he?'

'Your instruments went haywire, you said,' DuBrose suggested.

'Which is significant,' the little physicist agreed. 'Perhaps from where M-204's sitting, the earth *doesn't* revolve. But my instruments aren't able to register that; they were built on an earth that does revolve.' He laughed shortly. 'I'm so immersed in this business that I've forgotten my manners. Take off your cloaks. Drink? Deep Sleep?'

DuBrose demagnetized his throat-fastener and tossed his cloak towards a rack that caught it deftly. 'Thanks, no. We won't keep you long. We're – '

'I'd have solved the equation before this,' Pastor said, 'if the big shots hadn't moved me out of Low Manhattan. They found out some bombs were exploding and figured I might wreck the cave. So I came up here. If I do detonate, the force-field will limit the casualties.'

Pell said, 'Those bombs could penetrate force-fields, couldn't they?'

'They could indeed. Come in here.' Pastor herded them into a cluttered laboratory, much of it singularly unorthodox and jerry-built. He searched a messy table for a photostat blueprint. 'Here's a diagram of the bomb's mechanism. Know anything about electronics?'

'Very little,' Pell said, while DuBrose merely shook his head.

'Oh. Well. Anyhow, see this tricky business? It'll work on one type of circuit, but not on another. This other gadget will work on the other type of circuit only. But they're both functioning perfectly on the same circuit. We've tried reversing them, we've tried standing on our heads and looking cross-eyed, but the fact remains. Two mutually incompatible elements are functioning beautifully together. It can't be. But it is.'

Pell started at the diagram. Pastor said, 'What do you think of that?'

'I think it's tough on the engineers who had to figure out how and why the bombs got through force-fields.'

The physicist said, 'The equation, as far as I can tell yet, is founded on something like variable logic. It's full of mutually incompatible basics.'

'Two and two make five?' DuBrose said.

'Two and whee make diddle plus,' Pastor corrected. 'It can't be expressed in basic English. A semantics expert would give up in disgust. It says here' – he indicated a paper – 'that a free-falling body accelerates at the rate of five hundred feet a second. Later on in the equation that body is accelerating at nine inches a second. And *that's* a basic!'

'Does it make any sense at all to you?' Pell asked.

'There are glimmerings,' Pastor admitted. He went to a basin and began washing his hands. 'I'm going to knock off for a bit. I could use some Deep Sleep – but we can talk first. Though I don't know what I can tell you yet.'

Pell hesitated. 'These variables – our science takes certain constants as foundation-stones, truisms on which that science is built.'

'What is truth?' Pastor asked, rinsing his hands. 'Sometimes I wonder. Anyhow – '

They went back into the big, cluttered room. The physicist wandered over to the Fairyland control panel, idly touching the studs. 'I don't know,' he said. 'I'm trying to keep an open mind. It certainly isn't logical that bombs could penetrate force-fields, especially bombs that can't possibly work.'

DuBrose said, 'Could this have any connection with the Duds? They're supposed to be enemy weapons that failed. And they're unbreakable force-fields.'

Pastor didn't turn. 'Unbreakable, yes. Force-fields – I'm not so sure. I was on a couple of commissions delegated to study the Duds, and I had a theory or two nobody wanted to accept. Of course twenty-two years ago my mind was more elastic – ' He grinned. 'If you go through the files on that business, you'll find a man named Bruno said he'd detected hard radiations from one of the Duds.'

Pell leaned forward on the couch. 'Matter of fact, I did run across that reference. But it wasn't too detailed.'

'There was no proof,' Pastor said. 'The radiations lasted for about an hour, Bruno's instrument was the only one set up at that time, and you can't chart a graph from one point. The radiations formed a pattern of sorts, though. Bruno thought it might be an attempt at communication.'

'Yes, I know,' Pell said. 'The report stopped there.'

'The rest was guesswork. Who'd use hard radiations to communicate?'

DuBrose was remembering Billy Van Ness, with his closed eyes and his rasping '*K-k-k-kuk*!' noise. Warping of the basic genes, latent until delayed maturity, emerging as a so-far inexplicable psychopathic condition – '

He said, 'There's no radiation from the Duds now?'

'We can't detect any.'

Then why did cases like Billy Van Ness rouse from their stupor when they were near one of the tattered silver domes? Scarcely recognition, even through ESP. Such a memory would have to be acquired, not hereditary.

Pastor said, 'Oh, I suppose there's some sort of energy, or the Duds wouldn't still be impermeable. But we can't detect it. I doubt if the Duds can be connected with – this equation.'

'As long as you solve it – ' Pell said. 'There is an occupational hazard, you know.'

'Insanity. Want to test my knee-jerks?'

'As a matter of fact, I would,' the aide said. 'Got any objection?'

'None at all.'

'Ben.'

This was routine. DuBrose made notes and watched as Pell questioned the physicist, apparently irrelevant questions that all made sense in the aggregate pattern. Finally they had finished, and Pastor sat back grinning.

'Normal enough. You're an asocial type anyhow.'

'But not antisocial. I've a wife and two kids' – he pointed to tri-di cube portrait of transparent plastic – 'and I adjust all right, with one thing and another.'

Pell said, 'I've never seen such a complicated Fairyland set. Use it much?'

'Often.' Pastor went to the controls. 'I got away from the company patterns years ago. I create my own systems and paradoxes – '

Flashing bands and streaks of colour flamed across the screen. They almost made sense.

The physicist said, 'In this sequence, I've assigned human

emotions to colours. I make up the plot as I go along.'

For a while they watched the coruscating screen. Then Pell stood up.

'We'll leave you to Deep Sleep, Dr Pastor. Will you call us if anything breaks?'

'Sure.' Pastor switched off the Fairyland. 'But I'll have that equation solved within a few days. I'm certain of it.'

'How certain?' DuBrose asked later in the helicopter.

'I don't think he's whistling in the dark. But he's juggling plenty inside that head of his. A queer fish, Ben.'

'No sense of esthetic values.'

'I wonder. His own, maybe. I want a detailed psych report on Pastor from what we've observed tonight. Wax it and let me have it for additions as soon as you can, will you? If Pastor solves the equation, everything's fine. But if he doesn't – '

'Do you think he's a psychopathic type?'

'Everybody can go crazy, in one way or another. He's not potentially suicidal or homicidal. Possibly schizophrenic – I don't know. We'll head back to Low Chicago now. If we can integrate enough dope by morning, we can put it on the chief's desk.'

DuBrose pulled out a smoke-tube from the instrument panel and inhaled deeply. His mouth was tight. Pell chuckled.

'Getting you, Ben?'

'A little.' More than that, really, when the diaphragm is stiff and unsteady, and invisible bugs are crawling along the skin. DuBrose moved uneasily in the cushioned seat, while cogs slipped together without meshing in his thoughts.

'*Cui bono?*' Pell said. 'It's not our responsibility, remember.'

'Isn't it?'

'We can't solve the equation. We can't find the man who can – unless Pastor's the one. Only the chief is qualified to integrate the final factors.'

'Yeah,' DuBrose said, while the little bugs crept down his arms.

5

Ripples broadened in the mirror. Concentric circles fled out from the locus, distorting Cameron's face. He moved aside, watching the ripples gradually subside.

Then he moved again, directly before the mirror. When the image of his face hit the glass, the ripples started once more. He waited. They lessened and stopped.

Each time he blinked, however, minor circles began, one for each eye, spreading out over the smooth surface.

The angle of incidence is equal to –

Cameron looked at the tired face under its thatch of grey hair. He tried to keep his eyelids immobile.

Blink.

Ripple.

Quite impossible.

He turned away. He looked around the room. It was no longer a room to be taken for granted. Not the room he had known for years, in this house he had known for years. If the mirror betrayed him, so might the contoured, yielding floor. So might the billiard table. So might the glowing ceiling, and –

He turned sharply and mounted the stairs, without touching the escalator control. He wanted solidity under his feet, not the soft sliding motion that reminded him the earth was no longer quite as firm as usual.

His whole body jolted violently. Only rigid control kept him from –

It had been nothing much. He had mounted a top step that wasn't there. That could happen.

Had he *seen* that intangible top step? He tried to remember and couldn't.

This wasn't the first time. When he was off guard, when he had forgotten, then that top step that wasn't there would be there. Not tangibly. Not even visually, perhaps.

The visor was humming. Cameron reached it before Nela did. She shrugged and turned away, her sleek dark head suddenly terrible. Cameron stood with his hand on the switch, watching Nela walk back to her seat. He was wondering what he would do if a face, Nela's face, should suddenly appear on the back of her head.

Or not Nela's face.

He waited. He was afraid to stop looking until she had turned around. But it was Nela, with her cool, amused dark eyes and her tilted nose. He was glad she had never undergone rejuvenation. Old, wise eyes were wrong, somehow, in too young a face. Attractive as Nela was, her face was mature, and very comforting now.

'Well?' she said, lifting her eyebrows. 'Are you taking it?'

'Eh? Oh – ' Cameron pressed the switch. The blunt, dark face of Daniel Ridgeley, the courier, checkered in, wrist raised to show the identification disc.

'Priority. Message from the Secretary of War – '

Cameron said coldly, 'Seth Pell will receive it.'

Something exultant and gleeful flickered in those jet eyes. 'The Secretary insists, sir – '

Cameron snapped the switch. The screen blanked. After a moment the humming started again. Cameron turned off the set.

He put an elbow on the mantel and looked at nothing. His elbow slowly began to sink through the wood. He jerked away, glancing hastily at Nela. She was patting pillows into shape on the couch behind her.

She hadn't noticed. No one noticed, ever. You couldn't expect them to notice.

'You're nervous,' Nela said. 'Come and lie down here.'

'You're the only one who's seen it,' Cameron said. 'Nela, I – '

'What?'

'Well – nothing. I think I'm overworked a bit. I'll furlough pretty soon.'

He walked to the one-way windows. He could see out, into the moonlight speckling the tree-shadowed hillside, but no light filtered through those panes to attract enemy aircraft. If any aircraft *could* get past the coast barrages.

'Come and lie down.'

If he did, the couch might melt away beneath him. This room was too familiar. It was charged with latent horror. The familiar things were the ones that had betrayed him.

Better to be among unfamiliar things. If they behaved strangely, he might not notice it so easily. Was that fallacious reasoning? Too specious? At least it was worth acting on.

He came behind the couch and kissed the top of Nela's head. 'I'm going out for a bit. Don't wait up.'

'The boys called today. You haven't seen the recording.'

'It'll keep. How do they like the school?'

'They kicked, as usual. But they like it. They're growing, darling. In those school uniforms – ' Nela laughed softly. 'Remember?'

He remembered. Twins, fourteen years ago. They'd both been surprised. But they'd made plans, long-range plans –

He kissed Nela again and went out quickly. The copter took him to a Gate. A pneumocar shot him to Low Chicago, but not to his office. That, too, would have been familiar.

He found a valve and went out into the Spaces, automatically taking a light-tube from its rack, but slipping the cylinder into his pocket. Behind him the giant artery of the Way was a great Midgard Serpent coiling into the darkness.

Low thunders muttered around him. Under his feet the ground was gritty and hard. He went on slowly, staring around at the titans that served the city.

The pumps sighed and coughed; the heart of Low Chicago beat through the crimson gloom. Near him a mechanism of some sort rose and was lost in the shadow above. Out of blackness a piston, fifty feet in diameter, drove at him, hesitated, and shot back again. Forward it came, and back, forward and back, forward –

Lightning crawled across the vaulted ceiling that sheathed Low Chicago.

Br-r-rooom – *thlock*!

That was the piston.

Whssssss . .

Compressed air.

Whroooom . . . whroooom.

Pump.

His feet scuffed through dusty slag. Something was moving down there. He crouched, staring at the things that slipped swiftly and noiselessly through the cinders, red and black –

Chessmen.

His hand went through them.

Subjective. *The chessmen were walking about two by two.* A projection of his thoughts, preoccupied with a land beyond the looking glass, where the expected did not always happen. They were not there . . .

He did not look down again to make sure. Cameron swung around and walked hurriedly towards the nearest Way, not hearing the low thunder of the Spaces re-echoing all around him.

A valve opened; he stepped through and found a seat in one of the belts. His hand lay open on the padded arm. Suddenly something was thrust against his palm; instinctively his fingers tightened.

A metal cylinder.

He looked back. Already his chair was ahead of the seat on the slower belt that had briefly adjoined his. Daniel Ridgeley, the courier, was sitting there, jet eyes burning with excitement.

Cameron raised his arm and threw the cylinder straight at Ridgeley.

The courier lunged aside and caught it. His mouth opened in a soundless laugh.

The director's fingers touched a stud; the chair slid aside. Instantly Cameron was out of it, a reasonless cold panic filling him. Now he wanted familiar things, not the dim, strange vastness of the Spaces. And here was the infirmary annex to his own department, a refuge against –

Against what?

He looked over his shoulder, but Ridgeley had vanished. The panic had not gone, though. Cameron stepped into a lift and got off without noticing the floor. He stood looking into a dim, quiet room where a dozen beds made pale oblongs.

He came forward a few steps and paused, absorbing the peace that brimmed the room.

A nurse's voice said, 'All right?'

'All right,' Cameron said. 'It's the director.'

'Yes, Mr Cameron – '

The lift sighed. A low humming began; that meant unauthorized intrusion. The nurse's televised voice began to speak and broke off. Cameron swung around and began to back up.

He felt a door panel behind him. He groped for the knob, and it bent like putty beneath his fingers. Someone was coming along the hall outside, someone who was making staccato, harsh noises in his throat.

But at the other end of the room the lift's barrier slid aside, and the stocky, hunched form of the courier stood there, shapeless in silhouette.

Behind Cameron, in the hall, someone was going, '*Kuk-k-k-k-k-k.*'

Ridgeley came on. Cameron could see the cylinder in his hand.

The director let go of the useless doorknob. 'You're not allowed in here,' he said thinly. 'Get out.'

'I've my orders. Priority.'

'See Seth Pell.'

'The Secretary of War told me to deliver this to you personally.'

With part of his mind Cameron realized how irrational this nightmare was. All he had to do was to take the message and give it, unopened, to Pell. As simple as that. But somehow it didn't seem quite so simple, with that bulky, squat figure plodding relentlessly forward.

'*K-k-k-k-kuk*!'

Ridgeley put the cylinder into Cameron's hand.

The door behind the director opened, letting a shaft of pale light in. Cameron turned his head, blinking. Pell's white hair gleamed as he stood staring, his hand tight on the shoulder of a young man wearing an infirmary bedsuit. The boy was shaking from head to foot, his eyes were closed, and the rasping, harsh noise was coming from his throat.

DuBrose was there, too, his young face strained. He pushed past Cameron into the dormitory.

Pell said, 'Easy, Ben. Chief – '

'You'd better take this,' Cameron said, holding out the cylinder. 'Kalender's courier – '

The patient stopped shaking. The rattling clatter died in his throat. Without inflection, in a rapid, staccato voice, he said.

'Everyone is too short, flat people, but this new one . . . I saw him before . . . he reaches in the right direction, long, long, longer by far than anyone else here . . . not as long as the shining things but he is more complete in his duration – '

The boy stopped. DuBrose, facing Ridgeley, caught a new expression on the man's face – something like wild, inexplicable delight.

'Sorry if I caused any disturbance,' the courier said smoothly. 'But my job's done. I'll go now.'

Nobody stopped him.

An hour later Cameron was in Deep Sleep in his office, and DuBrose and Pell were working over Billy Van Ness. The boy was in third-stage hypnosis, and fragmentary words were beginning to emerge from the jumble of noises. But it took a long time before any coherent pattern became evident.

DuBrose spun the semantic integrator dial on the dictagraph and watched words form on a lighted screen. His lips moved as he read. He could hear Pell's soft, unhurried breathing behind him.

'It isn't ESP, then,' Pell said. 'It's ETP. Extra-temporal perception. That explains something that's puzzled me. The patterns cases like Van Ness follow when they walk. Certain symptoms of disorientation. They're just avoiding chairs that aren't there at the moment, but either were or will be. They reach for objects that were moved a week ago. They're disoriented in time – because they can sense duration.'

'It's crazy,' DuBrose said.

Pell watched the screen. 'See how this sounds. Some race far away in time made an expedition. I don't know why. They must have been pretty unthinkably inhuman. Fifty million years in the future – or a hundred million. Maybe they faced extinction and took refuge in time instead of in space. They came here, twenty-two years ago, in the Duds. They didn't survive. While they did, for an hour, they – talked? – in their particular way. Not with sound waves. Not with vibrations. With hard radiations. Or perhaps they always emitted those radiations.'

DuBrose looked at the hypnotized boy and swallowed dryly. Pell's cold, steady voice went on.

'Hard radiations. Genes getting knocked around – mutation. But a very queer kind of mutation. The only kind possible. It was a sort of biological meeting of two utterly unlike species. Mental. Genus homo and genus – X!'

They were perhaps the ultimate adaptation of life on earth. Their race had never been human; they had sprung from other seeds in their own unthinkably long ago. And they could move through time, in their own way. Not easily, for only under certain specialized, nearly unique conditions, could they exist at all.

Seventy-four temporal protective domes sprang into existence in the world of genus homo. From within those shells, genus X looked at a planet fantastically alien to them, as a human might regard the boiling gneiss raging across the seething crust of a molten earth.

And the hard radiations came out from the domes for an hour, radiations that were an integral part of the basic matrix of genus X. Human gene plasm responded. And was altered.

Before genus X passed, it had bequeathed to a few unborn specimens of genus homo certain latent abilities, wild talents not to be perceptible until the delayed maturation. And even then the powers of genus X would be all but useless to a merely human race.

The legatees could sense duration. But, by the time they were able to do that, they were hopelessly insane.

Pell said, 'Some sort of energy must maintain what's left of the Duds. These mutants sense that. Or else they see – '

'What about Ridgeley?'

'I've checked the records. This is actually the first time any of these cases has ever roused from his lethargy except when near a Dud. Remember what this boy said when he saw . . . sensed . . . Ridgeley?'

'It's integrated with the other stuff,' DuBrose said. 'There are several possible conclusions.' He nodded towards the screen.

'Yeah. To somebody who can see duration, a baby must look plenty flat. No, I'm wrong. That would depend on the baby's longevity. If he grew up to be a hundred, he wouldn't seem flat. But Billy said *everyone* was too short except Ridgeley. Ridgeley reaches in the right direction, longer than anyone else who was in the infirmary then – but not as long as the shining things.'

'The Duds. Wait a minute, Seth. If Billy here can sense duration, that might just mean that Ridgeley's going to live to a ripe old age.'

Pell grunted. 'Do you realize from how far in the future the Duds must have come? You can't compare the heights of ants when you use Everest as the measuring stick. If Ridgeley's duration is noticably long to Billy's perception, he must reach plenty far along temporal lines.'

'You're jumping at conclusions. There's not enough data – '

'You heard me question this boy. You heard the answers. Look how the integrator figures 'em!' Pell jerked his thumb towards the screen. 'What about that list? I asked our patient what he – senses – in this room, and – '

The list was complete and inaccurate. It included present furnishings, equipment that hadn't been here for years, a diatherm that was scheduled to arrive next week, a centrifuge that had been on order for a month, and a great deal of material that wasn't expected at all, including some gadgets that probably weren't invented yet.

'*Now* doesn't mean much to Billy Van Ness,' Pell said. 'He's told us what he senses in this room in the past, present and future. Look at the word association conclusions. It all points to duration, and Ridgeley's tied up with it. I asked those questions with a purpose, Ben.'

DuBrose moistened his lips. 'Well, then – what?'

'My guess is that Ridgeley may have come from the future. Not from the incredibly distant future of the Duds, but from one closer to us.'

'Seth, for Pete's sake! There's nothing to prove – '

'No proof at all. I know. And the only proof I may ever be able to get will probably be empirical. But it's the only answer that fits all the terms.'

'You could pluck an answer out of the air for any problem,' DuBrose complained, 'if you ignore probabilities. You could say Ridgeley's a goblin who's found Aladdin's lamp!'

'I'm not saying anything definitely. This is a theoretical solution. Nothing more. Billy Van Ness has ETP. His duration comparisons indicate that Ridgeley doesn't compare with radium half-time but about equals iron. If the boy were a metallurgist I could earn more. I don't know what grade of iron he has in mind. But, roughly, the life expectancy of ordinary iron equals Ridgeley's duration, as Billy's ETP sees it.'

'How long does iron last?'

'Find out. Come in my office, will you?'

There Pell put in a televisor call, a request for information on Daniel Ridgeley. 'Now we'll wait and see. Sit down, Ben. What do you think?'

DuBrose dropped on cushions. 'I still think you're jumping at conclusions. There might be other explanations. Why jump at the wildest possibility?'

'Yet you didn't cavil at the idea that the Duds might come from the future.'

'That's different,' DuBrose said illogically. 'They don't *do* anything. What's Ridgeley trying to do? Upset the apple cart? Is he following Kalender's orders?'

'The Secretary of War is a brass hat, but he's no traitor. Ridgeley could be – probably is – acting on his own initiative. He may be in enemy pay. All along, Ben, I've been puzzled by one point: how the Falangists could have worked out this equation. *They're* not from the future. Their technology isn't much more advanced than ours, if at all. We live on this side of the world; the Falangists live on the other; but we're contemporaries. They're neither supermen nor are they from a super future. They're people like us. But Ridgeley – well, I think he's from the future, and he's butting into a fight that doesn't concern him. Or maybe it does, somehow. I don't know.' Pell grimaced. 'Well, I'm hungry. Let's order up some chow. We've been running around all night, and it's 3 a.m.' He spoke into the mike, after switching off the force-field that guarded his desk.

'As for the report we're going to hand in to the chief,' he said, fingering a fresh bundle of papers and spools before him, 'it's integrated and ready, I think. We've taken out the dangerous stuff. Quite a job.'

'About Ridgeley, Seth – '

'One thing at a time. I believe Ridgeley ties in with this equation business. He's been trying to give dangerous information directly to the chief. Well, we'll guard against that from now on. This latest message from the Secretary of War – seven more technicians have gone insane. Not Pastor; he's still working away up in his hideaway in the Rockies. But the danger is clearer now. The equation *must* be solved before the enemy solves it.'

'Every technician in the country may go crazy,' DuBrose said.

'Only top-flight men can work on a thing like this. The others aren't qualified. But those men are the ones who keep the war from being lost. They're the ones who think up offensives and defensives fast. If our best technicians are insane – and the list is growing – we're caught flat-footed if the enemy launches an assault. There's one thing in our favour. Those insane technicians can be cured.'

DuBrose thought it over. 'Uh . . . yeah, I get that angle. They took refuge in insanity because they couldn't solve the equation, and the responsibility was too much for them. Show them the solution to the equation, and they'll snap out of it. Right?'

'Near enough. None of these case histories' – he tapped the pile on the desk – 'indicate noncurable pathological states. Once we – ' He stopped, looking past DuBrose.

'Hello, Ridgeley,' he said.

DuBrose found himself on his feet, swinging to face the courier. Ridgeley was standing against the closed door, his eyes blazing, his face impassive as ever. In a lifted hand he held something so bright and glittering that DuBrose could not see it clearly.

'It's too easy,' Ridgeley said.

'And you prefer it the hard way, is that it? I don't think you'll find it so easy.'

'No?'

'How did you check up on us? Some sort of scanning ray?'

'Something of the sort,' Ridgeley admitted. The thing in his hand trembled slightly; dazzling rays momentarily blinded DuBrose.

Pell said, 'So we're right. You're from the future.'

'Yes.'

DuBrose snarled, 'Why don't you go back there?'

For the first time he saw expression on those blunt features – something very much like fear. But Ridgeley only said, 'No, I like it here. I'd rather no one knew as much about me as you two know. So – '

DuBrose glanced towards Pell, waiting for a signal. But the aide hadn't even risen from his seat. He smiled at the courier and said, 'You turned off your scanner too soon. I've put in a routine check query on the visor. Querying you, Ridgeley. If we're found dead, or disappear, somebody will start wondering why the last time I used the visor, I asked about you.'

'You wouldn't be found,' Ridgeley said, but his voice wasn't quite as certain. He hesitated.

Tension grew in the room. Suddenly that burning, joyous excitement leaped again behind the courier's eyes.

'All right,' he said. 'We'll do it the hard way.' He fumbled behind him, opened the door, and slipped out. DuBrose sprang forward, but Pell's quiet voice halted him.

'Hold it, Ben. No heroics. You haven't even got a gun.'

DuBrose made an impatient noise. 'Well, let's do something! Can't we have that . . . that guy picked up? Or – '

'I'll think about it,' Pell chuckled. 'Take it easy. You're flying off the handle. Here.' He tossed a blue plastic key on the desk. 'Why not knock off for a few hours?'

'I . . . what is it?' DuBrose picked up the key and examined it.

Pell said, 'Not many people have those, Ben. They open the door to supercharged hedonism. Show that key at Blue Heaven in Low Manhattan, and you'll get the most thorough dose of extroversion you can imagine. Useful when hypertension creeps up. Try their Creepies – it's a catharsis. Go on, get out of here. That's an order. You need something like – a blue key.'

DuBrose said, 'What about you? If Ridgeley comes back – '

'He won't. Go away. I'll expect you back in the morning, bright-eyed and ready for anything. *Outside*!'

DuBrose went away.

6

Across the curve of the world dawn came, rose and grey, the laggard sun behind. The cool light brightened on a quiet land. Tiny hamlets speckled the continent, and only a few flaming streaks that might have been meteors gave any hint that the peace was deceptive. Even across the grey scars of the cities, New York and Detroit and San Fransisco, the reclaiming green crept out from the wilderness that had been the city parks.

Helicopters with their glider-trains troubled still air. The rising sun glittered here and there on a few silvery, tattered shells, the monuments of genus X. Warmen began to drift towards the pneumocar terminals.

Before dawn –

Three more technicians had gone insane, two of them irreplaceable key men in electronics.

Midmorning. Pell came into DuBrose's office, smiling and cheerful.

'Use that key?'

'Uh . . . no,' DuBrose said. 'I was dead beat. I took Deep Sleep. Feel better now.'

'Suit yourself,' Pell said, shrugging. 'I got that report on Ridgeley. He's a highly confidential and trustworthy Secret Service man. Not just a courier. He's been responsible for several fast deals but benefitted our side. He's been on the job for seven years. Every once in a while he disappears. No reason given. Unorthodox, but – he's valuable.'

'To whom?' DuBrose asked. 'The enemy?'

Pell looked puzzled. 'He's been valuable to us, Ben. That's what throws me. He dug up plans for some gadgets we found mighty useful. There's never been any question as to his loyalty.'

'Do anything about it?'

'Not . . . yet,' Pell said slowly. 'Except to put a few papers in my safe, just in case. The chief has the combination. Remember that.'

DuBrose turned the subject. 'How is the chief?'

'Jumpy. Nervous. I don't know why. I handed him the stuff on the equation a couple of hours ago – along with allied problems I dug up, to keep him from smelling a rat. I've handled it as semitheoretical material. I couldn't tell him how urgent it was – if he knew that, he'd realize its significance. But I loaded the other items with key words he'll subconsciously shy away from – the wrong emotional indexes for his personality. He'll study the equation dope first.'

'Won't he wonder about Ridgeley?'

'I blamed that on the brass hats. I said Ridgeley was just trying to do his duty – deliver his message to the Director of Psychometrics. Dunno if the chief swallowed it, but I gave him something else to think about – a few hints he'll chew on. Just in case he starts wondering too much why I wanted to isolate him and act as filter. I fixed it. Pretty soon he'll decide the enemy are trying to kill him. Simple assassination attempt. Toxin probably. Let him figure it out. A personal menace like that won't worry him in the least.'

'Oh. Well – I've got nothing new. Billy Van Ness is completely passive now. Force-feeding, as usual. And I took a call from Dr Pastor, up in the Rockies. He says he'll have the equation solved before the day's over.'

'Good. How did he look?'

'Not too well. I notified Wyoming Emergency to stand ready. Though there wasn't any definite symptom. He talked a little too fast – but nothing psychopathic. The responsibility didn't seem to bother him.'

'Fair enough,' Pell said. 'Now come along. The chief wants to see me about the equation – '

'Already?'

'He's a fast worker.'

Cameron sat behind his desk and watched it rain. He thought that if he could get through the door, the rain might stop; but he wasn't having any. He'd tried it already. Wading through knee-deep invisible water wasn't a pleasant experience.

The slanting veils of rain made the walls grey and shadowy. He felt the drops tap softly on his bare head and against his face and on his hands. With tremendous effort he remained motionless. Within his skin he was twisting and writhing.

There was, he thought, a gauge in his head, and a needle that had risen dangerously close to the red mark. He couldn't stand much more of this. What was keeping Pell?

As the door opened the rain stopped. Cameron looked at the backs of his hands; they were quite dry. So was the surface of his desk, and the carpet.

His head pounded.

He was rather sorry Pell and DuBrose had come in. That meant he had to do something. As long as he remained perfectly motionless, trying not to think, he could not easily be betrayed. Rain might fall, but the objects he reached for wouldn't slide away or collapse into blobs as long as he refrained from reaching.

Cameron drew in a long breath.

His voice came out more steadily than he had expected.

'Ben?'

'I wanted him to hear this,' Pell said. 'Got an answer for me?'

Cameron said carefully, 'I think so. You didn't give me all the necessary factors, but there may be a way. What's this for?'

'I'd rather not say just yet. It's semitheoretical anyhow.' Pell sat down; DuBrose followed his example.

'I'd say it's completely theoretical. Look here. You've got an equation based on constants gone variable. You want to know its probable effect on various types of trained personalities – scientifically trained. And you stipulate that the solution of the equation is a high-powered survival factor – the individuals *must* solve it. Is that correct, Seth?'

Pell nodded and crossed his legs, his eyes half-closed.

'Correct,' he said casually. 'What do you think?'

'You left out one point. If the technicians fail to solve the problem, they'll go insane, under the circumstances.'

'Mm-m. That's obvious, chief.'

Cameron looked at something on his desk, hesitated, and seemed to lose the threat. 'So . . . uh, well, the sort of equation you presuppose implies the use of truth itself as a variable. Or rather several sets of truths – all logical and accurate. Under certain conditions, let's say, an apple falls to the ground; under other conditions, it flies upward. In the first case the familiar law of gravitation holds good. In the second, it doesn't; an arbitrary basic is substituted, but a true one.'

'Can mutually contradictory truths coexist?' Pell asked.

'It isn't likely,' Cameron said. 'I'd say no. However, let's take it for granted that such an equation does exist – for the sake of the theory. The ordinary technician, trained to intricate work, has had a sound groundwork in basic physics; he takes some things for granted. Like the law of gravitation. Or – conduction of heat. If he dips both hands in boiling water and his right hand is burned while his left freezes, he won't be able to understand it. If enough things like that happen – ' Cameron paused.

Pell said, 'Yeah?'

'Oh . . . he'll find refuge in insanity. His imagination, his mind, won't be sufficiently elastic to embrace a whole new set of variable truths. It would be like going through the looking glass. Alice did it without trouble, but she was a child. An adult would have gone insane.'

'Every type of adult mind?'

Cameron said thoughtfully, 'Lewis Carroll could have solved this hypothetical equation of yours, Seth. Yes, I'm sure of it.'

Pell nodded. 'A thoroughly elastic mind, one that isn't bound too much by familiar values, the sort of guy who invents woolly dog stories. Is that it?'

'A man who makes up rules of his own. That's it, all right.'

'I want to find some men like that and chart their psychology,' Pell said. 'Got any suggestions?'

'Offhand, no. The average scientifically trained mind is inelastic by definition; it's fan-shaped. It's imaginative at the wide part of the fan, but it's rigidly censored by the narrow part – the accepted basics. I'll see if I can think of a screening process for you, Seth.'

'All right,' Pell said, rising.

Back in DuBrose's office, the two looked at each other blankly. Pell chuckled.

'So far, so good, at least. Find a man like Lewis Carroll. Can you think of a candidate?'

'Not without a screening process. Are there any mathematicians today who write fairy tales?'

'Not a one. And there aren't any fairy tale writers who make math their avocation. Not that Alice is a fairy tale, Ben.'

'What is it? Allegory?'

'Symbolic logic, beautifully worked out from arbitrarily assigned basics. Pure fantasy – the purest kind. Well, we'll have to try screenings. Maybe the chief will think of something. Meanwhile, screen technicians by avocation; use the big files downstairs. I'll try for psychological patterns that might fit.'

'O.K.,' DuBrose said.

Twenty minutes later he was at the dictograph when the visor hummed. The wrinkled, gnomish face of Dr Emil Pastor checkered in.

DuBrose pushed a button that would summon Pell as he jumped up. 'Dr Pastor. Glad you called. Anything new?'

The tousled head nodded. Something flickered in the blue background; it looked like a bird. Blue background? What –

'I have finished with it,' Pastor said. 'Understanding it showed me the unreality of all things.'

'You solved it, then?'

'Solved the . . . equation? Not all of it, no. But enough. Enough to show me the way. I can solve the rest now, if I wish. Ah, Mr Pell.'

'Hello, doctor,' Pell said, stepping into the scanner's range. 'I asked Mr DuBrose to call me when you vised. Thanks, Ben. Now have I missed anything?'

'Dr Pastor says he can solve the equation,' DuBrose said.

'But I won't,' Pastor said, blinking.

Pell didn't show surprise. 'Mind telling us why not?'

'Because nothing matters any more,' Pastor explained. 'I've found that out. It settled *my* problem. Everything is hollow, like a soap bubble. Maintained in existence simply by a certain coherence of will, the acceptance of the expected.'

Insane.

DuBrose saw Pell's shoulders slump a little.

'I'd like to discuss that with you personally' he said. 'May I fly in to your hideout? If you'll shut off the forcefield when I – '

'Oh, it's gone,' Pastor said mildly. 'I stopped believing in it and it disappeared. My house is gone, too – most of it. I let the televisor stand and part of the wall, because I'd promised to call you. But now . . . I don't know. What would we have to talk about?'

'The equation?' Pell suggested. A shadow crossed Pastor's face.

'No, I don't want to discuss that.'

DuBrose saw Pell's hand move. He said, 'Excuse me,' and slipped quickly out of the office. It took him three minutes to vise Wyoming Emergency and have an ambulance copter dispatched to the peak where Pastor was now.

DuBrose went back into his office, and moved up behind Pell. Pastor was still talking.

' . . . couldn't explain the theory to you very well. It deals with certain variables I'm sure you wouldn't accept. But they're surprisingly effective in practice. I simply used will power on my house and it was gone.'

'And that's an integral part of the equation?'

'Oh, yes.'

'I don't see.'

'Like this,' Pastor said. His wrinkled face twisted into an agony of concentration. He lifted his hand and pointed. DuBrose felt a sudden tension knot along his spine.

'You don't exist,' Pastor said to Pell.

Seth Pell vanished.

In his office Cameron was about to eat lunch. The laden tray was on the desk before him. He dipped the soup spoon into onion broth and lifted it towards his mouth.

The edges of the spoon thickened, curled, spread into cold metallic lips.

And kissed him.

7

The office had not changed. That seemed a minor miracle, somehow. The desk might have sprouted wings, the televisor could have scampered off on its bulky plastic base, and the White Queen should have jumped into the soup tureen. But the office was the same. The familiar logic. Emil Pastor's gnomish face blinked at DuBrose from the visor screen, and beyond it Pell's door stood half open.

'Like that,' Pastor said quietly. 'That's how I do it, Mr DuBrose.'

Psychosis unclassified – but a tentative prognosis was possible. The impossible part of it was that Pastor's psychosis was founded on paradox. He was insane and believed he could make things stop existing by applying will power.

He could do it, too. Seth Pell had – blinked out.

DuBrose didn't want to move. The numbness of shock held him. But slowly his mind began to work again, and to see the danger. If someone came into the office now – the director, or anyone at all – Pastor's precarious balance might be upset. The man was responsible, and he held a bomb that could blow up – All creation?

Habit takes over when the planning faculty is paralyzed. Dimly

DuBrose sensed that there were a dozen things to be done, but first of all it would be necessary to pacify Pastor. Though it had been years since his internship in Psychometric Base and the sanatoriums, old habits came to his aid. He knew he was facing a patient.

Deliberately DuBrose let his mind go blank. He studied Pastor's face. Visible symptoms? Case history? That eyrie lab in the Rockies, with its clutter of ill-assorted furniture, the nonconventional colour 'stories' on the Fairyland projector, the very fact that Pastor had settled on this particular wild talent of controlled obliteration out of the variety of powers the equation apparently could bestow – adding up to what? There was a key to the man's personality somewhere, a familiarity he had not sensed until now.

Sentiment. That picture of Pastor's wife and children – an emotional appeal?

Essential amorality, lack of empathy, tremendous egotism, that could enable Pastor to wipe a man out of existence with utter casualness. As a child destroys a toy.

A child is to a toy as Dr Emil Pastor is to mankind –

That was it. The subconscious motive. The murderous quintessence of rationalization. A madman will believe himself to be Christ, wound himself with the stigmata, and thereafter sincerely believe that the scars have appeared spontaneously and miraculously. Corroborative evidence. But Pastor's mind had worked more clearly. First he had chosen and acquired the power that would prove the reality of his rôle; as yet he might not even have realized consciously that he was God.

The ultimate paranoid egotism. Perfectly rationalized insanity!

Pastor said, 'Didn't you see what I did? You weren't watching – '

DuBrose was rather surprised that he spoke instead of screaming. 'Oh, I saw it. It surprised me, that was all. My reaction was pretty complicated. There's an instinctive attempt at rationalization.' He was choosing carefully the words with useful emotional indexes.

Pastor looked surprised. 'But rationalization with what? You can't do it. Only I can. You can't possibly perceive that everything's hollow as a soap-bubble. You instinctively accept the expected. I'm able to do this because I'm sceptical.'

'That's true, I guess,' DuBrose said. Too facile agreement would strike the wrong note; but provoking an argument would be dangerous, because the physicist could so convincingly demonstrate the truth of his argument. 'Anyway,' he went on, 'I'm glad you remembered to vise me. You've an almost miraculous power. Or – is it miraculous?'

Pastor smiled. 'I don't know. I'm still surprised. I don't really know the extent of my power.'

'It's a responsibility, I can see.'

The physicist didn't quite like that. He scowled a little. DuBrose went on quickly, 'I'm not presuming to inquire about your plans – ' He had almost used the word *advise*. But he had suddenly found a key to Pastor's personality; there was a parallel of sorts in history – an isolated mountain retreat, cluttered with disorganized and tasteless furniture – a magpie's nest – and a man who studied occultism instead of composing unorthodox colour-treatments. Dr Emil Pastor had much in common with the German Hitler.

Pastor said doubtfully, 'My plans? I don't want – ' He hesitated.

'I'm extremely interested,' DuBrose said. 'You can do miraculous things, Dr Pastor. But you know much more about the possibilities than I do. You remember you showed me one of your Fairyland compositions?'

'Yes,' Pastor said. 'You didn't pay much attention, though.'

'I wanted to see more, but I knew you were busy. I did see enough to realize what sort of creative mind you must have. And now you'll be able to compose on an indefinitely larger scale.'

Pastor nodded. 'I've just been destroying some things so far. Do you think that was wrong? I don't know if I can *create* –'

'Right and wrong are arbitrary values. They can be transcended.' Dangerous words, but necessary. DuBrose was trying to work on Pastor's subconscious, which knew it was God, even though the conscious mind had not yet felt the impact of that delusion. 'As I said, I'm very glad you vised me. I appreciate it. And, while I don't know what you intend, I'm sure it will be – remarkable. I'll be expecting an extraordinary composition.'

Pastor said helplessly, 'But I haven't made any plans yet.'

'The power is still new to you. You'll need to learn how to handle it to the best effect, I suppose – is that right? Even if you make a few mistakes through being hasty, it won't matter – right and wrong are arbitrary. But I would like to see what you'll do. Would that be possible?'

The flood of words had disconcerted Pastor. 'You're seeing me now.'

'The visor screen's limited. Would you let me come to your lab by copter? Don't forget,' DuBrose said, 'you can do exactly as you want. Nobody can stop you now. Forget my ideas if you don't like any of them. I can't help being enthusiastic. Sometimes I talk before I think. I've often jumped the gun and regretted it. If I were smart, I'd plan my moves in advance. But – ' he shrugged.

'Planning's wise,' Pastor said. 'Yes, it is! I want to think.' The screen suddenly went blank.

DuBrose took a few steps and caught the edge of his desk. His whole body began to shake uncontrollably.

He got that under control and vised Wyoming Emergency again. The same medic in charge came on.

'Has that ambulance copter gone out for Pastor yet?'

'Hello, Mr DuBrose. Yes, we sent it out stat. You said emergency.'

'Recall it. Double emergency. Don't let your men get near Pastor.'

'But if he's psychotic – is he a violent case?'

'He's homicidal en masse,' DuBrose said grimly. 'But as long as he's sitting on top of the Rocky Mountains, it's OK. I hope. I don't want him disturbed. *He mustn't be disturbed*. Recall that copter!'

'Right. I'll call you back.'

DuBrose said, 'Yeah,' broke the connection, and put in a call to the Secretary of War. When Kalender's heavy, hard face appeared on the screen, DuBrose was ready.

'I need help,' he said. 'You're the only man who can authorize this, Mr Secretary. It's extralegal. But it's absolutely vital.'

'You're Ben DuBrose,' Kalender said. 'Well? What is it?'

'Dr Pastor – '

'Has he solved the equation?'

'He's gone insane,' DuBrose said. Kalender grimaced.

'Like the others. Well – '

'Worse than the others. You remember that sanatorium case – M-204? The one who could nullify gravity. Pastor's got hold of a power a lot more dangerous.'

Kalender's harsh face changed. Brass hat though he was, he was competent in his job.

'How dangerous? Where is he?'

'His Rocky Mountain lab. I just talked to him on the visor. I think he'll stay put for a little while anyhow, making plans. And he's expecting me. A copter can rocket down and blast him before he has time to retaliate.'

'Retaliate how?'

'By making the copter disappear,' DuBrose said carefully. 'By making the Rocky Mountains disappear or by making the whole world disappear.'

Kalender's lips parted. His eyes tightened.

DuBrose said, 'I'm not insane. I haven't been working on the equation myself. Pastor showed me proof, that's all. Put a scanning ray on him, but be careful he doesn't detect it. He's destroyed most of his lab already.'

'That's fantastic,' the Secreatary of War said.

The visor hummed. DuBrose twisted a dial, saw a cameo face blink into view at one corner of the screen, and instantly snapped it blank again. He nodded at Kalender.

'Pastor. Calling me back. Oversee this.'

Kalender's face faded as Pastor's gnomish features checkered into a recognizable pattern. 'Mr DuBrose?'

'You just caught me. I was about to leave – '

'Don't come. I've changed my mind.'

'What?'

'I thought it over,' Pastor said slowly, 'and I saw the possibilities. I hadn't quite realized before. I was intoxicated. At first. But when I sat down and tried to make plans, I realized what having this power means. I'm not going to use it. I'm not meant to use it.'

DuBrose said, 'You've decided that?'

'Don't you agree?'

'I can see you must have your reasons. May I hear them?'

'I think this may be – a test of humility. I know I have the power. That's enough. I know all things are hollow. That's enough too. On this mountain I have been shown the kingdoms and powers of the world. I have been tempted. But I'll never use the power again.'

'What do you intend to do?'

'Think,' Pastor said. 'Thoughts are the only real things in a hollow world. Gautama knew that. I'm wiping out my past. I was too much concerned with the hollow things . . . technology – ' He smiled slowly. 'So I won't need to use my power. It was given to me as a test. And I survived that test. I know that meditation is more important than anything else.'

DuBrose said, 'You're wise, I think. I agree with you.'

'You can see why I mustn't use the power again.'

'Yes,' DuBrose said, 'you're right. And it's symbolic that you destroyed your laboratory. It was the symbol of your past, and I believe you were meant to destroy just that much.'

'Do you think so? Yes, I suppose . . . yes. My past has vanished. I can go forth without chains to a new life of meditation.'

'Did you destroy all the past?'

Pastor brought his eyes into focus. 'All my – what?'

'The laboratory. If you leave one part of your past still alive, it'll be a bond, won't it? And the lab is the symbol.'

Pastor said, 'One wall still stands.'

'Should it stand?'

'But I swore never to use the power again. It won't matter.'

'The symbol represents the truth,' DuBrose said. 'It will matter. You must start fresh. A single bond now – '

'I won't use the power again!'

'You haven't completed your task. The power was given to you so you could destroy the symbol of your past. Until you fulfill that command you won't be free. You won't be able to enter into your new life.'

Pastor's mouth twisted. 'I . . . must I? Do you believe . . . that was what was meant?'

'You know it was. The last symbol. Destroy it. *Destroy it*!'

'All right,' Pastor said. 'But it's the last time I'll ever use the power.'

DuBrose said, 'Push the visor away so I can see the wall go, will you? I want to be sure of your complete success.'

Pastor's face slid aside; there was a shifting panorama, and then the half-ruined wall of the laboratory stood against a cold grey sky. DuBrose said, 'Stand where I can see you. Now.'

'Well . . . but . . . DuBrose, must I – '

'You must.'

Pastor looked at the wall.

The wall vanished.

'Good,' DuBrose said. 'The last symbol is gone.'

Pastor's face was puzzled. 'No. I forgot – '

'What?'

'The visor. *That's* the last – '

The screen went blank.

Kalender's face came back. The Secretary of War was sweating.

'You're right. DuBrose. That man can't stay alive.'

'Then have him killed. But be careful. You'll have to catch him by surprise.'

'We'll manage.' Kalender hesitated. 'Why did you talk him into destroying that wall? Just to convince me?'

'Partly.'

'But he was determined not to use the power again – '

DuBrose said angrily, 'I had to be sure. He meant it then. But how long could he have held out? If I was able to talk him into using the power, the devils in his subconscious mind would eventually have done the same thing. If he had refused to destroy that wall, no matter how much I urged him, I might have figured it would be safe to let him live. Though even then – '

'He can destroy – anything?'

'Anything at all,' DuBrose agreed. 'Or everything. And since he's broken his word to himself once, he'll do it again. Kill him. Fast. Before he can get off that mountain.'

'I'll send a warplane from Denver,' Kalender said. 'I'd like . . . there's no time now, though. Goodbye.'

As his face faded, the medic at Wyoming Emergency called.

'I recalled the hospital copter, Mr DuBrose – '

'In time?'

'Yes. They'd gone only a few miles. But have you made other arrangements, or – '

DuBrose said, 'Other arrangements have been made, yes. Forget the affair. Goodbye.'

He clicked the visor off.

The room as empty and silent. The window ports showed the blue sky and sunny meadows of the hillside landscape miles above Low Chicago. Time slowed down and stopped.

Then he knew that Seth Pell was gone.

8

No one else must know. Seth's disappearance must be explained away, somehow, for a while. Because no hint of the real problem must reach Cameron; the director had to be shielded from realization of his responsibility, or he would go mad.

There was not even time for grief.

DuBrose went into Pell's office and stood silent, considering. The room's vacancy chilled him. An hour ago Seth had been sitting on that desk, swinging his heels and talking in his lazy, casual voice. Suppose DuBrose, not Pell, had been Pastor's victim? How would Seth have reacted?

With competence, anyhow.

DuBrose fumbled out a cigarette, stared at the desk, and tried to imagine Seth sitting there, white hair gleaming under the pale lights, youngish face faintly amused.

'How about it, Seth?'

'How about what?' Yes, that was it. Careless, casual, but –

'You know what. You're dead.'

'OK. So you're in charge. Take over, Ben.'

'But how? One man can't – '

'Oh, stop worrying. You'll do all right. It's only that sense of responsibility that can break you. You had one idea already. The chief mustn't know I'm dead.'

'He'll want to know – something!'

'Well, tell him something. Use your memory. Didn't I anticipate trouble?'

'Not this trouble. You did with Ridgeley.'

'So?'

'Yeah. You said you'd put some papers in your safe, just in case. And the chief's got the combination.'

'Smart boy. This is a good trick, you know. You're so used to kicking ideas around with me that it's hard for you to think on your own. OK. Imagine me any time you want. Put words in my mouth. It'll help a bit.'

It had helped. Seth wasn't sitting on the desk. He hadn't been sitting there. But, briefly, DuBrose had recreated Seth Pell as surely as Pastor had destroyed him.

DuBrose headed for the director's office. Cameron was at the window; he had slid aside the pane and was watching the shadowy, red-lit darkness of the Spaces. Thunder of the great machines came through the port. DuBrose saw that Cameron's luncheon hadn't been touched.

'What is it, Ben?'

'I'd like you to open Seth's safe.'

Cameron turned. His face was under iron control. 'Why? Where's Seth?'

DuBrose said carefully, 'I just got a message from him. He wants you to open his safe. That was all.'

Cameron hesitated, smoothed back his grey hair, and grimaced. Without a word he went past DuBrose into Pell's office. The safe was a dual-controlled, attuned to open only to the radiation pattern of Pell's brain or Cameron's.

The panel slid aside. A bulky envelope was propped up against a shelf. It was addressed to Cameron, who slit it open and took out a paper and another thick, sealed envelope.

The director's eyes moved swiftly across the letter. He handed it to DuBrose.

DuBrose read:

Bob,

I've been called away. Can't tell you details yet. Till I get back, let Ben take over. He knows the set-up. Give him full charge. If he isn't available, open this envelope yourself. See you later.

Seth.

Cameron held out the envelope. 'Here it is. Now – what is all this funny business?'

DuBrose said, 'First of all, you are going to do what Seth wants?'

'Yes. He knows what he's doing.'

'He gave me my orders.'

Cameron smiled. 'I'm in danger of being assassinated? Is that the answer?' Pell had led the chief to think that, DuBrose knew, to keep him from guessing the truth. As a red herring, it might prove useful.

'It might be the answer. Or it might not.'

'I'm not a child, Ben.'

'Chief, I'm just following Seth's orders.'

'All right,' Cameron said abruptly. 'Go ahead and follow them. Let me know any time you want my resignation.' He took a folder out of the safe and said, 'I'd meant to ask for this back. That new propaganda line . . . it may need some work.'

Harmless stuff. DuBrose knew what it was. He watched Cameron's broad back out of the room.

The director had forgotten to close Pell's safe. DuBrose shut the panel himself, frowning speculatively. The action wasn't at all like Cameron. He was meticulous about details. And he was a hearty eater.

Yet he hadn't touched the luncheon tray.

Had Cameron learned the truth, somehow, after all? Was an anxiety neurosis beginning to work?

Symptoms: absent-mindedness, loss of appetite –

Cameron glanced at the papers outlining the new indoctrination lines, but he couldn't focus on them. His mind wasn't under its usual tight control. He was conscious of the luncheon tray on the desk, and the soup spoon that had behaved so – abnormally.

Automatically he scrubbed the back of his hand across his mouth.

There was a pattern to all these things. All these hallucinations.

They were aimed at making him feel insecure.

Aimed?

A directive purpose?

Persecution, then. Why dodge the word? A persecution mania. What would a psychiatrist say?

It was either hallucination or it wasn't. If it wasn't, it was persecution. Or –

It was difficult to think clearly when at any moment the floor might tilt unsteadily beneath your feet.

Impossible to work on the propaganda papers now. Cameron shuffled them back into their folder and went to his own wall safe. He opened it.

There was an egg in the safe.

Cameron knew he hadn't put it there.

It wasn't a real egg either, because, as he reached for it, it went away – somewhere.

Seth had written:

Ben,

Anything can happen now. Ridgeley's found out we know he's from the future, and he's plenty dangerous. I'm allowing for the possibility that I'll be killed and you'll survive. If we're both killed – well, you won't be reading this.

But play it this way. The equation's got to be solved, and the chief's probably the only one who can find somebody to solve it. Maybe Pastor will do the trick. Maybe he won't. He's got further than anyone else so far. Keep screening, and do your best for the chief.

And don't let this throw you. In a few million years, what will it matter? Luck, though!

Seth.

The other papers in the envelope were the equation itself and the research material Pell had gathered on it. None of it was new to DuBrose. He sat back and considered.

Seth was dead. (I'll mourn you later.)

Daniel Ridgeley was alive. DuBrose had almost forgotten the courier. At the moment, he could be discounted, though not permanently. The Secretary of War might help on that score. Ridgeley might be in the pay of the Falangists. Though why a man from the future would bother with temporal-local wars DuBrose could not imagine. Why did Ridgeley apparently feel *pleasure* when he faced enemies? It had been that, an odd, illogical delight that had flamed behind the courier's dark eyes when DuBrose had pulled a vibro-pistol on him, and when Pell had managed that business last night, when Ridgeley had been dissuaded from murder.

Billy Van Ness and his ETP – extra-temporal perception; could Billy, in his few lucid moments, help? How? By locating Ridgeley? Finding the courier wouldn't be enough; DuBrose thought the key would be motivation. And that motive might lie thousands of years in the future, in the world from which Ridgeley had presumably come.

Well, then – the Duds? The monuments of that lost race from the inconceivably far future, now tattered, dissolved domes of impermeable force? Nothing there.

The equation.

Pell had proposed it to the chief as a casual theoretical problem. Who could solve a formula based on variable logic? And Cameron had named Lewis Carroll – a thoroughly elastic mind, one not bound by conventional values.

But no mathematicians existed today who wrote fairy tales of symbolic logic. DuBrose had already used the big files for a screening on technicians by a vocation. He hadn't found much. One mathematician seemed a possibility; he was a sculptor of mobiles, but he was also one of the men who had gone insane while studying the equation.

Pastor had gone further than most. DuBrose decided to attack the problem from a new angle. If he could pick out the factors that had made Pastor nearly successful in his attempt, there might be an answer there.

He made a psycho-chart, omitting the name, and noted a few questions. Cameron could probably get something out of this pattern. But DuBrose dared not take the chart in now. The director would certainly smell the concealed rat.

He shoved the chart among some other routine folders waiting Cameron's decision and sent them into the director's office. Now he could only wait – on that point anyway.

'What next, Seth?'

'I can't tell you anything except the words you put in my mouth. You know that. Remember me. Visualize me. Think what I might say.'

'I'm trying to.'

'Get drunk. Eat some Kix. Take Deep Sleep for a year. Use that blue key I gave you. Try some high-powered hedonism; it opens the right doors for that.'

'Escapism. I'd be trying to dodge responsibility.'

'Semantic trouble. Your responsibility's limited to keeping the chief on the beam. He's the guy who can keep the works from blowing up. But don't let him know that.'

'Maybe if I checked out over those screenings again – '

'Maybe.

DuBrose did that. He drew up some charts, ran off several lists, and studied them. Avocations: badminton, baseball, bowling. Cards – a whole sub-group. Oil painting, surrealistic, classic, tri-dimensional. Writing Creepies, the sensory 'movies' of the period. Chess, several varieties. Were there several varieties? What was fairy chess, anyhow? Rabbit raising. Hydrosphere exploration. Adagio dancing. Dipsomania.

DuBrose thought the dipsomaniac sounded like the best bet.

Then Kalender vised. He had bad news. The warplane sent to blast Dr Pastor had failed; Pastor couldn't be located.

DuBrose began to feel like a target aimed at by a dozen expert archers. 'I won't ask if you've done everything possible, Mr Secretary. You know the importance of this as well as I do.'

'We've put scanning rays on the whole area, and psycho-radar detectors, tuned to the frequency of the adult mind. No response.'

'Pastor's instruments didn't work on M-204. It's possible that Pastor's mind is running on a different frequency now.'

'Well – we've done infrared aerial pix, and picture-series to check on ground movement. Nothing but deer and a few pumas. There's a copter registered to Pastor. It can't be located. Did he have it on the mountain with him?'

'Maybe. He might have destroyed it. You've sent out an alarm?'

'A kill-on-sight priority alarm, Mr DuBrose. It's a general alert.'

'The first shot must be mortal, you know. If Pastor retaliates – '

'I've seen what he can do,' Kalender said, moving his mouth stiffly. 'What I want now is suggestions. Let me talk to the director.'

DuBrose said, 'I can't. I'm sorry. He gave orders, you know – '

'But this is emergency!'

'I know it. But it's equally vital that Mr Cameron be kept isolated from such things for a while.'

Kalender flushed darkly. After a moment he said, 'Then put on Seth Pell.'

'He's unavailable. I'm in charge in his absence.' DuBrose went on without waiting for an explosion. 'Pastor might head for his home. I think he's emotionally attached to his family. He may go there either to be with them, or to destroy them. They're symbols of his past, too. He promised not to use his powers again, but . . . I suggest spotting some logicians with your blasting crews, in case of trouble. Pastor's weakness seems to be metaphysics. A good logician might be able to argue him out of retaliating. Though the only safe way is to kill him on sight.'

'Mm-m – That makes sense. All right.'

'One more thing.' DuBrose had made his decision. 'Record this, please. Daniel Ridgeley's a spy.'

Kalender jerked back. 'What? I'm – '

DuBrose's back stopped crawling. 'Wait,' he said, letting out his breath. 'I had to get that recorded fast. I didn't know if Ridgeley might kill me before I could get the words out. But it's on the record now. If he murders me, you'll get on his trail.'

The Secretary of War said slowly, 'Mr DuBrose, what's the matter with your department? Are you having mass hallucinations in Psychometrics? Ridgeley has been invaluable to us – '

'Hallucinations? Is Pastor's power imaginary? What's so fantastic about Ridgeley's being a Falangist spy?'

'I – *know* Ridgeley. I trust him completely. You don't know what services he's rendered – '

'Will those services save us from the Falangist equation? Sure you trust him. That's what he was after. Remember those occasional periods when he drops out of sight? Do you know what he does during those times?'

'Of course . . . eh?'

'Remember this,' DuBrose said. 'Ridgeley is a lot more dangerous than Pastor. I can't ask you to pick him up or have him killed. I don't think it would be possible. But I'd like you to stand ready. Locate Ridgeley; don't let him know he's spotted. Put a scanner on him and keep it there.'

Kalender rubbed his jaw. 'We can't take chances. So I'll do as you suggest. But – when can I talk to the director?'

'You'll be the first one to talk to him, as soon as it's safe. Right now he must be kept isolated. It's a security precaution. You know the effect the equation has on people – '

The Secretary was finally beginning to understand. 'There's been another suicide. An electronics man. And two more insanity cases. Not counting Dr Pastor.'

'The equation should be suppressed till we – '

'Impossible. It must be solved. You don't know your office will succeed. As long as there's a chance that someone may solve that – thing, we've got to take the chance.'

'Even if it drives every technician in the country crazy,' DuBrose said.

'I don't like it either. Keep in touch with me.'

That was all. DuBrose eyed the window port. Claustrophobia touched him chokingly. At any second, all this might dissolve –

Pastor was loose – somewhere. And until his brain was blasted into nothingness, there would be no safety for anything or anyone, anywhere.

He sent another batch of material in to Cameron and tried to conjure up the image of Seth, without too much success.

'What now?'

'How should I know?'

'I can't rush the chief – '

'Naturally. He mustn't suspect the importance of the equation.'

'What about Pastor?'

'Done everything you can?'

'I'm not equipped to find him. I've condemned him to death already. Isn't that enough?'

'What about Ridgeley?'

'Oh. Well, the more information I can get about that guy – '

Billy Van Ness had a private room in the infirmary. DuBrose went there to study the boy's chart and examine the patient. The excitement caused by Ridgeley's arrival last night had worn off. Van Ness was in a passive state, eyes closed, thin face relaxed.

ETP. Extra-temporal perception might prove valuable in dealing with a man from another time-sector. Pell has spoken of hypnosis, had tried it on the boy, with some success. DuBrose ordered gadgets brought in and used mechano-suggestion on Van Ness. When that failed, he had recourse to an injection.

'*K-k-k-kuk*!'

The harsh, unpleasant noise rasped out of the boy's throat. DuBrose remembered the palate deformation. Was this sound the equivalent of hard radiation emanations made audible – the probable method of communication used by that unknown race that had created the Duds?

He probed. This time it was easier to make Van Ness speak intelligibly. Pell had broken trail last night. But the temporal disorientation was still present. The mutant made no distinction between past, present and future. Some sort of temporal anchor was needed to pin down Van Ness' wildly oscillating perception. How strange the world must seem to this mutant who never used his eyes! He could see *duration* –

'– living and then backwards in long extension and stop . . . and again backwards, and again –'

Question.

'Shining. Bright domes. So long they reach to –'

Question.

'No word. There is none at the end. Or the bend, I mean. Where they doubled back. Came to look for –'

Question.

'There is no word. Back and back, searching.'

Question.

'Where are they now? . . . The end is now.'

DuBrose thought. Genus X, the race that had built the domes, that strange unimaginable people that had travelled back through time and left the shining, tattered Duds as their eidolons. He wondered. Searching for what?

For something necessary to their existence. And failing to find it. Back through time, in age-long leaps, back to this world that must have seemed so primevally alien to genus X. But the end is now.

'The man you saw last night, Billy –'

'*K-k-k-k-kuk*!'

Saw? Last night? To the mutant, the words were variables. DuBrose tried to frame his question more narrowly.

'The man. He reached in the right direction, remember?' Would it be memory or prescience to Van Ness' warped, expanded time-sense? 'He was longer than anyone else. Except the shining things. He was more complete –'

'Running, running . . . I saw him run. There was a fight.'

'A fight, Billy? What kind of a fight?'

'*K-k-k-kuk*! Too short to see – those big machines. Oh, big, big, but so short!' Immense machines of brief duration. What could they be?

'Noise. Sometimes. But sometimes silence, and a place where many lives were short – running, running, as they come . . . came . . . will come . . . *k-k-k-k-uk! K-K-K-K-KUK*!'

The first symptoms of convulsion began to appear. DuBrose hastily gave another injection and calmed the boy with deft hypnotic suggestion. The racking shudders died. Van Ness lay motionless, breathing shallowly, his eyes closed.

DuBrose went back to his office. He was in time to meet Cameron tossing some papers on the desk.

'I'm going home, Ben,' the director said, 'A bit of a headache. I couldn't do much with these problems. Managed a few. Where's Seth?' He watched DuBrose's face. 'Never mind. I – '

'Nothing's wrong, is there?'

'No,' Cameron said flatly. 'I'll see you later.' He went out, leaving DuBrose to wonder. Had Ridgeley got to the chief again?

Symptoms: headaches, nervousness, inability to concentrate –

DuBrose hurriedly leafed through the folders, looking for one in particular. He found it. But the dossier on Dr Emil Pastor had apparently not been touched. Maybe those other screening charts listing the avocations might –

Nothing there either. Or wait. Opposite one name there was a lightly pencilled check mark.

Eli Wood, Low Orleans, mathematician; home, 108 Louisiana B-4088; avocation, fairy chess –

9

None knew him. He was grateful; he felt deep humility because he could walk through the Ways of Low Denver and not be recognized for what he was. The Ways swept past, crowded with warmen, but no one watched the small, quiet figure strolling on the stationary central path. This was the second test, and probably a more difficult one than the first. Destroying the symbols of his past had been dangerously easy. The temptation had been there. Because he knew, now, that all things were hollow, he also knew how easy it would be to prick the world bubble.

For he could not die. His thought would live on. In the beginning was the Word, and in the end would be the Word, too.

He had wanted to go home, but this test must come first, and Low Denver had been the nearest cave city. His credentials had enabled him to enter. He had used those credentials just as though he were an ordinary man. And he would go on pretending that, in all humility. Only his thoughts, the thoughts of God, would blaze between the stars, the hollow stars, into the hollow universe that he could destroy –

That was the test. He must never use the power again. How often the other God must have been tempted to erase the universe He had made! But He had refrained, as Dr Emil Pastor must refrain.

He would still call himself Dr Emil Pastor. That was a part of the programme of humility. And he would never die. His body might, but his thought would not.

All these warmen on the Ways – how grateful they would be if they knew they continued to exist only by the loving-kindness of Dr Emil Pastor. Well, they would never know. Pride was a snare. He didn't want altars.

The firmament was an altar revealing the glory of Dr Emil Pastor.

An ant crawled out of a crevice and raced towards the Ways. Pastor chased it back to safety. *Even an ant* –

How long had he stayed here? Surely there had been time enough. He had passed *this* test of humility; nothing had tempted him to reveal himself to the warmen of Low Denver; he wanted to go home. He hoped his wife would not realize the change. She must always continue to believe that he was Emil-dear, as the children must never guess he was anyone else but Dad. He could play the role. And he felt a surge of tenderness towards them because he knew that they were hollow.

They could vanish – if he willed it.

So he must never will it. He would be a kindly god. He believed in the principle of self-determination. It was not his task to interfere.

Time enough had passed. He stepped on a Way and was borne towards one of the pneumocar stations. In the car, he clutched a strap – the acceleration always did odd things to his stomach – and leaned back, waiting for the brief blackout to pass.

It passed. Fifteen minutes later he stepped out at a Gateway. A group of uniformed men were standing waiting. At sight of him an almost imperceptible tension touched them. But they were well trained. Not a hand moved towards a pistol.

God walked towards them.

Cameron was dining with Nela. He watched her calm, friendly face and knew that there was no sanctuary even there. As he watched, the flesh might melt from her skull and –

Music murmured from an audio. Fresh pine-scent filled the room. Cameron picked up a spoon, dropped it again, and reached for a water goblet.

The water was warm and brackish. The shock to his taste buds was violent. But he managed to set the glass down without spilling more than a few drops.

'Jitters?' Nelas asked.

'Tired. That's all.'

'You were like this last night. You need a furlough, Bob.'

'Maybe I'll take one,' Cameron said. 'I don't know – '

He tried the water again. It was freezingly cold and very sour.

Abruptly he pushed back his chair. 'I'm going to lie down for a bit. It's all right. Don't get up. A bad headache is all.'

Nela knew how he hated fussing. 'Call me if you want,' she said, as Cameron went out. 'I'll be around.'

And then upstairs, in the bed that at first was pleasantly soft and relaxing, and then too soft, so that he kept sinking down and down into a feathery, pneumatic emptiness, with that nausea in his stomach that droppers always gave him –

He got up and walked around the room. He didn't look into the mirror. The last time he had done so, his image had made ripples in the glass.

He walked.

He was walking in circles. But presently he noticed that he was always facing the same spot, the same picture on the wall. He was on a turntable.

He stood motionless, and the room tilted. He found a chair, closed his eyes, and tried to shut out all sensory impressions.

Hallucination or reality.

If reality, then it was more dangerous. Were Seth and Ben DuBrose involved? Their hints about assassination were palpable red herrings. He might have believed them under other circumstances. But these *hallucinations* –

It was difficult to think clearly.

Perhaps that was the intention. Perhaps he wasn't intended to think clearly.

Half-formulated thoughts swam into focus. He had to pretend to believe that these – attacks – were purely subjective. He had to pretend that they were succeeding in their purpose –

But he knew that the psychic invasion was objective.

He knew that he was being persecuted. Others might not notice the things that had been happening to him. The persecutors were clever. They were determined to drive him mad – well, why? Because he possessed information of value? Because *he* was a valuable key man?

And that argument added up to one thing. Paranoia, with systematized delusions of persecution.

Cameron got up carefully. He winced. Once again it had happened. And, as usual, the unexpected.

He went downstairs, walking slowly and awkwardly, his face drawn and grey. Nela caught her breath at sight of him.

'Bob. What's wrong?'

'I'm flying to Low Manhattan,' he said through stiff lips. 'A doctor there I want to see – Fielding.'

She came swiftly towards him. Her arms slipped around his neck.

'Darling, I won't ask any questions.'

'Thanks, Nela,' Cameron said. He kissed her.

Then he went out to the copter, walking unsteadily and remembering the fairy tale of the little mermaid who exchanged her fish-tail for human legs. There had been a price exacted. Ever after that, the little mermaid walked on sharp knives, no less painful because they were imaginary.

Wincing at every step, Cameron walked towards the copter's hangar.

'I don't drink,' the mathematician said, 'but I've some brandy I keep for guests. Or do you prefer Pix? I've got some somewhere. I don't use them either, but – '

'Never mind,' DuBrose said. 'I just want to talk, Mr Wood.' He laid the portfolio across his knees and stared. Wood sat rather uneasily in a plain relaxer chair, a tall, thin man with old-fashioned noncontact spectacles and a thatch of neatly-combed, mousy hair. The room was meticulously, fussily clean, an odd contrast to Pastor's cluttered, garish eyrie lab.

'Is it war work, Mr DuBrose? I'm already working in Low Orleans – '

'Yes, I know. I've investigated. Your record shows you're extremely capable.'

'Why – thanks,' Wood said. 'I . . . thanks.'

'This will be confidential. We're alone here?'

'I'm a bachelor. Yes, we're alone. I gather you're from Psychometrics, though. That's rather out of my line.'

'We have our fingers in a lot of pies.' Watching the man, DuBrose found it difficult to believe how many degrees Wood held and how many papers had been published under his name – some of them advancing remarkable theories of pure mathematics. 'Here it is. You're interested in fairy chess, aren't you?'

Wood stared. 'Yes. Yes, I am. But – '

'I've got a reason for asking you. I'm not a chess player. Can you give me some idea of what fairy chess is?'

'Why . . . certainly. You understand this is merely a hobby of mine.' DuBrose thought Wood blushed slightly as he reached for a pile of chessboards and laid them out on a table. 'I don't quite know what you want, Mr DuBrose – '

'I want to know what fairy chess is. That about covers it.'

Some of Wood's shyness was dissipated. 'It's a variation of ordinary chess, that's all. About 1930 a number of players got interested in the possibilities offered. They felt there wasn't enough scope in orthodox chess, with its variation of problems – two-man moves and so on. So fairy chess was created.'

'And – ?'

'Here's a regulation board – eight squares by eight. Here are orthodox chessmen, king, queen, knight, bishop, castle, pawn. Knight moves two squares in one direction and one at right angles, or one and two. Castle in straight lines, bishop – diagonally in any direction on a single colour. The idea, of course, is to checkmate. There've been a great many variations, but some themes are simply impossible on the regulation board, especially certain geometrical themes.'

'You use a different board?'

'In fairy chess, you may have men of different powers and boards of different types. Modified space compositions – here's one.' He showed DuBrose an oblong board, eight squares by four. 'Here's another, nine by five; here's a larger one, sixteen by sixteen. And here are fairy chessmen.' DuBrose stared at unfamiliar pieces. 'The grasshopper. The nightrider – though that's merely an extension of knight's move. Here's the blocker, which can block but never capture. Here's an imitator.'

'What does that do?'

'When any man moves, the imitator must move for the same number of squares in a parallel direction. It's rather difficult to explain unless you're familiar with chess principles, I'm afraid.'

'Well – I gather it's chess, with a new set of rules.'

'Variable rules,' Wood said. DuBrose leaned forward sharply. 'You may invent your own men and assign them arbitrary powers. You may design your own boards. And you can have rule games.'

'Meaning?'

'Here's one.' Wood set up a few pieces. 'Let's say, on this, that black never plays a longer move than his previous move. A one-rule game.'

DuBrose studied the board. 'Wait a moment. Doesn't that presuppose a certain arrangement of men?'

Wood smiled, pleased. 'You might make a good player. Yes, you'd automatically have to assume that black's longest move is always available to begin with. Here's another. Black helps white mate in two moves. Oh, there are plenty of problems, the castling mutation, the camel-hopper, the actuated revolving centre, checkless chess, the cylinder board – the variations are endless. You can have irreal men. The possibilities are endless.'

'Assigning these arbitrary values – wouldn't that bother a man who'd been trained with orthodox chess?'

'There's been a minor war since 1930,' Wood said. 'The orthodox players, some of them, call fairy a bastard and unacceptable form. Still, we have enough fairy chess players to hold tournaments once in a while.'

A thoroughly elastic mind . . . one that isn't bound too much by familiar values . . . a man who makes up rules of his own.

Jackpot!

But DuBrose kept his fingers crossed as he opened the portfolio.

Three hours later Eli Wood pushed his spectacles up on his forehead and laid down a curve-stemmed pipe. 'It's fascinating,' he said. 'Most extraordinary thing I've ever encountered.'

'But it's possible? You can accept – '

'I've been accepting ridiculous things all my life,' Wood said. 'I've seen some peculiar things.' He didn't elucidate. 'So your equation is founded on the variability of truths.'

'It's far over my head. But – several sets of truth.'

'Certainly. Several sets.' Wood searched for his spectacles, found them, and pulled them down into place. He blinked at DuBrose through the lenses. 'If mutually contradictory truths exist, that proves they're not contradictory – unless,' he added mildly, 'they are, of course. That's possible, too. It's simply fairy chess, applied to the macrocosm.'

'If I remember right, part of the equation says that a free-falling body accelerates at the rate of five hundred feet a second. Later on the body is accelerating at nine inches a second.'

'Black never plays a longer move than his previous move.

Remember? That's the rule in this part of the equation, I'd say.'

'Presupposing a certain arrangement of men.'

'Which would be the constant factor. I don't know what it is; this will take a great deal of study.'

'You can nullify gravity, then – '

'Some themes are impossible on a regulation board. Set up the equivalent of a board in which the rule is – no gravity – and you've got it.'

A macrocosmic board, one of the conditions of which is that the earth doesn't revolve. Within the limits of that board *–it doesn't*. Nevertheless it doesn't move. Galileo was wrong.

'Can you solve this equation?'

'I can try. It'll be a fascinating problem.'

There was more to discuss, but finally DuBrose was satisfied. He left, having secured Wood's promise to consider the problem top priority. At the door DuBrose, troubled by doubt, turned.

'You're not – bothered – by the idea of variable truths?'

'My dear man,' the mathematician said mildly. 'In *this* world?' He chuckled, bowed, and let the door panel slide shut.

DuBrose went back to Low Chicago.

10

Two visor calls were waiting. DuBrose turned on the playback attachment. The Secretary of War should have come first, but he listened to Nela Cameron instead.

'Ben. I tried to get Seth, but he's out. I'm worried about Bob. He's gone to New York to see a Dr Fielding. He's . . . I don't know. It's probably something at the office. Call me if there's anything I should know, will you? That's all.'

Dr Fielding. DuBrose knew him; a psychiatrist. Mm-m.

The Secretary of War said that there had been an inexcusable mistake. Dr Emil Pastor had been located leaving Low Denver. He had been wounded – but not killed.

Result: that whole group of intercepter guards had disappeared.

There was no trace of Pastor. He couldn't get far. Kalender had ordered double precautions. Pastor must be killed on sight without mercy.

Any suggestions?

DuBrose could think of none. Kalender had muffed the job. Anything could happen now.

He left messages and headed for Low Manhattan. No use calling Dr Fielding. It might be better if Cameron had left before DuBrose arrived. That way, DuBrose might get some valuable information from the psychiatrist.

Very definitely, something was wrong with the chief.

Flying southeast, DuBrose thought of Eli Wood. Could the mathematician solve the equation? A man trained to the variables of fairy chess – well, the very fact that Wood had taken up fairy chess showed the elasticity of his mind. DuBrose remembered that Pastor had composed unorthodox stories of his own on the Fairyland gadgets. Why hadn't the War Office given Wood the equation already?

The answer was obvious. Only the top-flight men had been selected to solve the equation. Wood was competent enough, but his record lacked the brilliance necessary to impress the brass hats. And he didn't, after all, have one of the Bib Jobs.

Would the mathematician go mad, like the others?

No use putting all the eggs in one basket. There might be other technicians who played fairy chess – or the equivalent.

The copter roared towards the nearest Gateway to Low Manhattan. DuBrose tried to visualize Seth.

'Something's wrong with the chief.'

'Has he got wind of what's going on, Ben?'

'I don't know. I wish you weren't dead. If I could only be sure what's the best thing to do – '

'You've got Eli Wood on the job. That's something. As for the chief, he may be the Civilian Director of Psychonamics, but he's got a colloid in his head. You're a psychotechnician. Get busy.'

'I'll try. But I'm walking six tightropes at once – '

Only one God has ever died . . .
Only one God has let his side . . .
Be wounded by a soldier's spear!

What was that? Some old poet; he couldn't remember the name.

Trying to kill me! Trying to kill their God!

He had acted instinctively. Self-preservation was almost a taxis.

Coincidentally with the burning agony in his shoulder, he had used the power. They had vanished.

Now his left arm hung withered and useless. The pain throbbed in dizzying rhythms through his head and body. He kept walking. The stars glared, coldly and unapproachably, but he could quench them if he wanted. He could turn that blazing vault black for ever and ever.

Dr Emil Pastor. Dr Emil Pastor. Emil-dear. A name, a word, a spot of cool, friendly light in the raging turmoil –

But what was Dr Emil Pastor? What was Emil-dear?

If he could find his way to that spot of light –

Where was it? There was only the dark here, and night winds, and grass that rustled under his feet. A tree loomed up before him. He destroyed it without thinking. Realization came back then. There was some reason why he mustn't use the power.

Good intentions. The other God had had good intentions, too. But they had tortured him, hated him . . . What about the Deluge?

Emil-dear. That meant something. It meant peace and safety, words he had almost forgotten. He didn't want to be God, really. He hated being God. If he could get to the place where he had left Dr Emil Pastor, he could slip out of that incarnation and find rest once more. But he didn't know where it was.

Colorado. He was somewhere in Colorado. But that told him nothing. Without transportation or communication, he was lost, even He.

The woman –

He was going to her. To find the Dr Emil Pastor he had left with her. She could help him. He was going to her.

Nothing was going to stop him!

DuBrose met the Director of Psychometrics outside Dr Fielding's office. Cameron's face was haggard, his grey hair rumpled, and his eyes had lost their steadiness. A nerve jumped in his cheek.

He said, 'What do you want?'

'We got trouble,' DuBrose said shortly.

'Nela told you I was here?'

'Right. She said you were going to see Fielding.'

'Didn't you wonder why?'

'It's not unusual for our department to consult a psychiatrist sometimes,' DuBrose said. 'But you've been acting funny. So, since you ask – yeah, I wondered why.'

Cameron's gaze flicked past DuBrose's shoulder. He gave a low exclamation, turned, and nodded for DuBrose to follow. As they walked, he said, 'Was that Ridgeley?'

'Yes.'

To DuBrose's surprise, the director exhaled with relief. 'Not a hallucination, anyhow. I've been seeing him everywhere tonight . . . I've been on the run through Low Manhattan, trying to dodge him. Haven't seen Fielding yet. I don't know – '

DuBrose guided Cameron on to a Way. The courier, he saw, was still following, though at a distance.

'What's up?'

'I've been out in the Spaces,' Cameron said dully. 'Trying to dodge him. It's getting so I can't – ' He paused. His questioning gaze probed DuBrose's. 'Where's Seth?'

'I can't tell you, chief. I only wish I could. Why not trust me?'

'It's – Ridgeley. Why should he be following me? I've spoken to guards twice. Each time, when they looked for Ridgeley, he was gone.'

DuBrose said, 'I asked the Secretary of War to check on him. We think he's in Falangist pay.'

'A Falangist?'

'No-no. But in their pay.'

'Assassination doesn't worry me too much,' Cameron said. 'It's this other – ' Again he stopped. DuBrose glanced at an overhead marker and urged the director to a crosstown Way. Low Manhattan was crowded, even at this late hour. On a full-time production schedule, even the graveyard shift roared.

'Ben. Are you trying to dodge Ridgeley?'

'I know a place where we can get away from him. I hope.'

Blue Heaven was mildly notorious. At its garish portals DuBrose took out a blue key and used it as a passport, while Cameron frankly stared. 'I didn't know you went in for these diversions,' he said.

'Seth gave me this key,' DuBrose explained. 'He thought I needed an emotional catharsis. Ever been here?'

'No. Seth's told me about it. Rather – high powered, I gather. But – ' He peered along the Way. There was no sign of the courier.

DuBrose said, 'He can't walk through walls. It'd take him a while to get hold of one of these keys, and I don't know for sure that he can.' They went along a mirrored hall through pale clouds that glowed faintly. Some energizing radiation pulsed through the dim air. An attendant appeared.

'Your pleasure? What type of enjoyment would you prefer? We have a new pattern for Creepies – '

'That'll do,' DuBrose said. 'Where is it?'

Clouds billowed up and surrounded them; they were conscious of smooth motion through that warm opacity. They were relaxed upon padded cushions before they quite realized that the movement had stopped. The soft voice of the attendant said, 'The clouds will thicken a little. We don't bother with awkward neural attachments here. The water vapour is the conductor.'

'Wait a minute,' DuBrose said. 'Suppose we want to take a break? How do we turn off the program?'

'This lever, at your right hand. Now – '

The clouds thickened. DuBrose was not sure the attendant had gone. He waited. The first tingling vibrations of a Creepy neuro-pattern began to whisper through him. He felt drowsy, comfortable, infinitely relaxed. Images moved slowly through his mind.

Greek theatres had been one of the early forms of audience-projection. Later the cinema had expanded the scope, and television. All these art-forms had been aimed at making the receptor identify himself with the artist – and the Creepies, with their delicate patterns of pure sensory impressions, were the current development. DuBrose had felt Creepies before – you didn't see them – and knew they were excellent in entertainment-value. But this semi-bootlegged stuff was different.

It was rough!

Shock – shock – *slam*! Through the drowsy inertia the racing sensory currents plunged into DuBrose's brain, with a violence that sent adrenalin pumping into his blood. Fear, hatred, passion – these emotions and others, stepped up abnormally, mingled in a cacophonic symphony that melted him horribly. His hand twisted the lever. Instantly the nerve-racking violence stopped, but he was sweating.

The fogs faded. Beside him, Cameron grinned faintly.

'Better than a Turkish bath,' he said. 'But leave it off. I want to be able to see if Ridgeley shows up.'

DuBrose took a few deep breaths. 'Any idea why he's chasing you?'

'I might have. But do you?'

'I told you. He's probably in Falangist pay. Why don't you tell me the real trouble, chief?'

'I can't. Not yet. Unless . . . answer a question for me. Has anything turned up that might make me . . . indispensable?'

DuBrose thought that over. He was a psychotechnician; he could see how close Cameron was to the verge. If he could take the risk now, it might solve a good many problems.

'Well – answer a question for me first.' He'd chance it – with his fingers crossed. 'Remember that hypothetical equation we were talking about yesterday?'

'The truth-variable? I remember.'

'Could a guy who plays fairy chess solve that equation? Or would he go insane?'

Cameron sensed the significance of the query. His eyes narrowed. But he took a long time to answer.

'He could solve it. If anybody could, I imagine.'

DuBrose swallowed. 'And . . . if he couldn't . . . you'd still have enough dope to find somebody else who could, I suppose. I . . . I'll answer your question, chief. I don't want to. But I'm afraid. I'm afraid of what's happening to you. You're screwed up, and you won't tell me what it is, and I'm betting it's tied up with – this business.'

'Ridgeley?'

'He's part of it. Seth and I couldn't tell you before because we were afraid the responsibility would – have bad results. But you know the answer now.'

'*What answer?*'

'That equation isn't hypothetical,' DuBrose said. 'The Falangists have got it and have solved it. They're using it against us. We've got it, but we haven't been able to solve the thing. Our technicians have been going nuts. It's been your job to find a type of mind that could solve the equation.'

Cameron hadn't moved. 'Keep talking.'

'Seth and I had to keep the knowledge of that responsibility from you. You understand why now, don't you, chief?'

The director nodded slowly. But he didn't speak.

'We had to present the problem to you as theoretical. We were afraid you'd catch on. But I saw that fairy chess man tonight, and he's certain he can work out the equation. Even if he can't, we know, now, the type of man who can handle truth-variables. It's a matter of selection. If you fail, it's because the right man can't be found. But that won't be your fault. You know what sort of mind to look for.'

'It's close to casuistry,' Cameron said. 'But it's sound logic. Only I don't know enough about the set-up. Tell me. Where's Seth?'

'Dead.'

Silence. Then –

'Start at the beginning. Let's have it, Ben. And fast.'

Nearly an hour later Cameron said, 'If I'd known this from the beginning, I wouldn't have had my own trouble. But if you'd told me the set-up, the responsibility would probably have driven me insane. Listen.' He told DuBrose about the rippling mirror, the soft doorknob, the mobile spoon, the shifting floor. 'All aimed at my sense of security, you see. Trying to make me incapable of decisions. Building up an anxiety neurosis – to say the least. I knew it was impossible, except through science we haven't attained yet. But – '

DuBrose's throat was dry. 'Lord! If you'd told us!'

'I didn't dare. I was mixed up at first. I thought it was all objective and tried to find explanations. There weren't any. There were two possible answers. I was going insane. Or I was the victim of a planned campaign. In the latter case, there was some motive – I didn't know what. But I guessed that it was to drive me insane by artificial means. I decided to string along. I knew there might be scanning rays on me. Any word I said might be picked up by – the Falangists, or whoever was attacking me.'

Cameron sighed. 'It wasn't easy. I decided I could learn more by pretending to believe the manifestations were subjective. That way, the enemy might discount me, and I might find out what they were after. I knew you and Seth were up to something, and I guessed it was connected with this business – my hallucinations – but I trusted Seth. More than I trusted you, Ben. Till now.'

DuBrose said, 'You've been playing along, then – '

'It sounds easy, doesn't it? But a man can never be sure whether or not he's going insane. I haven't been sure. My mind . . . well, I've been in a genuine psychotic state, artificially induced. They succeeded in that. Tonight I had to have some help. I had sense enough not to tip my hand by seeing you or . . . Seth. I thought if I talked to a psychiatrist, I could get the value of catharsis, anyhow, without giving away what I suspected. But now it doesn't matter. Even if there's a scanner on me now – the Falangists can't make use of any information they gather. Because they can't stop us.'

'Don't underestimate them,' DuBrose said. 'They've solved the equation. They can use it as a weapon. They know how to make bombs that can penetrate our forceshields, for one thing. And I'll bet that isn't all.'

Cameron closed his eyes. 'Let's see. First, the equation must be solved. That'll put us on even terms with the Falangists. Second, a counterequation must be solved. But I don't know if even a fairy chess player could work that out.'

DuBrose blinked. He hadn't foreseen this possibility. It was an entirely new and unexpected responsibility – the need for finding a man who could not only solve the equation, but nullify its effect.

'Eli Wood's a fine mathematician – '

'Of this era. He can break down the equation; I'm willing to accept that. It's easier to analyse than to create. Ben, don't you realize yet where that equation must have come from?'

'The Falangists – '

'All right,' Cameron said. He got up. 'We've work to do. But I feel better. I . . . *know* now, that I'm not going insane, or going to be driven insane. For a while I was beginning to feel like a medieval peasant, attributing everything to my personal gods and devils. Now – '

He turned towards an arched opening visible through the thinning mists. 'Now we'll find a visor – fast. Then we'll start integrating. Come on, Ben. You'll have to be ready to take over for me – in case.'

'But you're all right now, chief. You know what the Falangists were trying to do to you.'

'I know,' Cameron said coldly. 'But you've forgotten one thing. Even now, they could succeed. They could drive me insane through sheer pressure. They can use that equation on me till my mind cracks and retreats into insanity as an automatic defence measure.'

'It's still happening?'

'Centipedes,' Cameron said. 'Little bugs. Spiders. If I took my tunic off and looked, I wouldn't see them, so there's no way of knowing what they are. But they're crawling all over me, and insanity would be a relief, Ben.'

He shivered.

11

At a public visor they called Kalender. The Secretary of War wasn't at GHQ, but it didn't take long to get the beam relayed.

The strong, harsh face showed strain and annoyance. 'So you've finally decided to talk to me, eh? I appreciate it, Mr Cameron.'

'Mr DuBrose was acting under my instructions,' Cameron said briefly. He didn't want to quarrel now. 'It was important that I be kept incommunicado while I worked on a certain matter. The slightest distraction might have been fatal.'

'Fatal?'

'Yes. What's the latest on Dr Pastor? DuBrose has kept me posted on current stuff.'

'Have you solved the equation? Or found anyone who can?'

'Not yet,' Cameron said. 'I'm doing my best. But what about Pastor?'

'Oh . . . well, nothing. We've a dragnet out. Your man DuBrose thought he might head for his home. We've a cordon there. Enough camouflaged equipment to blast him into electrons. Or quanta. We haven't told his wife anything. If he shows up – '

'He's left no trail?'

'Of . . . obliteration, you mean? No. I doubt if he's using the power.'

'You're doing all you can,' Cameron said. 'Now what about Daniel Ridgeley?'

Kalender said, 'It's ridiculous. The man's invaluable to us. DuBrose must be wrong.'

'Did you check his case history?'

'Naturally. And it checks.'

'Could it have been faked?'

'Not easily.'

'But it could have been, eh?'

'He can't be a Falangist,' the Secretary of War snapped. 'If you knew the valuable information his espionage work has given us – '

'A lot of good that will do you now,' Cameron said. 'The equation can simply wipe us out, and you know it. Have you put a scanner on Ridgeley?'

'Haven't been able to locate him. I called him on his private wave length, but he's turned off his receiver.'

The director didn't comment on that. 'He's in Low Manhattan. Put a scanner on me. Here's the visor number where I am now. I think Ridgeley may try to get in touch with me; if he does, scan him. And don't lose him! Better put three or four beams on the man.'

DuBrose whispered something; Cameron nodded. 'Ben DuBrose is with me. Scan him, too. We can't miss a bet on picking up Ridgeley.'

Kalender said, 'Do you want shadows?'

'No guards, no.' Cameron thought for a moment. 'All I want is to have Ridgeley under close supervision. But don't restrict his movement. That's important. I've got an idea.'

'You're scanned,' the Secretary said, after nodding to someone off-screen. 'Both of you. Anything else?'

'Not now. Luck.'

'Luck.'

DuBrose said, 'You told him we hadn't found anybody to solve the equation.'

'Well, the beam might have been tapped. We don't want Wood murdered. I'm probably scanned already by Falangists. Otherwise they wouldn't have been able to direct their mumbo-jumbo so accurately. It never happens when anyone else could notice.'

'They're still . . . working on you?'

'Yeah,' Cameron said. 'Well, I'll call Nela. Then – '

He did.

'Then what, chief?'

'Seth had an apartment not far from Low Manhattan. I want to see if he left anything.'

'What about Ridgeley?'

Cameron met DuBrose's eyes and grinned. What about Ridgeley? The courier was almost as much of an unknown quantity as the equation itself.

They found a pneumocar.

Seth Pell's 'apartment' was really a cottage, a unit affair aimed at convenience amounting practically to hedonism. Cameron had the key-combination. The tinted fluorescents went on automatically as they entered, and the aerothermo-adjusters began to murmur softly. DuBrose looked around the big, pleasant living room. He had never been here before.

'Seth used this as a hideout,' Cameron said. 'Here.' He went to a night battle scene on the wall. As he approached, rhythmic motion rippled across the panel. The white streaks of rockets flared up, two by two; the pulsing of scarlet-tinged smoke clouds throbbed gently. Cameron watched the scene, waited briefly, and whistled a few bars. The wall opened.

Cameron took out two vibropistols, handed DuBrose one, and walked to the other end of the room. 'It's not a duel,' he said. 'Let's say it's a trap. Just in case. Ridgeley would catch up with us sometime, and this is the first time we've been away from crowds since I got to Low Manhattan. Stay the room's length away from me.'

DuBrose nodded. He balanced the pistol. He had never fired one in his life, but that wouldn't matter. Aim and press. That was all. He glanced at the doors.

Cameron had opened another panel, and then a safe behind it. Finally he switched off a force-shield. 'Nothing, I guess,' he said, hunting through papers. 'I didn't expect to find much here. Seth seldom brought work to this hideout.'

DuBrose studied the room. It was a unit, well furnished, with none of the bad taste that had marked Pastor's magpie eyrie. Thousands of books filled the shelves, both ancient and modern; and there were cases of ribbon-volumes, recorded on wire tape. A pillow on a low relaxer still held the impress of Pell's head.

'Seth told me once that he was a misogynist,' DuBrose said.

Cameron nodded. 'I suppose he was. He didn't make many friends. You had to earn his friendship. You'd think he'd have been an antisocial type. But he wasn't; he adjusted surprisingly.'

'He liked his work.'

'Seth would have adjusted to any kind of work. He was – ' Cameron pulled out a book, examined it, and thrust it back. 'He had a theory that wars were inevitable. He said they were extensions of the individual life pattern. Most people go through a series of personal wars, emotional, economic, and so on. A maturing influence, if they survive. Perhaps not strictly necessary, but Seth thought inevitable, according to the general pattern of existence. Survival of the species and self-preservation – the main factors. Reflected, *in petto*, by individual wars and by national ones.'

'That sounds like a morbid philosophy.'

'Not if you don't expect happy endings. Ben, when this war with the Falangists is over, that won't bring the millennium. Seth would have said that each war is a hammer blow forging a sword into shape. Tempering it. It works that way on the individual, when the sword isn't spoiled or broken. Perhaps it works that way with the race. A people who'd always lived in Utopia wouldn't have much survival value. Your gun, Ben.'

DuBrose didn't have to elevate the muzzle more than an inch. He kept it aimed steadily at the sturdy, bronze-haired figure standing by the door. Ridgeley's brown-and-black uniform was spotless; the lapel insignia gleamed under the tinted fluorescents.

DuBrose studied the man. Neckless, compact, very strongly muscled, but built for speed as well as strength. There was nothing to mark the courier as an envoy from another time-period. Unless that glowing exultation deep in the black eyes meant anything.

Ridgeley held no weapon, but DuBrose remembered the cryptic, glittering gadget the courier had once aimed at him.

Cameron said quietly, 'I don't know your potentialities, Ridgeley. You might be able to kill both of us before we could kill you. But you're in danger of cross-fire. You're between DuBrose and me.'

Ridgeley's face was impassive. 'Why, you might kill me,' he said pleasantly. 'I admit that possibility. But I like taking risks.'

'You intend to murder us?'

'I'll try to, anyhow,' the courier said. DuBrose moved his pistol a little. Ridgeley wasn't infallible. By this time the scanner was focused on him. Did he know that? In any case, he himself had admitted that these odds might be too heavy.

A man from the future wasn't necessarily a superman. He had his own limitations.

'I've an ace up my sleeve,' Cameron said. 'So don't begin till we've finished talking. I think I can make you change your mind.'

'Do you think so?'

'First – what about trading information?'

'There's no necessity.'

'Will you tell me what you want?'

Ridgeley didn't answer, but the quizzical mockery darkened behind his eyes.

DuBrose watched the courier with one eye and Cameron with the other, trying to anticipate a signal. None came. He could feel perspiration trickling along his ribs.

'DuBrose and I both want to stay alive,' Cameron said. 'So do you. This particular combat can come now or later. Is that right?'

'Why not now?'

'Because it may not solve anything. Do you know what happened to Dr Pastor?'

'No,' Ridgeley said. 'I've been out of touch lately. I thought it wiser. Pastor – wasn't he working on the equation?'

Yes – the courier had his limitations. DuBrose watched, trying to find some clue behind those impassive features, while Cameron explained what had happend to Pastor.

'So that's the immediate danger,' he finished. 'We might kill you, you might kill one or both of us, or both. Pastor's still free, somewhere. Do you see the latent trouble?'

Ridgeley apparently had already made his decision. 'Pastor must be killed. The Secretary of War might fail. In that case . . . yes, he's the immediate problem, Cameron. There'd be little satisfaction in killing you if Pastor destroyed the world afterwards.'

'Hold on,' DuBrose said. 'Don't you *know* whether or not Pastor used his power – is going to use it – that way? Unless time's a variable – '

'I don't know,' Ridgeley said. 'So I can't take chances. I'll see you later.'

He backed out of the room. DuBrose moved forward and closed the door. The window ports were one-way, so privacy was insured.

'We're letting him go, chief?'

Cameron was rubbing his forehead. 'We'd better. He might do the job for us – get rid of Pastor. And that *must* be done. A gun battle now wouldn't have meant a final decision. Ben – he said he didn't know.'

'What? Oh. That was odd. If he's really from the future, if he's mastered temporal travel – he ought to know.'

'Yes, he should. At least he should know whether or not time's inflexible or whether there are temporal probability lines. Mm-m. Let's try Kalender.'

Kalender said there were now five scanning rays impinging on Daniel Ridgeley, and that the courier was heading by copter north-west. Also a technician, studying the equation, had suddenly giggled, shrunk to nothingness, and vanished. Microscopic examination revealed nothing but a pinpoint hole in the floor. Presumably the technician had dropped clear to the centre of gravity.

There had been three more cases of straight insanity as well.

Cameron switched off the beam and nodded at DuBrose. 'Try Eli Wood. See how he's getting on. Perhaps I'd better stay out of range.' The director listened closely from his vantage point.

Wood's mild face was ink-stained, but his placidity seemed unruffled. 'Oh, Mr DuBrose. I'm glad to see you. I thought of trying to reach you at Psychometrics, and then – well, you said this was highly confidential.'

'It is. How're you doing?'

'Nicely,' Wood said. 'It's fascinating work. But it's much more complicated than I expected. Sometimes it's necessary to work on two or three problems simultaneously, in view of the temporal variation. If I could have access to some integrators – '

'Head for Low Chicago,' DuBrose said, in response to a nod from Cameron. 'We'll authorize you to use the Integrators. You can have a staff – '

'Fine. I'll need men, too – trained men.'

DuBrose hesitated. 'Won't that be dangerous? For them?

'I don't think so. I simply want certain problems solved fast. I'll give them the material to work on. And I'll want some mechanics. There are a few changes I'd like to make in an Integrator. I've worked out the method, but I don't know how to rig wires.'

'OK. Any idea when you'll be finished?'

'I can't tell you.'

'Well – go ahead.'

'Oh – one more thing, Mr DuBrose. I've never been to the integrator rooms. Will it be all right if I smoke there? I can't work very well without my pipe.'

'It'll be all right,' DuBrose said, and watched Wood's calm face fade away. Cameron chuckled.

'He's the right type, I think.'

'What about those helpers he wants?'

'They won't go insane. It isn't their responsibility. They delegate that to Wood. Well, let's head for Low Chicago ourselves. I want to see that mutant boy – Van Ness? If we can get some information about Ridgeley out of him, that'll help.'

'It won't be easy. He's badly disoriented.'

'I know,' Cameron said. 'But we've got to fight Ridgeley some time. I'd just like to know why – that's all!'

DuBrose nodded, thinking that if the courier's motivation could be discovered, a good many problems would be automatically solved. However, matters seemed to be approaching a climax. From now on, these final steps would, at least, be extraordinarily interesting. It would certainly be exciting –

But it wasn't. It was routine.

12

Wars are not won by battles. Before the battle must come gruelling, intensive preparation, in which every contingency must be planned and charted. In this particular case the unknown quantities had to be found, and there were many of them. Item: Who was Ridgeley? What did he want? What powers did he possess?

'We can't find out through his War Department record,' Cameron said, studying graphed psych-lines. 'He'd built up an assumed personality for that role. We've got to study his environment, his actions and reactions – and Billy's very useful on that score.'

DuBrose watched the mutant, sleeping quietly under hypnosis, an encephalogram charting his brain-waves. 'We've found that temporal anchor, anyway.'

It was merely a sea anchor so far, with guided hypnosis to aid. The radiation-pattern of Van Ness' brain had showed distinctive variations under certain stimuli. By leading the mutant to concentrate his EPT upon the time-sector they wanted, by checking, on the chart, the stimuli that distracted him or, conversely, helped him to focus, it had been possible to learn something of Ridgeley's past – in the future. But it was always necessary to allow for a margin of error, due to Van Ness' confusion over duration. Thus there were blanks and snarls in the story; some of these could be straightened out by applying the yard-stick of familiar experience, but when that failed, the unknown *x* had to be supplied.

It took days.

Meanwhile nothing had been heard from Dr Pastor. Cameron had finally decided to use guards. Low Chicago was on alert. Only the most necessary warmen were allowed into the cavern that teemed with guards and specialized technicians. In the Integrator rooms, Eli Wood and his staff of co-ordinators worked at top speed, though the mathematician did not seem to be affected by the tension. Puffing thoughtfully at his pipe, he wandered through the forest of huge semicolloid mechanical brains, making notes on his cuff when he couldn't find a pad, and occasionally discussing his progress with Cameron and DuBrose.

'Won't we need machines?' DuBrose had asked once. 'To utilize the equation once we crack it, I mean? Some sort of transmitter – '

'Probably,' Wood said. 'Though I'm not sure even of that. You see, this thing is working out as a group of variable truths, so *very* variable that we can't anticipate what we'll need to harness it. That mental case of yours – he used mental energy, and he neutralized gravitation. I might find one basic, arbitrary truth that would presuppose the transmission of controlled variable-truths through the medium of a lead pencil or a block of iron. Or a hair follicle,' he added, blinking mildly.

'But you're getting it?'

'Why sure. However, the counterequation is 'way beyond me. I *might* crack that too, but it would take months.'

'Can we wait months?' DuBrose said, and answered his own question. 'No. We've a chance now to smash the Falangists. Their chief weapon is controlled use of the equation. More of those bombs of theirs have penetrated our shields. If they launched an all-out invasion now – '

'Their robots might win,' Cameron broke in. He stared at the huge Integrator pulsing softly in the distance. 'That was their plan. The bombs were nothing. They were aiming at the technicians.'

Wood said, 'There can't be more than a hundred top men in this country. Electrophysicists, electronic engineers – and so on. Men who are trained to think up fast countermoves – '

'It's a technological war,' Cameron agreed. 'Once they drove our best technicians insane, we'd be as helpless as the blood-stream without a liver. In a position where we needed new ideas fast –we'd go down. Because the men who could supply those ideas would be insane.'

'Even when we crack the equation, though,' DuBrose said, 'it'll be deadlock.'

'Yeah – We'll be on even terms with the Falangists again.' Cameron moistened his lips; without a counter-equation, there would be no help for him. The psychic assault had not halted. An hour ago, in his office, he had watched a lighted cigarette crawl out from between his fingers and loop up his forearm like an inchworm, burning his skin as it moved.

DuBrose was watching the director. 'We'll manage it,' he said. 'Somehow. There's got to be a way. We've enough resources – '

Cameron nodded. 'I finally got Kalender to stop all research on the equation. All but yours, Wood. So that'll save some technicians – but the top ones are either dead or insane already.'

DuBrose said, 'We can't get back the dead ones, but we can cure the others. Just show them the solution to the equation.'

'Not quite as easy as that, Ben – but that's the cure. They went insane because they couldn't shoulder their responsibility. If we can make 'em realize there *is* no more responsibility along that line, they should snap out of it fast.'

'Well, I've got to get back to work,' Wood said, rekindling his pipe. 'All this, you know, is a form of fairy chess in which the rules aren't clearly stated.' He blinked at the great Integrator. 'Amazing things. I don't understand – ' He went off, shaking his head thoughtfully.

'He'll crack it,' DuBrose said confidently.

'Yeah. When? Let's look up Billy.' Flanked by guards, they returned to the psychometrics sanatorium and another session with the mutant. Bit by bit, more notes were being added to the file on Daniel Ridgeley.

Van Ness could be no more than a spectator. He saw duration, but he was a psychotic case himself, and had the reactions, though not the vocabulary, of a child. He would answer questions and tell what he saw, but no more than that. And, while he had learned to identify Ridgeley easily because the courier's protracted duration-line was perceptible to him, a chronological charting was obviously impossible. He skipped; in one sentence, Ridgeley would be seen as an infant, in another an adolescent, in a third, a mature adult, and in a fourth, an invisible something suspended in what must have been a pre-birth incubator, though it seemed extraordinarily complicated.

And very slowly, very faintly, the picture of Ridgeley's own world began to swim out of the clouded vistas of time.

It took shape. Like a land seen from above, fog-shielded, peaks and rises gradually emerged from that misty dimness. It was possible to assign a tentative chronology, too, by making Van Ness describe Ridgeley's appearance thoroughly. Lines of experience appear and deepen on a man's face as he grows older.

Routine. Tedium. Anxiety, as the days dragged past and the *status quo* held. Dr Emil Pastor stayed invisible. Cameron's hallucinations continued, till he allowed DuBrose to dope him whenever that drastic step was necessary. The insane technicians stayed insane. M-204, in his sanatorium, was still Mohammed and remained afloat a few feet above his bed, ignoring the undignified force-feedings as he passively ignored everything else.

Unofficially, GHQ moved to Low Chicago. A concentration of equipment and men began to flow into the cavern city. No one knew what might be necessary, but everything was made as available as was possible.

Ridgeley, they learned from the scanners focused on the courier, was moving through the country, sometimes by copter, sometimes afoot, using something resembling a directional compass. He was obviously trying to locate Dr Pastor. When he did, GHQ would know it.

Cameron came in one day nervously excited. DuBrose looked up from the papers on his desk, automatically expecting trouble.

'Anything wrong?'

'Found Pastor yet? No? Well, listen in on this. I've got an idea.' He used DuBrose's visor to get Eli Wood. The mathematician, as quietly imperturbable as ever, nodded at them from the screen.

'Morning. We're coming along nicely. I just found out that people ain't. According to that particular truth, it's quite accurate. We're reaching the end, incidentally.'

'And you're still OK? But I can see that you are. Listen, Wood – check with me. How does this sound? We're assuming that Ridgeley brought the equation with him when he hopped back through time. He gave it to the Falangists. Well, the mutant Van Ness is giving us some of Ridgeley's background, and he comes from a remarkably advanced world – technologically speaking. The equation is used there. I can't pump out too much from Van Ness, but I gather it's a war weapon – not *the* one, just one of 'em. Wouldn't the counter-equation, the nullifying factor, have been known to Ridgeley's contemporaries?'

Wood pursed his lips. 'Seems like it would. Can't you get that through your mutant?'

'He's a superficial observer. Even if he saw the counterequation used, he couldn't describe the set-up clearly enough. He'd miss too much. Besides, we can't guide him easily – and if we could, we wouldn't know what to look for. But assuming that Ridgeley knows the answer to the equation and how to handle it, can't we also assume he knows the counterequation?'

'Seems like. You've got scanners on him.'

'That,' Cameron said, 'is what I mean. He's looking for Pastor.

And Pastor's got that obliterative power that's part of the equation. Ridgeley must know how to protect himself against Pastor.'

'The only protection would be the counterequation.'

'If he uses it against Pastor – '

'The application,' Wood said thoughtfully, staring at his pipe bowl. 'I see. If he should do that, we could break down whatever he does into the counterequation. If a scientifically trained observer sees a gun go off for the first time, he should be able – theoretically, anyway – to work out a formula for gunpowder. Huh. I'd suggest cameras equipped for quantitative analysis keep them focused on Ridgeley through the scanners. Attach ultra-violet, infrared and any other stuff you can think of. That'll do to start. If Ridgeley does use some application to the counterequation against Dr Pastor, we can crack that problem, too.'

As Wood checkered out, Cameron turned to DuBrose. For the first time in weeks, the chief's eyes lost their tight fixity.

'You know what it would mean?' he asked softly.

'Yes. You wouldn't be . . . haunted . . . any more.'

Cameron shrugged. 'Natural for me to think of the personal application first. But it would also mean we could smash the Falangists. They don't have the counterequation. Because Ridgeley wouldn't have given it to them. The counterequation is his own life insurance. In his position, he's automatically a target for assassination – because the Falangists can't trust him.'

'Wouldn't he be too valuable to them?'

'More dangerous than valuable. He gave them a weapon that could win the war, in exchange for . . . something. I don't know what. But if they should win, what use would they have for Ridgeley? And suppose Ridgeley sold out to us? A mercenary will change sides if it's profitable enough. The Falangists may be afraid of Ridgeley, they may find him tremendously useful, but they can't possibly trust him. He could win the war for either side, from the Falangist point of view. So Ridgeley would know enough not to trust his allies, and he wouldn't sell 'em his armour as well as his weapon.'

'Sounds sensible,' DuBrose admitted. 'But suppose he doesn't find Pastor?'

'Mm-m. Cheerful, aren't you? Let's try Billy again.'

The pattern emerged.

There had been war in Ridgeley's time, too. But an absolute war. One that was served by the mightiest technological system the planet had ever seen.

It had gone on for a long time. It had sealed its impress into every part of the socio-economic system. Before birth, the sensitive germ-plasm was impregnated with radiations that would permit the later development of certain necessary talents. Ridgeley's people were warriors in bone, sinew, nerve, and brain. Psychologically they were beautifully equipped for their job.

And, in that time, there was but one job. War.

Exquisite muscular co-ordination blended with a super-fine neural structure. Ridgeley had whiplash responses. He could make split second decisions. He was the embodiment of Mars.

He had been trained to fight and conquer, with all the tremendous facilities of his time-era. To fight and win.

But only that.

In Cameron's office –

'You started the wheels going around in my head,' Wood said, 'when you suggested that Ridgeley wouldn't trust his Falangist allies. He wouldn't give them the counterequation. But the big point – the one that was holding me up – is something else. There's been a certain screwiness to the equation itself.'

'The whole thing's screwy,' DuBrose said. 'That's the basic idea, isn't it?'

Wood blinked. 'Nevertheless I was assuming the gambits were all there. Until yesterday. Has it occurred to either of you that the Falangists aren't making full use of their weapon?'

Cameron said slowly, 'Our technicians are going insane – '

'A few factors of variable logic have been used. All that *can* be used by application of the incomplete equation.'

'*Incomplete*!' DuBrose said.

Wood tapped ashes from his pipe. 'It is. It's beautifully disguised, camouflaged so that it *almost* seems like a complete equation, but there's a factor missing. I didn't realize that till I realized the possibility of its absence. A jig-saw puzzle with a piece missing. If you know that, if you fit the rest together, you can see the shape of the missing piece. In its present incomplete form the equation's applications are limited.'

'But why?' Cameron asked.

DuBrose said, 'By God, I know the answer to that! The complete equation must be dangerous to Ridgeley! It could be used against him! Naturally he wouldn't trust *that* to the Falangists, or to anyone.'

The Director studied his hands. 'We've been assuming that the

Falangists have the . . . the complete weapon. Whereas you say they probably have the bomb but not the bomb-sight. Eh?'

Wood nodded. Cameron went on:

'Well . . . the Falangists aren't fools. They have good technicians. They'd have discovered that the equation isn't complete.'

Wood nodded again. 'They've had time enough.'

'But they haven't found the missing factor, or they'd have used it against us in an all-out attack. I'm assuming that the completed equation, in practical application, would be rather invincible.'

'Can't be sure. I'd say it might be. Except, of course, against the counterequation.'

Cameron smiled. 'Then the Falangist technicians would be working on the problem, too. They'd have an occupational illness too. They'd *have* to get the missing factor, for fear we might get it first, and for fear of Ridgeley. I wonder how many top Falangist technicians are insane by now?'

DuBrose said excitedly, 'It's a two-edged sword. It must be. If Ridgeley – '

The Director grunted. 'Can you find that missing factor?'

'I think so.'

'Then why couldn't the Falangists?'

'A racial psychological handicap, perhaps,' DuBrose suggested. 'They've always been reactionaries. Their culture as a unit is fairly new, but it's based on very old, established lines. They –'

'They don't play fairy chess,' Wood said. 'Oh, it's possible they might get the answer, but they couldn't have done it yet, or we'd be smashed. That's how powerful the complete equation can be. Here's another point.' He chuckled. 'If I should fail, I know I won't be shot or have to commit honour-suicide. The Falangists have a strict, arbitrary code of ethics. They serve the State, but they worship it too. Failure to them is unthinkable.'

Cameron seemed to agree. 'The Danes conquered the Saxons plenty of times, but Alfred and his men kept coming back. When the Danes were defeated at Ethandune, they were psychologically broken as well. The Falangist culture is inflexible. It had to be, in the beginning, or it would have broken up. But now . . . yeah, our technicians worry if they can't solve the equation; and they go insane. But a Falangist technician would be conditioned to worry a lot more. Cultural handicap.'

Wood said mildly, 'I'm having fun. I just don't have time to worry. So I may crack the equation, missing factor and all, quite soon.'

Cameron looked at him. 'We can win the war. We've the chance to do so. But if we do, I'll always wonder why Ridgeley joined the losing side?'

'He wouldn't,' DuBrose said, 'if he knew. So he couldn't have known. Maybe no records survived to his time-period. There'd be only a vague legend that there *was* a war about now. But the legend might not say who won. Even if there were records, they might be so incomplete that – '

'Incomplete or incorrect,' Cameron said. 'Then there's another possibility. Alternative time-lines. In Ridgeley's original past, the Falangists might have won. But by coming back in time, he changed the set-up and switched the historical line across to an alternative future.'

The mathematician got up. 'I must get back to work. Now that the matter is clarified somewhat, perhaps – '

Cameron didn't hear from him, then, for three days.

In the cool of the evening God, né Emil Pastor, walked through the wheat fields of Dakota. A small, slight figure, he trudged on, while the silvery ocean of wheat rippled softly around him in the moonlight. He was following his shadow.

The shadow is the reality; the reality, shadow. Under his feet the hollow earth boomed deeply, and the sound crashed again and again into his aching head. He hated to stop. There had been enough delay. The sooner he reached his goal, the sooner his questions would be answered.

God should be omnipotent. That was the trouble. He was a dual personality. He had a dim, uneasy feeling that he might be not only God, but Apollyon. He might not be God at all. He might be merely the demon of destruction.

Why hadn't he been able to heal his own arm?

The neural tissues had been burned out. The pain he felt in that arm was imaginary, a familiar phenomenon in amputation cases. He had bound the withered member to his body; the loose swinging distracted him.

Physician, heal thyself. God, heal Thyself. Apollyon –

He was very, very puzzled as he slowed to a halt and stood silent in the great quiet wheat field, staring at his black, one-armed shadow. But far away and dimly he could still remember something called Emil-dear, and that meant safety, and his shadow would take him to that sanctuary.

There he could learn his name. God or Apollyon. That would tell him his destiny. God must rule with justice and forbearance. Apollyon must destroy.

Something was moving in the wheat.

No – it was the wind.

He willed the pain to stop, but it did not stop.

Slow, helpless, easy tears spilled down his cheeks, and he did not see the movement coming quietly through the wheat, under the white, relentless moonlight.

The iconoclast slipped noiselessly towards God.

'What about the application?'

'Simple enough. It's like this, Mr Cameron. You can't play fairy chess unless you've got a board, the pieces, and unless you know the rules. Now we've cracked the equation, we know the rules.'

'The board, though? And the pieces?'

'All around us. Matter, light, sound – things you wouldn't ordinarily think of as . . . uh . . . machinery. Ordinarily they're not. In orthodox chess you can't use a nightrider or a grasshopper. In orthodox logic you can't use a . . . a cigarette as a machine. But even a cigarette can be assigned arbitrary powers when you assume variable truths. This space-time continuum and its properties are the board and the men. By working on certain irreal space-time assumptions, you alter the shape of the board. And when I say irreal, I mean irreal by orthodox standards.'

'But the practical application!'

'A gas engine could give us the initial power, or simple nervous energy would do as well. There are vast sources of energy all around us, Mr Cameron. In a world of orthodox logic we can't tap that energy, or we can't do it without specialized machines, anyhow.'

'You've got the *complete* equation? That missing factor – '

'I found it. It fits. We've got something even the Falangists don't have. But even so it isn't unlimited. The variable-truth microcontinuum can be maintained only as long as there's a sufficient energy output effectively tapped and directed. Which may be lucky, or the universe could go hog-wild. There *are* limitations. Even mental radiations can't be maintained indefinitely. But a thought can start the ball rolling.'

DuBrose came into Cameron's office.

'Pastor's dead,' he said flatly. 'Ridgeley killed him. But he didn't use the counterequation.'

The director put his hands flat on the desk and studied them carefully. A muscle jumped in his cheek.

'That,' he said, 'is unfortunate.'

'How . . . how is it?'

Cameron lifted a ravaged face. 'What do you think? They've been hammering at me without a let-up for – a million years! I. . . I. . . give me a shot, Ben.'

DuBrose carried a narcotic kit in his pocket these days. He put the sterilized needle deftly into Cameron's arm and let ultraviolet glow briefly on the skin. A moment later the director settled back, the tic in his cheek subsiding.

'Better. Can't stand much of this. Can't think too clearly in this dreamlike state.'

'It keeps the bugs away, chief.'

'Not bugs now. Something new – ' Cameron didn't elucidate. 'Tell me – what you want to.'

'The scanner's been on Ridgeley, you know. He located Pastor in Dakota ten minutes ago. He sneaked up and killed him with that little crystal gadget of his. Indian stuff. Pastor never saw him coming. Ridgeley crawled to within range and let go. I don't think any civilized man of this time could have done it.'

'Ridgeley – trained for war. All kinds.'

'Yeah. Well, he didn't have to use the counterequation. The whole thing was recorded; Wood's looking at the play-back now. But I'm sure he won't find anything.'

Cameron slowly indicated a paper on his desk. 'Been psyching Ridgeley. Read it.' He settled back, closing his eyes, the lines of strain still twisting his face. DuBrose studied the director anxiously, knowing that Cameron couldn't stand much more of this. From the moment the doorknob had opened a blue eye and stared at Cameron, the man had been under relentless attack for nearly two weeks. The anxiety neurosis was building up to a true psychosis. Yet if the pressure could be removed, the cure would be speedy.

By the time Eli Wood appeared, DuBrose had finished the paper. He handed it silently to the mathematician.

Wood read it. He nodded at Cameron.

'Doped up, eh? Well, I guess you need it. Ridgeley didn't use the counterequation; did DuBrose tell you?'

'Even if he had,' Cameron said rather thickly, 'we might not have been able to break it down.'

Wood shook his head. 'Fallacious logic. We've got the original solved equation as a model now. And it's possible to analyze anything. Just let Ridgeley try that counter-equation where I can see him, and I'll guarantee to give you the answer within a few hours, probably. The Integrators are already adjusted for variable logic.'

'He might . . . not know it, after all.'

DuBrose picked up the paper again. 'But he might, chief. If we could force him into a position where he *had* to use it . . . mm-m. What dope have we got on him, anyway?'

'He came from . . . a world geared to total warfare.'

Wood said, 'Did you get all that stuff from your mutant?'

DuBrose smiled faintly. 'By major operations. This data has been boiled down from eighty thousand words of extraneous material. But as for Ridgeley – we've learned some of his limitations. He's the last of the worriers.'

Not quite as simple as that. Picture a world geared to absolute warfare, a world so technologically advanced that interdoctrination could begin before birth. And visualize the planet shaking beneath the conflict of two nations, two races, that had been locked in a death-struggle for generation upon generation. By comparison the war with the Falangists seemed brief.

The matrix was war. That was the basic pattern, and all else had to integrate and co-ordinate. The psychology was more easily understandable than the science of that time.

Indoctrination, then, until the individual was a perfect machine for fighting and winning. But only that.

Necessarily the faculty for compromise, for flexibility, had been rigidly trained along certain military lines. Daniel Ridgeley, since his embryonic period, had been shaped to conquer and rule. Even before his conception, the basic genes and chromosomes had been carefully chosen for heredity value.

And Ridgeley's nation had lost the war.

Of the defeated, many died, and very many more submitted and were absorbed into the social scheme of the victors. But Ridgeley was a war criminal. Not a major one; when he disappeared, no one troubled to search through time for him. He was gone – *and he could not come back* – so he was forgotten.

Temporal travel was beginning to be understood in Ridgeley's period. So he had taken that way of escape. He could not have stayed in his own time-world, because his psychological pattern could not conceivably have fitted into a scheme of failure. He was a machine built for one purpose.

Tigers by heredity and environment are carnivores. On a diet of grass they would die. If they possessed the delicate nervous organisms of men, they might go mad.

Carnivores rule; herbivores submit. The meat of battle – successful war – was necessary to Ridgeley's existence. So, deprived of his natural diet, he had sought it elsewhere.

'Some of this is theoretical,' Cameron said slowly.

DuBrose nodded at Wood. 'We don't know from how far in the future Ridgeley comes. You'd think he could have referred to a history book and found out whether or not the Falangists will win this war. He'd never choose the losing side.'

'Maybe he didn't,' Cameron said.

'We worked out another answer, chief. Remember? Histories of this era may not have survived in Ridgeley's time. Perhaps all he had to work on was the knowledge that there *was* a war around this period. Then, again, time may be flexible after all, so the future can be changed by switching off into different probability lines. But I dunno. The big thing – ' He watched Wood. 'Listen to this. Time travel was understood by Ridgeley's nation, and a number of people had tried it then. But none of them ever came back, from either the future or the past.'

The mathematician blinked. 'Why not?'

'We don't know, yet. Don't forget, our mutant contact is technically insane. He's temporarily disoriented, which is enough to drive anybody batty, I'd say. Those creatures that lived in the Duds might have been able to use ETP and stay sane – but they weren't even remotely human, so normal standards of sanity can't be applied to them. When Billy matured and acquired ETP, he went crazy.'

Cameron said, 'Can anbody – use the equation?'

'Under guidance, yes,' Wood told him. 'And it'll be easier as soon as my gadgets are finished.'

Cameron closed his eyes. 'Deadlock now. We've solved the equation but so have the Falangists. If we get the counterequation, Ridgeley might give it to the Falangists – and it'd be deadlock again. Ben, we'd better mobilize. Get ready for an all-out attack on the Falangists. See Kalender. Is Ridgeley still scanned?'

'Yes.'

On the desk Cameron's hands tightened into fists. 'Use the equation on him. Hammer him. Give him the same treatment the Falangists are giving me. But worse. An assault that will tie his nerves into bowknots. Don't let up for a second.'

Something crawled down DuBrose's spine and exploded into elation. '*Force him to use the counterequation*?'

'In self-protection. It won't be easy. He's resourceful. But there's only one shield against the equation, and if we can drive Ridgeley into using it – '

'OK, chief. Can do, Wood?'

'Can do,' the mathematician said laconically. 'But – '

'But what?'

'God help Ridgeley.'

13

'Ready?'

'Ready.'

The copter was over a mile away. But he could reach it. That was the first step. The second would be to reach the Falangists. With the equation, it should be simple to pass the coastal force-shields. Grey mists of dawn hung over the wheat fields. A few stars faded before the encroaching, pearly light. Under his feet the ground winced and screamed like living flesh.

He blocked his mind.

Concentrate on the single purpose; that was it. Ten minutes to the copter, moving fast. That wouldn't end it. Under his hands the controls might squirm and twist; the variable truths, controlled now by his enemies, could hammer relentlessly at him.

But not effectively.

In his own time-era he had been trained to meet such assaults. Usually they were easy to neutralize with the counterequation – which was so simple. He couldn't use it now. There were scanners on him, and avid eyes watching, ready to study and analyze.

Reach the Falangists and give *them* the counterequation. They wouldn't be too grateful, probably, but he could protect himself. And he would be one of the conquerors.

Drops of oily, thick liquid crept down his face and crawled towards his mouth and nostrils. He exhaled more strongly. He kept his mind blocked. Expecting the unexpected was the way to fight such an assault as this. And years of indoctrination and training had showed him the way.

He adjusted his pace as the ground changed its texture, now rough as broken rock, now slick as smooth ice.

The wheat fields sank. He stood on a pinnacle at the edge of an abyss.

He began to descend, iron face impassive, the exultant glow of excitement burning behind the black eyes. He was trained for battle. This was war. Only in the face of dangerous odds could he feel this blazing delight.

His mind had been trained to react unusually to adrenalin. He could feel caution, but fear was usually alien to him.

The ground billowed like an ocean.

It slid away from under him. He had been walking for more than ten minutes. The copter was nowhere in sight, nor the grove of trees that sheltered it.

He paused to consider, still keeping that tight rein on his mind. The block held. The invasion glanced off harmlessly.

The landscape had shifted. The copter was over towards the left. He walked in that direction, a sturdy, reckless man trudging through wheat fields –

His eyes shot out on stalks.

'No luck yet.'

'Let me try.'

The eyes retracted. Before him stretched a Gargantuan chessboard. He felt a compulsion to move towards one square, but he did not turn from his course. The copter –

Here came the chessmen, bizarre, fantastic shapes, leaping in crazy patterns skyward and down again. But he had seen stranger creatures on the bio-labs of his own time-era.

He walked on.

'Three hours, Wood! But at least we've kept him away from his copter.'

'He can cope with the imaginations of normal minds, apparently. He's been conditioned –'

'How about psychotic patients? Could you guide their thoughts – project them?'

'It might work. You'll have to help me. Hypnosis, and suggestion. You handle the patients, I'll handle the equation. We'll try it, DuBrose. Can't we get Cameron to help?'

'He's asleep. Drugged. I had to.'

Hiding around nonexistent corners the shapes of terror gibbered at him. The slow nightmare flight of white birds painfully laboured past. A melting face repeated meaningless rhymed phrases. Red and yellow and spotted imps told him he was guilty and had sinned.

Hallucinations of insane minds, given objective reality by the variability of truth. The properties of energy and matter were altered, on the fairy chessboard, so that these arbitrary chessmen assumed form and substance.

The fairy chessmen screamed at him, laughed at him, sobbed and whistled and clicked and gasped –

Lurking, hating shadows. The phantoms of irrational fear and hatred and elation. The world of the insane.

He went on towards the copter. His eyes flamed with their terrible, burning delight.

Seven hours.

'I've got one answer,' Wood said.

DuBrose turned a white, strained face and mopped sweat from his forehead. 'To what?'

'Time travel, I think. Had you realized that Ridgeley could have escaped very easily by moving a few days away in time? But he hasn't done that. I've been tying it in with other factors; the fact that in Ridgeley's period nobody ever returned from a temporal trip. And the Duds, too. Our tentative theory about them is that they came back through time searching for something – we'll probably never know what. And they gave up and died right here.'

DuBrose kindled a cigarette, noticing that his hand shook uncontrollably. 'What does that add up to?'

'One-way time travel,' Wood said. He screwed up his face and studied the air. 'I've only worked it out in my head, but it adds up. You can move in only one direction temporally. Into the future or the past. But you can't come back.'

'Why not?'

Wood gestured. 'Why wasn't Ridgeley pursued by his enemies? He's a war criminal in his own period. But he was allowed to escape through time, and he's extremely dangerous. Suppose he'd gone onto the future, far in advance of his own time, picked up some super-weapons, and returned to his period with them? You don't let a criminal run loose if he has access to a vibropistol.'

'Unless he can't *get* back,' DuBrose said, frowning. 'You mean Ridgeley's exiled?'

'Voluntarily. The creatures in the Duds couldn't retrace their steps either. You can move – and continue to move – in only one temporal direction, either future or past. But you can't return. You'd meet yourself coming back.'

'*What?*'

'It's a one-way track,' Wood said. 'Two objects can't exist in the same space-time.'

'You mean two objects can't occupy the same space at the same time.'

'Well? An extension of Ridgeley exists from now to his own period, along the time-line. He can't go home. He'd bump into himself. He'd explode or something.'

DuBrose scowled. 'Uh. It's a bit hard to swallow. The Duds – '

'They gave up, I suppose. They knew it was no use searching further. So they – died.'

'Wait a minute. Why hasn't Ridgeley tried to escape our attack by going into the past? He could do that, couldn't he?'

'He could, but would he? You're the psychologist.'

'Yeah . . . he wouldn't. He can't give up a fight until he knows he's licked. Suppose he decides he is licked and escapes into the past again? Without using the counterequation?'

'Would he? Even if he has to let that information fall into our hands, he's not lost his private war. He may have other aces up his sleeve.'

'We've got to break him down. He's resisted all our assaults so far. He's conditioned to the unexpected or something. Even those projections of objective insanity haven't cracked him. What would?'

The mathematician grimaced. 'I don't know. If we keep pounding at him – '

A vagrant thought moved in DuBrose's mind. He caught at it.

'The mutant . . . yeah! Billy Van Ness! Wood, could we use him against Ridgeley?'

'Why – how? We're using psychotic projections now.'

'Ordinary insanity,' DuBrose said quickly, stubbing out his cigarette. 'Van Ness has got something special. ETP. He's a mutation of a nonhuman race, a totally alien one. They gave him a legacy that drove him insane as soon as he could use it. The extra-temporal perception was latent in him till he matured. Then – retreat to insanity. I don't think even Ridgeley's mind could stand ETP.'

'We don't want to drive him insane.'

'Don't forget his trigger responses. He'll know what we're trying to do. He'll use the counterequation – he'll have to. There won't be time for him to work out other possible solutions. If the ETP is as dangerous as I think it is, Ridgeley will get one whiff of it, panic, and give us the information we want. But – can we transmit Van Ness' ETP?'

'Not according to orthodox logic,' Wood said. 'Only we'll use a truth-variant in which psychic transmission of the faculty is possible. We can try it.'

'If it works, we'll have to be ready.' DuBrose spoke into a visor. 'Instant mobilization. At the word, smash down on the Falangists with the equation applications we've already charted. Get me Kalender . . . Mr Secretary? Hold ready. The word may come at any time now. An all-out robot assault on the Falangists.'

'We're mobilized for that,' Kalender said tautly. 'What about defence?'

'When we get the counterequation, we can handle it from here. Wood and his staff will tackle it instantly. OK?' DuBrose turned from the visor, a tight, cold feeling in his stomach.

He was afraid of what he was going to do.

They kept up the unrelenting attack on Ridgeley as they prepared. But the courier, by sheer, dogged nerve – or lack of it – had nearly reached his copter. As Wood rechecked and diagramed the factors of the equation that they would have to use, DuBrose put the mutant under hypnosis and made sure that the warped, half-alien mind was sufficiently under his control.

The scanner showed Ridgeley trudging on, his eyes blazing with the joy of conflict that was his reason for being, while around him the materialized madness of variable truths raged unceasingly.

To render Ridgeley en rapport with Billy Van Ness – that was the plan. If it could be done –

Finally:

'*Ready, DuBrose*?'

'*Ready.*'

This was the lance that could pierce his armour. He saw it coming. In that single moment while Ridgeley saw and understood what weapon they were using against him, he analyzed the chances, made his decision, and acted.

He used the counterequation.

Around him the turmoil died. The wheat fields lay placid under the afternoon sun. A hundred feet away was the grove of trees that shielded the copter.

He was armoured now. The equation could not harm him. But his enemies had forced him to reveal the nature of the counterequation. Very well. He could still fly to the Falangists –

Luckily he had protected himself before there had been full rapport with that mutant. Even the brief glimpse he had had was disturbing, a small, latent seed buried deep in his brain.

A seed? *Latent*?

But what was this thing that grew, that uncoiled, that spiralled out and out through his consciousness as though a spark had ignited the whole heap of gunpowder? One cell in his brain, one thought – but from the thought the contagion leaped faster than light, giving Ridgeley the extra-temporal perception that had come from an alien race of the ultimate future.

Delayed reaction. Time-bomb. The brain-colloid had to adjust itself to ETP –

The grove of trees was in violent movement. No, that was illusionary. There were hundreds, thousands of trees, superimposed in space but conjoining in time, and the line of their duration stretched like a network, with offshoots of germination that ended in other trees –

Masonry loomed before Ridgeley.

Tepees stood there.

Future and past –

Limited spatially to this area, but without temporal limits. Everything that had been or was to be, Ridgeley perceived in a shifting, monstrous kaleidoscope that became clearer as his perception sharpened. It was not merely sight. ETP is something else, a consciousness of the objective that goes beyond vision and sound and hearing.

Spatially the manifestation was limited to a small area immediately surrounding Ridgeley, but he was oddly certain that he could expand the range at will. He made no effort to do that. He stood motionless, his head sunk between his heavy shoulders, veins throbbing on his forehead.

Suddenly he closed his eyes.

The disorientation grew worse. A dozen, a hundred, a thousand material objects occupied the same space in which he existed. An illusion. But he knew that two objects cannot concomitantly occupy the same space-time.

In the past and future, at this spot, there had been catastrophes. The land-surface of the earth is not large. And, in all time, there had been opportunity for lightning to strike near here, for quakes to rock the ground and for trees to crash down on the spot where Ridgeley stood.

The veins throbbed faster on his forehead. Teeth clenched, he bowed his head as though fighting a storm of sleet, while the ETP natural to a nonhuman race channelled through his brain, opening unimaginable doors.

Van Ness and the other mutants had learned to perceive duration – and they had gone mad. Disorientation was terribly inevitable. Only by retreating into insanity had they been able to survive at all, in a world of complete flux, of utter incoherence to any mind that instinctively expected a logical pattern. This was not even variable truth. It was fairy chess with a board extended to the end and the beginning of time, and on that incalculably vast chessboard the innumerable pieces were moving . . .

A player can see the board and the pieces and comprehend the pattern. But if a pawn – or, in fairy chess, a night-rider – could see the board from the viewpoint of a player – what would be his reaction?

Ridgeley drew in upon himself, tighter and tighter. The impingement was becoming unendurable.

His legs bent. He sank down.

Keeping his eyes squeezed shut, he drew up his knees, crossed his clenched fists, and bent his head forward. He remained motionless in the foetal position.

He was not dead. He breathed.

But that was all.

A month later Cameron sat at his desk and stared defeat in the face. Not national defeat. Victory was three weeks old already, but how ephemeral a victory only Cameron knew.

The long, routine years had been merely preparation; the attack, invasion and conquest of the Falangists had been blitz. The counter-equation was a sword that nothing could turn. Or rather, a shield the enemy did not possess. Under Eli Wood's direction the disorganization of the Falangists had progressed with unbelievable speed.

And here was peace.

Everywhere but in this room, this head, this foreboding mind. The counterequation was simple to apply, and Cameron still kept its effect in use around him. He had a reason. He was still shaky from his long ordeal, but no variable-truths could penetrate the armour of the counter-equation even if any fugitive Falangists were still able to operate from hiding. Cameron was safe from that.

From himself he was not safe. He sat quite still, his back to the door, and a conversation from a few days past drifted through his mind. He did not want to remember it, but the sentences beat inexorably in his ears.

DuBrose: 'Here's some indoctrination stuff for the Falangists. Needs your OK, chief.'

Cameron: 'I'll tend to it. How do you feel, Ben? Want a furlough?'

DuBrose: 'Lord, no. The work's too fascinating. Even Ridgeley – though, of course, he's incurable. And a good thing.'

Cameron: 'Good? Well, necessary. But not just, Ben.'

DuBrose: 'Not just? For my money, it was a beautiful case of applied justice. He started this mess through time-travelling, and ETP smashed him.'

Cameron: 'You think Ridgeley started it? He didn't. His psychological pattern was set long before his birth, before his conception. He acted in the only way he possibly could have acted. You can't hold a man responsible for the things that happened before he was born. The real culprits were the ones who made Ridgeley's indoctrination along those lines necessary – and possible. Do you know who those culprits were, Ben?'

DuBrose had looked bewildered. 'Who?'

Cameron tapped the papers on his desk. 'What's this stuff? Indoctrination plans. We've got to use them. We've got to train our own men along supervised military lines or the Falangists may start another war. Preparedness is necessary. A vital survivor-factor. But in the end – Ben, the end of it will be Ridgeley. Ridgeley's civilization. The seeds of that culture are right here, in these papers, in us, and what led to us out of our own past. We're the culprits, Ben.'

'Casuistry,' DuBrose had said.

'Yes, maybe. Anyhow, it's got to be done.'

'Don't think about it,' DuBrose advised. 'That's one responsibility you can't change. You aren't responsible for what happened in your past any more than Ridgeley was for his. Forget it.'

'Yes, but you see, I *know*. The men who evolved our work for us and taught us didn't know. They hadn't seen what I've seen – the ultimate end. But when you *know*, and can't do anything but go right on with a thing whose end you've seen already – when you see a war fought and men going mad and man dying and Ridgeley punished as he was punished for a thing that can be traced straight back to me – *that* responsibility's hard to take, Ben.'

He had struck his desk a hard blow, and had time for a brief flash of irrelevant pleasure in the knowledge that it must remain a solid desk now the counterequation was on. Not a surface that would ripple under the blow, or open a wet mouth to engulf his fist.

DuBrose had said, 'You need a furlough worse than I do. I'm going to see you get one.'

Cameron went to a window port, opened it and watched the red gloom of the thundering Spaces outside. There was no escape. Every other nation was a potential enemy. From California to the Eastern Seaboard the nation had to remain a perfect war machine, ready to move into action at a second's notice. In such a machine, men are important cogs. And they must be cast of the right alloy, shaped to the right measure with precision skill, polished and tooled until they were –

Till they were men like Ridgeley.

And Cameron dared not change that process. He dared not even try, for fear of succeeding. What could he say? 'Disarm. Seek peace. Hammer your swords into plough-shares.'

And suppose they did? The enemy would strike again – and succeed, against an unprepared nation.

The thundering Spaces were before him, but all he saw was a race of circling thoughts made all but visible in the limbo of his mind.

'Forget it,' he said aloud.

But there must be an answer.

'Forget it.'

No problem is insoluble. There must be an answer.

'I've tried to find it for weeks. There is no answer. Forget it.'

There must be an answer. You're responsible. You created Ridgeley.

'Not I alone.'

But you have the knowledge the others don't have. You're responsible.

'Forget it.'

Tell them? Don't tell them? There must be an answer.

'This has been going on for weeks. The war's over – '

This war. You're responsible.

'Forget it. I'm going home. I'm going to take a furlough. I'm going to take Nela. We'll go up into the woods and relax.'

There must be an answer.

'So there'll be future wars. I . . . I'm no idealist. What can I do? Ridgeley's civilization – it's not pleasant. It may end in extinction, or a race of semirobots. Or the race may achieve peace finally.'

But you're responsible. You can't dodge that. You made Ridgeley. What can you do?

'I . . . there must be an answer.'

There must be an answer.

'There must be an answer.'

There must be an answer!

THERE MUST BE AN ANSWER!

THERE MUST BE AN ANSWER THERE MUST BE AN ANSWER THERE MUST BE –

DuBrose got into the pneumocar, adjusted the straps, and waited for the blankout. After it had passed, he settled back to fifteen minutes of idleness as the vehicle rushed towards Low Chicago. But his mind was active.

The past month had changed Ben DuBrose. He looked older than his thirty years now, perhaps because his blue eyes had acquired a new look of competence and his mouth was firmer. Seth Pell's death had left him as potential successor to the job of Director of Psychometrics, and a crown prince is usually conscious of his responsibilities. Always before, DuBrose had known that Cameron and Pell were, in effect, buffers. He was Number Three – not quite a third leg, but certainly a spare tyre. Now, however, Pell was dead, and Cameron had shown that he was not infallible. Some day the big job would devolve upon DuBrose, and he would be ready for it. Far more ready than he had been a month ago.

He had changed. His horizons had expanded. Eli Wood's conversation had done a good deal in that direction, and so had the very concept of variable logic. He was older, abler, and even wiser. He could see, for example, why the war time precautions had not been relaxed. The Falangists were defeated, but the location of Low Chicago and the other war-cities was still in the realm of military secrecy.

Preparedness was necessary, of course. Yet DuBrose thought that there would not be another war. He thought of the stars. And he thought of the mutant Van Ness, and of Ridgeley.

In Daniel Ridgeley's time there had been no interplanetary travel. There had been only global conflict that stretched back for unknown years, back along a time-track of conquest and defeat and deadlock, wars of attrition and red triumph and ash-tray failure, back to the war between America and the Falangists, and even before that. It was one road, the road that led to Ridgeley and his tremendous, futile culture.

One road out of many. No wonder, DuBrose pondered, that Ridgeley had chosen the wrong side when he came back through time. Had he thought that the Falangists were the ultimate victors? Or had he – not known?

Say he had not known. Or, if he had, he might have felt that his technological gifts could swing the balance in the direction he chose.

But there was another answer. Ridgeley's movement through time and his subsequent actions had affected time itself. Had switched the pattern of the future into a new path. Variable futures –

Again DuBrose remembered the mutant, and what Van Ness had revealed about that tremendous world that was now never to exist. For it was a world founded upon war, upon centuries and ages of continual battle, while the see-saw of victory swayed back and forth between the nations. War brings about technological progress, but only in certain specialized directions. Rocket-fuel, solar mirrors in superatmospheric orbits, antigravity may be perfected for use, somehow, against the enemy, but not for use against the stars.

In Eden, DuBrose thought, leaning back against the softly padded cushions – in Eden the trouble began. And even after that, Cain slew Abel. In every Paradise, there have been wars. But in the Polar cold, in the Sahara, in all inhospitable lands where men wrench a dangerous living from the hostile elements, there is comradeship and unity against the Enemy older than man, the universe in which he dwells.

And now? The earth was at peace for a little while. The weapons, the fuels, the technological miracles the world had perfected for destruction lay idle – and such things could not remain unused. Not while the stars hung in the skies, and the planets held their secrets – no longer unreachably far away. During the war no interplanetary travel had been attempted. The all-out effort had prevented such frivolous experiments.

But now the tools lay ready. Nations geared to the highest pitch of efficiency could not remain idle, could not rust in a lethargy that would be psychologically unendurable. There would always be an Enemy.

Not the Falangists. The Enemy stood at the gates of the sky, with the silent challenge it had given since man first raised his eyes from the ground. There would be new ships, DuBrose thought, a singing, joyous excitement in his blood – new ships like this pneumocar, but not burrowing through the dirt like moles. Ships to reach the planets.

There was the Enemy. The hostile universe that had always made man band together in a common unity. There lay the future that would wipe out Ridgeley's futile, tragic culture – because the future would slip into a new track now, one that led to solar – galactic! –

expansion rather than fatal interglobal conflict.

A thousand years might pass. Ten thousand. But even then, Ridgeley would never be born. The arid soil from which his culture sprang had been fertilized, enriched by a nutrient that would bring forth greater glories than Ridgeley had ever imagined.

For years man had had the bridge. But now he could use it. Now he could reach the stars.

They were the Enemy. The hostile, distant, alluring, secret stars. And they, too, would be conquered. But that would be no sterile victory.

DuBrose thought: *the old order changeth, giving place to the new.*

The pneumocar stopped. DuBrose stepped out into Low Chicago. 'I must tell the chief,' he thought, as he moved towards a Way, and then – 'Oh, well. He's probably figured it out for himself already.'

But the chief had not figured it out. He could not, now. For Robert Cameron had been fighting too long, and his battle had been waged with the resources of pure nerve. When tremendous tension is relaxed suddenly, the result is sometimes dangerous.

The chief was very vulnerable now.

Vulnerable to phantoms.

– THERE MUST BE AN ANSWER THERE MUST BE AN ANSWER THERE MUST –

Stop it.

He didn't want to stop. Even in that circling confusion was refuge of a sort, from this unbearable responsibility which was in itself a grim kind of justice. The guilty must be punished. He himself must be punished. He, Cameron, a war criminal beside whom Ridgeley was as innocent as a tank or a plane. He must go on. Answer or no, he must go on. His duty was to the living, not the unborn future.

Was it? Was it? He had not asked for this responsibility. But ignorance of the law excuses no man. Justice . . . Justice . . . If thine eye offend thee –

If thine eye offend thee –

Yes, there was one answer. Not a good one, but an answer. He had only to turn around to accept it.

He decided to turn around.

Automatically his hand reached out to close the window port. It did not shrink away from his touch. The metal remained firm and cool, as metal should. The counterequation still held him cradled in an unbroken shell of protection from all enemies. He knew that. No variable-truths could reach him here even if any enemies survived to hurl them at him.

He was shut in here with the one inescapable enemy.

He knew what was behind him. He had felt it a little while ago when he reached unsuspectingly for the door. There had been a strange, soft fluttering against his palm as he touched the knob. He had not looked down then. He had jerked his hand away and gone back to the desk. Now he would face it. Now he would look, and know, and accept the answer that would mean his own personal release, a laying down of the burden he had not asked for and could no longer carry. Now he could face the door.

The doorknob opened a blue eye and looked at him.

Camouflage

Talman was sweating by the time he reached 16 Knobhill Road. He had to force himself to touch the annunciator plate. There was a low whirring as photo-electrics checked and OK'd his fingerprints; then the door opened and Talman walked into the dim hallway. He glanced behind him to where, beyond the hills, the spaceport's lights made a pulsating, wan nimbus.

Then he went on, down a ramp, into a comfortably furnished room where a fat, grey-haired man was sitting in an easy chair, fingering a highball glass. Tension was in Talman's voice as he said, 'Hello, Brown. Everything all right?'

A grin stretched Brown's sagging cheeks. 'Sure,' he said. 'Why not? The police weren't after you, were they?'

Talman sat down and began mixing himself a drink from the server near by. His thin, sensitive face was shadowed.

'You can't argue with your glands. Space does that to me anyway. All the way from Venus I kept expecting somebody to walk up to me and say, "You're wanted for questioning." '

'Nobody did.'

'I didn't know what I'd find here.'

'The police didn't expect us to head for Earth,' Brown said, rumpling his grey hair with a shapeless paw. 'And that was your idea.'

'Yeah. Consulting psychologist to – '

'– to criminals. Want to step out?'

'No,' Talman said frankly, 'not with the profits we've got in sight already. This thing's big.'

Brown grinned. 'Sure it is. Nobody ever organized crime before, in just this way. There wasn't any crime worth a row of pins until we started.'

'Where are we now, though? On the run.'

'Fern's found a foolproof hideout.'

'Where?'

'In the Asteroid Belt. We need one thing, though.'

'What's that?'

'An atomic power plant.'

Talman looked startled. But he saw that Brown wasn't kidding. After a moment, he put down his glass and scowled.

'I'd say it's impossible. A power plant's too big.'

'Yeah,' Brown said, 'except that this one's going by space to Callisto.'

'Highjacking? We haven't enough men – '

'The ship's under Transport-control.'

Talman cocked his head to one side. 'Uh. That's out of my line – '

'There'll be a skeleton crew, of course. But we'll take care of them – and take their places. Then it'll simply be a matter of unhitching the Transplant and rigging up manuals. It isn't out of your line at all. Fern and Cunningham can do the technical stuff, but we've got to find out first just how dangerous a Transplant can be.'

'I'm no engineer.'

Brown went on, ignoring the comment. 'The Transplant who's handling this Callisto shipment used to be Bart Quentin. You knew him, didn't you?'

Talman, startled, nodded. 'Sure. Years ago. Before – '

'You're in the clear, as far as the police are concerned. Go to see Quentin. Pump him. Find out. Cunningham will tell you what to find out. After that, we can go ahead. I hope.'

'I don't know. I'm not – '

Brown's brows came down. '*We've got to find a hideout*! That's absolutely vital right now. Otherwise, we might as well walk into the nearest police station and hold out our hands for cuffs. We've been clever, but now – we've got to hide. Fast!'

'Well . . . I get that. But do you know what a Transplant really is?'

'A free brain. One that can use artificial gadgets.'

'Technically, yeah. Ever seen a Transplant working a power-digger? Or a Venusian sea-dredge? Enormously complicated controls it'd normally take a dozen men to handle?'

'Implying a Transplant's a superman?'

'No,' Talman said slowly, 'I don't mean that. But I've got an idea it'd be safer to tangle with a dozen men than with one Transplant.'

'Well,' Brown said, 'go up to Quebec and see Quentin. He's there now, I found out. Talk to Cunningham first. We'll work out the details. What we've got to know are Quentin's powers and his vulnerable points. And whether or not he's telepathic. You're an old friend of Quentin, and you're a psychologist, so you're the guy for the job.'

'Yeah.'

'We've got to get that power plant. *We've got to hide, now*!'

Talman thought that Brown had probably planned this from the beginning. The fat man was shrewd enough; he'd been sufficiently clever to realize that ordinary criminals would stand no chance in a highly technical, carefully specialized world. Police forces could call on the sciences to aid them. Communications were excellent and fast, even between the planets. There were gadgets – The only chance of bringing off a successful crime was to do it fast and then make an almost instantaneous getaway.

But the crime had to be planned. When competing against an organized social unit, as any crook does, it's wise to create a similar unit. A blackjack has no chance against a rifle. A strong-arm bandit was doomed to quick failure, for a similar reason. The traces he left would be analyzed; chemistry, psychology, and criminology would track him down; he'd be made to confess. Made to, without any third-degree methods. So –

So Cunningham was an electronics engineer. Fern was an astrophysicist. Talman himself was a psychologist. Big, blond Dalquist was a hunter, by choice and profession, beautifully integrated and tremendously fast with a gun. Cotton was a mathematician – and Brown himself was the co-ordinator. For three months the combination had worked successfully on Venus. Then, inevitably, the net closed, and the unit filtered back to Earth, ready to take the next step in the long-range plan. What it was Talman hadn't known till now. But he could readily see its logical necessity.

In the vast wilderness of the Asteroid Belt they could hide forever, if necessary, emerging to pull off a coup whenever opportunity offered. Safe, they could build up an underground criminal organization, with a spy-system flung broadcast among the planets – yes, it was the inevitable way. Just the same, he felt hesitant about matching wits with Bart Quentin. The man wasn't – human – any more –

He was worried on the way to Quebec. Cosmopolitan though he was, he couldn't help anticipating tension, embarrassment, when he saw Quent. To pretend to ignore that – accident – would be too obvious.

Still – He remembered that, seven years ago, Quentin had possessed a fine, muscular physique, and had been proud of his skill as a dancer. As for Linda, he wondered what had happened on that score. She couldn't still be Mrs Bart Quentin, under the circumstances. Or could she?

He watched the St Lawrence, a dull silver bar, below the plane as it slanted down. Robot pilots – a narrow beam. Only during violent storms did standard pilots take over. In space it was a different matter. And there were other jobs, enormously complicated, that only human brains could handle. A very special type of brain, at that.

A brain like Quentin's.

Talman rubbed his narrow jaw and smiled wanly, trying to locate the source of his worry. Then he had the answer. Did Quent, in this new incarnation, possess more than five senses? Could he detect reactions in normal man could not appreciate? If so, Van Talman was definitely sunk.

He glanced at his seatmate, Dan Summers of Wyoming Engineers, through whom he had made the contact with Quentin. Summers, a blond young man with sun-wrinkles around his eyes, grinned casually.

'Nervous?'

'Could be that,' Talman said. 'I was wondering how much he'll have changed.'

'Results are different in every case.'

The plane, beam controlled, slid down the slopes of sunset air towards the port. Quebec's lighted towers made an irregular backdrop.

'They do change, then?'

'I suppose, psychically, they've got to. You're a psychologist, Mr Talman. How'd you feel, if – '

'There might be compensations.'

Summers laughed. 'That's an understatement. Compensations . . . why, immortality's only one such . . . compensation!'

'You consider that a blessing?' Talman asked.

'Yes, I do. He'll remain at the peak of his powers for God knows how long. There'll be no deterioration. Fatigue poisons are automatically eliminated by irradiation. Brain cells can't replace themselves, of course, the way . . . say . . . muscular tissue can; but Quent's brain can't be injured, in its specially built case. Arteriosclerosis isn't any problem, with the plasmic solution we use – no calcium's deposited on the artery walls. The physical condition of his brain is automatically and perfectly controlled. The only ailments Quent can ever get are mental.'

'Claustrophobia – No. You say he's got eye lenses. There'd be an automatic feeling of extension.'

Summers said, 'If you notice any change – outside of the perfectly normal one of mental growth in seven years – I'll be interested. With me – well, I grew up with the Transplants. I'm no more conscious of their mechanical, interchangeable bodies than a physician would think of a friend as a bundle of nerves and veins. It's the reasoning faculty that counts, and that hasn't altered.'

Talman said thoughtfully, 'You're a sort of physician, to the Transplants, anyway. A layman might get another sort of reaction. Especially if he were used to seeing . . . a face.'

'I'm never conscious of that lack.'

'Is Quent?'

Summers hesitated. 'No,' he said finally. 'I'm sure he isn't. He's beautifully adjusted. The reconditioning to Transplant life takes about a year. After that it's all velvet.'

'I've seen Transplants working, on Venus, from a distance. But there aren't many spotted away from Earth.'

'We haven't enough trained technicians. It takes literally half a lifetime to train a man to handle Transplantation. A man has to be a qualified electronic engineer before he even starts.' Summers laughed. 'The insurance companies cover a lot of the initial expense, though.'

Talman was puzzled. 'How's that?'

'They underwrite. Occupational risk, immortality. Working in atomic research is dangerous, my friend!'

They emerged from the plane into the cool night air. Talman said, as they walked towards a waiting car, 'We grew up together, Quentin and I. But his accident happened two years after I left Earth, and I never saw him since.'

'As a Transplant? Uh-huh. Well, it's an unfortunate name. Some jackass tagged the label on, whereas propaganda experts should have worked it out. Unfortunately it stuck. Eventually we hope to popularize the – Transplants. Not yet. We're only starting. We've only got two hundred and thirty of them so far, the successful ones.'

'Many failures?'

'Not now. In the early days – It's *complicated*. From the first trephining to the final energizing and reconditioning, it's the most nerve-racking, brain-straining, difficult technical task the human mind's ever worked out. Reconciling a colloid mechanism with an electronic hookup – but the result's worth it.'

'Technologically. I wonder about the human values.'

'Psychologically? We-ell . . . Quentin will tell you about that angle. And technologically you don't know the half of it. No colloid machine, like the brain, has ever been developed – till now. And this isn't purely mechanical. It's merely a miracle, the synthesis of intelligent living tissue with delicate, responsive machinery.'

'But handicapped by the limitation of the machine – and the brain.'

'You'll see. Here we are. We're dining with Quent – '

Talman stared. '*Dining*?'

'Yeah.' Summers' eyes showed quizzical amusement. 'No, he doesn't eat steel shavings. In fact – '

The shock of meeting Linda again took Talman by surprise. He had not expected to see her. Not now, under these altered conditions. But she hadn't changed much; she was still the same warm, friendly woman he remembered, a little older now, yet very lovely and very gracious. She had always had charm. She was slim and tall, her head crowned by a bizarre coiffure of honey-amber coils, her brown eyes without the strain Talman might have expected.

He took her hands. 'Don't say it,' he said. 'I know how long it's been.'

'We won't count the years, Van.' She laughed up at him. 'We'll pick up right where we left off. With a drink, eh?'

'I could use one,' Summers said, 'but I've got to report back to headquarters. I'll just see Quent for a minute. Where is he?'

'In there.' Linda nodded towards a door and turned back to Talman. 'So you've been on Venus? You look bleached enough. Tell me how it's been.'

'All right.' He took the shaker from her hands and swirled the Martinis carefully. He felt embarrassment. Linda lifted an eyebrow.

'Yes, we're still married, Bart and I. You're surprised.'

'A little.'

'He's still Bart,' she said quietly. 'He may not look it, but he's the man I married, all right. So you can relax, Van.'

He poured the Martinis. Without looking at her, he said, 'As long as you're satisified – '

'I know what you're thinking. That it'd be like having a machine for a husband. At first . . . well, I got over that feeling. We both did, after a while. There was constraint; I suppose you'll feel it when you see him. Only that isn't important, really. He's – Bart.' She pushed a third glass towards Talman, and he looked at it in surprise.

'Not – '

She nodded.

The three of them dined together. Talman watched the two-foot-by-two cylinder resting on the table opposite him and tried to read personality and intelligence into the double lenses. He couldn't help imagining Linda as a priestess, serving some sort of alien god-image, and the concept was disturbing. Now Linda was forking chilled, sauce-daubed shrimps into the metallic compartment and spooning them out when the amplifier signalled.

Talman had expected a flat, toneless voice, but the sonovox gave depth and timbre whenever Quentin spoke.

'Those shrimps are perfectly usable, Van. It's only habit that makes us throw chow out after I've had it in my foodbox. I taste the stuff, all right – but I haven't any salivary juices.'

'You – taste 'em.'

Quentin laughed a little. 'Look, Van. Don't try to pretend this seems natural to you. You'll have to get used to it.'

'It took me a long time,' Linda said. 'But after a while I found myself thinking it was just the sort of silly thing Bart always used to do. Remember the time you put on that suit of armour for the Chicago board meeting?'

'Well, I made my point,' Quentin said. 'I forget what it was now, but we were talking about taste. I can taste these shrimps, Van. Certain nuances are lacking, yeah. Very delicate sensations are lost on me. But there's more to it than sweet and sour, salt and bitter. Machines could taste years ago.'

'There's no digestion – '

'And there's no pylorospasm. What I lose in refinements of taste I make up for in freedom from gastro-intestinal disorders.'

'You don't burp any more, either,' Linda said. 'Thank God.'

'I can talk with my mouth full, too,' Quentin said. 'But I'm not the super-machine-bodied-brain you're subconsciously thinking I am, chum. I don't spit death rays.'

Talman grinned uneasily. 'Was I thinking that?'

'I'll bet you were. But – ' The timbre of the voice changed. 'I'm not super. I'm plenty human, inside, and don't think I don't miss the old days sometimes. Lying on the beach and feeling the sun on my skin, little things like that. Dancing in rhythm to music, and – '

'Darling,' Linda said.

The voice changed again. 'Yeah. It's the small, trivial factors that make up a complete life. But I've got substitutes now – parallel factors. Reactions quite impossible to describe, because they're . . . let's say . . . electronic vibrations instead of the familiar neural ones. I *do* have senses, but through mechanical organs. When impulses reach my brain, they're automatically translated into familiar symbols. Or – ' He hesitated. 'Not so much now, though.'

Linda laid a bit of planked fish in the food-compartment. 'Delusions of grandeur, eh?'

'Delusions of alteration – but no delusion, my love. You see, Van, when I first turned into a Transplant, I had no standard of comparison except the arbitrary one I already knew. That was suited to a human body – only. When, later, I felt an impulse from a digger gadget, I'd automatically feel as if I had my foot on a car accelerator. Now those old symbols are fading. I . . . feel . . . more directly now, without translating the impulses into the old-time images.'

'That would be faster,' Talman said.

'It is. I don't have to think of the value of pi when I get a pi signal. I don't have to break down the equation. I'm beginning to sense what the equation means.'

'Synthesis with a machine?'

'Yet I'm no robot. It doesn't affect the identity, the personal essence of Bart Quentin.' There was a brief silence, and Talman saw Linda look sharply towards the cylinder. Then Quentin continued in the same tone. 'I get a tremendous bang out of solving problems. I always did. And now it's not just on paper. I carry out the whole task myself, from conception to finish. I dope out the application, and . . . Van, I am the machine!'

'Machine?' Talman said.

'Ever noticed, when you're driving or piloting, how you identify yourself with the machine? It's an extension of you. I go one step farther. And it's satisfying. Suppose you could carry empathy to the limit and be one of your patients while you were solving his problem? It's an – ecstasy.'

Talman watched Linda pour sauterne into a separate chamber. 'Do you ever get drunk any more?' he asked.

Linda gurgled. 'Not on liquor – but Bart gets high, all right!'

'How?'

'Figure it out,' Quentin said, a little smugly.

'Alcohol's absorbed into the blood stream, thence reaching the brain – the equivalent of intravenous shots, maybe?'

'I'd rather put cobra venom in my circulatory system,' the Transplant said. 'My metabolic balance is too delicate, too perfectly organized, too upset by introducing foreign substances. No, I use electrical stimulus – an induced high-frequency current that gets me high as a kite.'

Talman stared. 'And that's a substitute?'

'It is. Smoking and drinking are irritants, Van. So's thinking, for that matter! When I feel the psychic need for a binge, I've a gadget that provides stimulating irritation – and I'll bet you'd get more of a bang out of it than you would out of a quart of mescal.'

'He quotes Housman,' Linda said. 'And does animal imitations. With his tonal control, Bart's a wonder.' She stood up. 'If you'll excuse me for a bit, I've got some K.P. Automatic as the kitchen is, there are still buttons to push.'

'Can I help?' Talman offered.

'Thanks, no. Stay here with Bart. Want me to hitch up your arms, darling?'

'Nope,' Quentin said. 'Van can take care of my liquid diet. Step it up, Linda – Summers said I've got to get back on the job soon.'

'The ship's ready?'

'Almost.'

Linda paused in the doorway, biting her lips. 'I'll never get used to your handling a spaceship all by yourself. Especially that thing.'

'It may be jury-rigged, but it'll get to Callisto.'

'Well . . . there's a skeleton crew, isn't there?'

'There is,' Quentin said, 'but it isn't needed. The insurance companies demand an emergency crew. Summers did a good job, rigging the ship in six weeks.'

'With chewing gum and paper clips,' Linda remarked. 'I only hope it holds.' She went out as Quentin laughed softly. There was a silence. Then, as never before, Talman felt that his companion was . . . was . . . had changed. For he felt Quentin gazing at him, and – Quentin wasn't there.

'Brandy, Van,' the voice siad. 'Pour a little in my box.'

Talman started to obey, but Quentin checked him. 'Not out of the bottle. It's been a long time since I mixed rum and coke in my mouth. Use the inhaler. That's it. Now. Have a drink yourself and tell me how you feel.'

'About – ?'

'Don't you know?'

Talman went to the window and stood looking down at the reflected fluorescent shining in the St Lawrence. 'Seven years,

Quent. It's hard to get used to you in this – form.'

'I haven't lost anything.'

'Not even Linda,' Talman said. 'You're lucky.'

Quentin said steadily, 'She stuck with me. The accident, five years ago, wrecked me. I was fooling around with atomic research, and there were chances that had to be taken. I was mangled, butchered, in the explosion. Don't think Linda and I hadn't planned in advance. We knew the occupational risk.'

'And yet you – '

'We figured the marriage could last, even if – But afterwards I almost insisted on a divorce. She convinced me we could still make a go of it. And we have.'

Talman nodded. 'I'd say so.'

'That . . . kept . . . me going, for quite a while,' Quentin said softly. 'You know how I felt about Linda. It's always been just about a perfect equation. Even though the factors have changed, we've adjusted.' Suddenly Quentin's luagh made the psychologist swing around. 'I'm no monster, Van. Try and get over that idea!'

'I never thought that,' Talman protested. 'You're –'

'What?'

Silence again. Quentin grunted.

'In five years I've learned to notice how people react to me. Give me some more brandy. I still imagine I taste it with my palate. Odd how associations hang on.'

Talman poured liquor from the inhaler. 'So you figure you haven't changed, except physically.'

'And you figure me as a raw brain in a metal cylinder. Not as the guy you used to get drunk with on Third Avenue. Oh, I've changed – sure. But it's a normal change. There's nothing innately alien about limbs that are metal extensions. It's one step beyond driving a car. If I were the sort of super-gadget you subconsciously think I am, I'd be an utter introvert and spend my time working out cosmic equations.' Quentin used a vulgar expletive. 'And if I did that, I'd go nuts. Because I'm no superman. I'm an ordinary guy, a good physicist, and I've had to adjust to a new body. Which, of course, has its handicaps.'

'What, for example?'

'The senses. Or the lack of them. I helped develop a lot of compensatory apparatus. I read escapist fiction, I get drunk by electrical irritation. I taste even if I can't eat. I watch teleshows. I try to get the equivalent of all the purely human sensory pleasures I can. It makes a balance that's very necessary.'

'It would be. Does it work, though?'

'Look. I've got eyes that are delicately sensitive to shades and gradations of colour. I've got arm attachments that can be refined down until they can handle microscopic apparatus. I can draw pictures – and, under a pseudonym, I'm a pretty popular cartoonist. I do that as a sideline. My real job is still physics. And it's still a good job. You know the feeling of pure pleasure you get when you've worked out a problem, in geometry or electronics or psychology – or anything? Now I work out questions infinitely more complicated, requiring split-second reaction as well as calculation. Like handling a spaceship. More brandy. It's volatile stuff in a hot room.'

'You're still Bart Quentin,' Talman said, 'but I feel surer of that when I keep my eyes shut. Handling a spaceship – '

'I've lost nothing human,' Quentin insisted. 'The emotional basics haven't changed. It . . . isn't really pleasant to have you come in and look at me with plain horror, but I can understand the reason. We've been friends for a long time, Van. You may forget that before I do.'

Sweat was suddenly cold on Talman's stomach. But despite Quentin's words, he felt certain by now that he had part of the answer for which he had come to Quebec. The Transplant had no abnormal powers – there were no telepathic functions.

There were more questions to be asked, of course.

He poured more brandy and smiled at the dully-shining cylinder across the table. He could hear Linda singing softly from the kitchen.

The spaceship had no name, for two reasons. One was that she would make only a single trip, to Callisto; the other was odder. She was not, essentially, a ship with a cargo. She was a cargo with a ship.

Atomic power plants are not ordinary dynamos that can be dismantled and crated on a freight car. They are tremendously big, powerful, bulky, and behemothic. It takes two years to complete an atomic setup, and even after that the initial energizing must take place on Earth, at the enormous standards control plant that covers seven counties of Pennsylvania. The Department of Weights, Measures, and Power has a chunk of metal in a thermostatically-controlled glass case in Washington; it's the standard metre. Similarly, in Pennsylvania, there is, under fantastic precautionary conditions, the one key atomic-disrupter in the Solar System.

There was only one requirement for fuel; it was best to filter it through a wire screen with, approximately, a one-inch gauge. And that was an arbitrary matter, for convenience in setting up a standard of fuels. For the rest, atomic power ate anything.

Few people played with atomic power; the stuff's violent. The research engineers worked on a stagger system. Even so, only the immortality insurance – the Transplantidae – kept neuroses from developing into psychoses.

The Callisto-bound power plant was too big to be loaded on the largest ship of any commercial line, but it had to get to Callisto. So the technicians built a ship around the power plant. It was not exactly jury-rigged, but it was definitely unstandardized. It occasionally, in matters of design, departed wildly from the norm. The special requirements were met deftly, often unorthodoxly, as they came up. Since the complete control would be in the hands of the Transplant Quentin, only casual accommodations were provided for the comfort of the small emergency crew. They weren't intended to wander through the entire ship unless a breakdown made it necessary, and a breakdown was nearly impossible. In fact, the vessel was practically a living entity. But not quite.

The Transplant had extensions – tools – throughout various sections of the great craft. Yet they were specialized to deal with the job in hand. There were no sensory attachments, except auditory and ocular. Quentin was, for the nonce, simply a super spaceship drive control. The brain cylinder was carried into the craft by Summers, who inserted it – somewhere! – plugged it in, and that finished the construction job.

At 2400 the mobile power plant took off for Callisto.

A third of the way to the Martian orbit, six spacesuited men came into an enormous chamber that was a technician's nightmare.

From a wall amplifier, Quentin's voice said, 'What are you doing here, Van?'

'OK,' Brown said. 'This is it. We'll work fast now. Cunningham, locate the connection. Dalquist, keep your gun ready.'

'What'll I look for?' the big blond man asked.

Brown glanced at Talman. 'You're certain there's no mobility?'

'I'm certain,' Talman said, his eyes moving. He felt naked exposed to Quentin's gaze, and didn't like it.

Cunningham, gaunt, wrinkled and scowling, said, 'The only mobility's in the drive itself. I was sure of that before Talman double-checked. When a Transplant's plugged in for one job, it's limited to the tools it needs for that job.'

'Well, don't waste time talking. Break the circuit.'

Cunningham stared through the vision plate. 'Wait a minute. This isn't standardized equipment. It's experimental . . . casual. I've got to trace a few . . . um.'

Talman was surreptitiously trying to spot the Transplant's eye lenses, and failing. From somewhere in that maze of tubes, coils, wires, grids and engineering hash, he knew, Quentin was looking at him. From several places, undoubtedly – there'd be overall vision, with eyes spotted strategically around the room.

And it was a big room, this central control chamber. The light was misty yellow. It was like some strange, unearthly cathedral in its empty, towering height, a hugeness that dwarfed the six men. Bare grids, abnormally large, hummed and sparked; great vacuum tubes flamed eerily. Around the walls above their heads ran a metal platform, twenty feet up, a metal guard rail casually precautionary. It reached by two ladders, on opposite walls of the room. Overhead hung a celestial globe, and the dim throbbing of tremendous power murmured in the chlorinated atmosphere.

The amplifier said, 'What is this, piracy?'

Brown said casually, 'Call it that. And relax. You won't be harmed. We may even send you back to Earth, when we can figure out a safe way to do it.'

Cunningham was investigating lucite mesh, taking care to touch nothing. Quentin said. 'This cargo isn't worth high-jacking. It isn't radium I'm carrying, you know.'

'I need a power plant,' Brown remarked curtly.

'How did you get aboard?'

Brown lifted a hand to mop sweat from his face, and then, grimacing, refrained. 'Find anything yet, Cunningham?'

'Give me time. I'm only an electronics man. This setup's screwy. Fern, give me a hand here.'

Talman's discomfort was growing. He realized that Quentin, after the first surprised comment, had ignored him. Some indefinable compulsion made him tilt back his head and say Quentin's name.

'Yeah,' Quentin said. 'Well? So you're in with this gang?'

'Yes.'

'And you were pumping me, up in Quebec. To make sure I was harmless.'

Talman made his voice expressionless. 'We had to be certain.'

'I see. How'd you get abroad? The radar automatically dodges approaching masses. You couldn't have brought your own ship alongside in space.'

'We didn't. We got rid of the emergency crew and took their suits.'

'Got rid of them?'

Talman moved his eyes towards Brown. 'What else could we do? We can't afford half measures in a gamble as big as this. Later on, they'd have been a danger to us, after our plans started moving. Nobody's going to know anything about it, except us. And you.' Again Talman looked at Brown. 'I think, Quent, you'd better throw in with us.'

The amplifier ignored whatever implied threat lay in the suggestion.

'What do you want the power plant for?'

'We've got an asteroid picked out,' Talman said, tilting his head back to search the great crowded hollow of the ship, swimming a little in the haze of its poisonous atmosphere. He half expected Brown to cut him short, but the fat man didn't speak. It was, he thought, curiously difficult to talk persuasively to someone whose location you didn't know. 'The only trouble is, it's airless. With the plant, we can manufacture our own air. It'd be a miracle if anybody ever found us in the Asteroid Belt.'

'And then what? Piracy?'

Talman did not answer. The voicebox said thoughtfully, 'It might make a good racket, at that. For a while, anyhow. Long enough to clean up quite a lot. Nobody will expect anything like it. Yeah, you might get away with the idea.'

'Well,' Talman said, 'If you think that, what's the next logical step?'

'Not what you think. I wouldn't play along with you. Not for moral reasons, especially, but for motives of self-preservation. I'd be useless to you. Only in a highly intricate, widespread civilization is there any need for Transplants. I'd be excess baggage.'

'If I gave you my word – '

'You're not the big shot,' Quentin told him. Talman instinctively sent another questioning look at Brown. And from the voicebox on the wall came a curious sound like a smothered laugh.

'All right,' Talman said, shrugging. 'Naturally you won't decide in our favour right away. Think it over. Remember you're not Bart Quentin any more – you've got certain mechanical handicaps. While we haven't got too much time, we can spare a little – say ten minutes – while Cunningham looks things over. Then . . . well, we aren't playing for marbles, Quent.' His lips thinned. 'If you'll throw in with us and guide the ship under our orders, we can afford to let you live. But you've got to make up your mind fast. Cunningham is going to trace you down and take over the controls. After that – '

'What makes you so sure I can be traced down?' Quentin asked calmly. 'I know just how much my life would be worth once I'd landed you where you want to go. You don't need me. You couldn't give me the right maintenance even if you wanted to. No, I'd simply join the crewmen you've already disposed of. I'll give you an ultimatum of my own.'

'You'll – what?'

'Keep quiet and don't monkey with anything and I'll land in an isolated part of Callisto and let you all escape,' Quentin said. 'If you don't, God help you.'

For the first time Brown showed he had been conscious of that distant voice. He turned to Talman.

'Bluff?'

Talman nodded slowly. 'Must be. He's harmless.'

'Bluff,' Cunningham said, without looking up from his task.

'No,' the amplifier told him quietly, 'I'm not bluffing. And be careful with that board. It's part of the atomic hookup. If you fool with the wrong connections, you're apt to blast us all out of space.'

Cunningham jerked back from the maze of wires snaking out of the bakelite before him. Fern, some distance away, turned a swarthy face to watch. 'Easy,' he said. 'We've got to be sure what we're doing.'

'Shut up,' Cunningham grunted. 'I *do* know. Maybe that's what the Transplant's afraid of. I'll be plenty careful to stay clear of atomic connections, but – ' He paused to study the tangled wires. 'No. This isn't atomic – I think. Not the control leads, anyway. Suppose I break this connection – ' His gloved hand came up with a rubber-sheathed cutter.

The voicebox said, 'Cunningham – don't.' Cunningham poised the cutter. The amplifier sighed.

'You first, then. Here it is!'

Talman felt the transparent faceplate slap painfully against his nose. The immense room bucked dizzily as he went reeling forward, unable to check himself. All around him he saw grotesque space-suited figures reeling and stumbling. Brown lost his balance and fell heavily.

Cunningham had been slammed forward into the wires as the ship abruptly decelerated. Now he hung like a trapped fly in the tangle, his limbs, his head, his whole body jerking and twitching with spasmodic violence. The devil's dance increased in fury.

'Get him out of there!' Dalquist yelled.

'Hold it!' Fern shouted. 'I'll cut the power – ' But he didn't know how. Talman, dry-throated, watched Cunningham's body sprawling, arching, shaking in spastic agony. Bone cracked suddenly.

Cunningham jerked more limply now, his head flopping grotesquely.

'Get him down,' Brown snapped, but Fern shook his head.

'Cunningham's dead. And that hookup's dangerous.'

'How? Dead?'

Under his thin moustache, Fern's lips parted in a humourless smile. 'A guy in an epileptic fit can break his own neck.'

'Yeah,' Dalquist said, obviously shaken. 'His neck's broken, all right. Look at the way his head goes.'

'Put a twenty-cycle alternating current through yourself and you'd go into convulsions too,' Fern advised.

'We can't just leave him there!'

'We can,' Brown said, scowling. 'Stay away from the walls, all of you.' He glared at Talman. 'Why didn't you – '

'Sure, I know. But Cunningham should have had sense enough to stay away from bare wires.'

'Few wires are insulated around here,' the fat man growled. 'You said the Transplant was harmless.'

'I said he had no mobility. And that he wasn't a telepath,' Talman realized that his voice sounded defensive.

Fern said, 'A signal's supposed to sound whenever the ship accelerates or decelerates. It didn't go off that time. The Transplant must have cut it out himself, so we wouldn't be warned.'

They looked up into that humming, vast, yellow emptiness. Claustrophobia gripped Talman. The walls looked ready to topple in – to fold down, as though he stood in the cupped hand of a titan.

'We can smash his eye cells,' Brown suggested.

'Find 'em.' Fern indicated the maze of equipment.

'All we have to do is unhitch the Transplant. Break his connection. Then he goes dead.'

'Unfortunately,' Fern said, 'Cunningham was the only electronic engineer among us. I'm only an astrophysicist!'

'Never mind. We pull one plug and the Transplant blacks out. You can do that much!'

Anger flared. But Cotton, a little man with blinking blue eyes, broke the tension.

'Mathematics – geometry – ought to help us. We want to locate the Transplant, and – ' He glanced up and was frozen. 'We're off our course!' he said finally, licking dry lips. 'See that telltale?'

Far above, Talman could see the enormous celestial globe. On its dark surface a point of red light was clearly marked.

Fern's swarthy face showed a sneer. 'Sure. The Transplant's running to cover. Earth's the nearest place where he can get help. But we've plenty of time left. I'm not the technician Cunningham was, but I'm not a complete dope.' He didn't look at the rhythmically-moving body on the wires. 'We don't have to test every connection in the ship.'

'OK, take it, then,' Brown grunted.

Awkward in his suit, Fern walked to a square opening in the floor and peered down at a mesh-metal grating eighty feet below. 'Right. Here's the fuel feed. We don't need to trace connections through the whole ship. The fuel's dumped out of that leader tube overhead there. Now look. Everything connected with the atomic power is apparently marked with red wax crayon. See?'

They saw. Here and there, on bare plates and boards, were cryptic red markings. Other symbols were in blue, green, black and white.

'Go on that assumption,' Fern said. 'Temporarily, anyhow. Red's atomic power. Blue . . . green . . . um.'

Talman said suddenly, 'I don't see anything here that looks like Quentin's brain case.'

'Did you expect to?' the astrophysicist asked sardonically. 'It's slid into a padded socket somewhere. The brain can stand more gravs than the body, but seven's about tops in any case. Which, incidentally, is fine for us. There'd be no use putting high-speed potential in this ship. The Transplant couldn't stand it, any more than we could.'

'Seven G's,' Brown said thoughtfully.

'Which would black out the Transplant too. He'll have to remain conscious to pilot the ship through Earth atmosphere. We've got plenty of time.'

'We're going pretty slow now,' Dalquist put in.

Fern gave the celestial globe a sharp glance. 'Looks like it. Let me work on this.' He paid out a coil from his belt and hitched himself to one of the central pillars. 'That'll guard against any more accidents.'

'Tracing a circuit shouldn't be so hard,' Brown said.

'Ordinarily it isn't. But you've got everything in this chamber – atomic control, radar, the kitchen sink. And these labels are only for construction convenience. There wasn't any blueprint to this ship. It's a single-shot model. I can find the Transplant, but it'll take time.

So shut up and let me work.'

Brown scowled but didn't say anything. Cotton's bald head was sweating. Dalquist wrapped his arm about a metal pillar and waited. Talman looked up again at the balcony that hung from the walls. The celestial globe showed a crawling disc of red light.

'Quent,' he said.

'Yes, Van.' Quentin's voice was quietly distant. Brown put one hand casually to the blaster at his belt.

'Why don't you give up?'

'Why don't you?'

'You can't fight us. Your getting Cunningham was a fluke. We're on guard now – you can't hurt us. It's only a matter of time until we trace you down. Don't look for mercy then, Quent. You can save us trouble by telling us where you are. We're willing to pay for that. After we find you – on our own initiative – you can't bargain. How about it?'

Quentin said simply, 'No.'

There was silence for a few minutes. Talman was watching Fern, who, very cautiously paying out his coil, was investigating the tangle where Cunningham's body still hung.

Quentin said, 'He won't find the answer there. I'm pretty well camouflaged.'

'But helpless,' Talman said quickly.

'So are you. Ask Fern. If he monkeys with the wrong connections, he's apt to destroy the ship. Look at your own problem. We're heading back towards Earth. I'm swinging into a new course that'll end at the home berth. If you give up now – '

Brown said, 'The old statutes never were altered. The punishment for piracy is death.'

'There's been no piracy for a hundred years. If an actual case came to trial, it might be a different matter.'

'Imprisonment? Reconditioning?' Talman asked. 'I'd a lot rather be dead.'

'We're decelerating,' Dalquist called, getting a firmer grip on his pillar.

Looking at Brown, Talman thought the fat man knew what he had in mind. If technical knowledge failed, psychology might not. And Quentin, after all, was a human brain.

First get the subject off guard.

'Quent.'

But Quentin didn't answer. Brown grimaced and turned to watch Fern. Sweat was pouring down the physicist's swarthy face as he concentrated on the hookups, drawing diagrams on the stylopad he wore attached to his forearm.

After a while Talman began to feel dizzy. He shook his head, realizing that the ship had decelerated almost to zero, and got a firmer grip on the nearest pillar. Fern cursed. He was having a difficult time keeping his footing.

Presently he lost it altogether as the ship went free. Five space-suited figures clung to convenient handgrips. Fern snarled, 'This may be deadlock, but it doesn't help the Transplant. I can't work without gravity – he can't get to Earth without acceleration.'

The voicebox said, 'I've sent out an SOS.'

Fern laughed. 'I worked that out with Cunningham – and you talked too much to Talman, too. With a radar meteor-avoider, you don't need signalling apparatus, and you haven't got it.' He eyed the apparatus he had just left. 'Maybe I was getting too close to the right answer, though, eh? Is that why – '

'You weren't even near it,' Quentin said.

'Just the same – ' Fern kicked himself away from the pillar, paying out the line behind him. He made a loop about his left wrist, and, hanging in midair, fell to studying the hookup.

Brown lost his grip on the slippery column and floated free like some overinflated balloon. Talman kicked himself across to the railed balcony. He caught the metal bar in gloved hands, swung himself in like an acrobat and looked down – though it wasn't really *down* – at the control chamber.

'I think you'd better give up,' Quentin said.

Brown was floating across to join Fern. 'Never,' he said, and simultaneously four G's hit the ship with the impact of a pile driver. It wasn't forward acceleration. It was in another, foreplanned direction. Fern saved himself at the cost of an almost dislocated wrist – but the looped line rescued him from a fatal dive into uninsulated wiring.

Talman was slammed down to the balcony. He could see the others plummet to hard impacts on unyielding surfaces. Brown wasn't stopped by the floor plate, though.

He had been hovering over the fuel-feed hole when the acceleration was slammed on.

Talman saw the bulky body pop out of sight down the opening. There was an indescribable sound.

Dalquist, Fern, and Cotton struggled to their feet. They cautiously went towards the hole and peered down.

Talman called, 'Is he – '

Cotton had turned away. Dalquist remained where he was, apparently fascinated, Talman thought, until he saw the man's shoulders heaving. Fern looked up towards the balcony. 'He went through the filter screen,' he said. 'It's a one-inch gauge metal mesh.'

'Broke through?'

'No,' Fern said deliberately. 'He didn't break through. He went through.'

Four gravities and a fall of eighty feet add up to something slightly terrific. Talman shut his eyes and said, 'Quent!'

'Do you give up?'

Fern snarled. 'Not on your life! Our unit's not that interdependent. We can do without Brown.'

Talman sat on the balcony, held on to the rail, and let his feet hang down into emptiness. He stared across to the celestial globe, forty feet to his left. The red spot that marked the ship stood motionless.

'I don't think you're human any more, Quent,' he said.

'Because I don't use a blaster? I've different weapons to fight with now. I'm not kidding myself, Van. I'm fighting for my life.'

'We could still bargain.'

Quentin said, 'I told you you'd forget our friendship before I did. You must have known this highjacking could only end in my death. But apparently you didn't care about that.'

'I didn't expect you to – '

'Yeah,' the voicebox said. 'I wonder if you'd have been as ready to go through with the plan if I'd still had human form? As for friendship – use your own tricks of psychology, Van. You look on my mechanical body as an enemy, a barrier between you and the real Bart Quentin. Subconsciously, maybe, you hate it, and you're therefore willing to destroy it. Even though you'll be destroying me with it. I don't know – perhaps you rationalize that you'd thus be rescuing me from the thing that's erected the barrier. And you forget that I haven't changed, basically.'

'We used to play chess together,' Talman said, 'but we didn't smash the pawns.'

'I'm in check,' Quentin countered. 'All I've got to fight with are knights. You've still got castles and bishops. You can move straight for your goal. Do you give up?'

'No!' Talman snapped. His eyes were on the red light. He saw a tremor move it, and gripped the metal rail with a frantic clutch. His body swung out as the ship jumped. One gloved hand was torn from its grip. But the other held. The celestial globe was swinging violently. Talman threw a leg over the rail, clambered back to his precarious perch, and looked down.

Fern was still braced by his emergency line. Dalquist and little Cotton were sliding across the floor, to bring up with a crash against a pillar. Someone screamed.

Sweating, Talman warily descended,. But by the time he had reached Cotton the man was dead. Radiating cracks in his faceplate and contorted, discoloured features gave the answer.

'He slammed right into me,' Dalquist gulped. 'His plate cracked into the back of my helmet – '

The chlorinated atmosphere within the sealed ship had ended Cotton's life, not easily, but rapidly. Dalquist, Fern and Talman matched glances.

The blond giant said, 'Three of us left. I don't like this. I don't like it at all.'

Fern showed his teeth. 'So we're still underestimating that thing. From now on, hitch yourselves to pillars. Don't move without sound anchorage. Stay clear of everything that might cause trouble.'

'We're still heading back towards Earth,' Talman said.

'Yeah,' Fern nodded. 'We could open a port and walk out into free space. But then what? We figured we'd be using this ship. Now we've *got* to.'

Dalquist said, 'If we gave up – '

'Execution,' Fern said flatly. 'We've still got time. I've traced some of the connections. I've eliminated a lot of hookups.'

'Still think you can do it?'

'I think so. But don't let go of your handgrips for a second. I'll find the answer before we hit atmosphere.'

Talman had a suggestion. 'Brains send out recognizable vibration patterns. A directional finder, maybe?'

'If we were in the middle of the Mojave, that would work. Not here. This ship's lousy with currents and radiations. How could we unscramble them without apparatus?'

'We brought some apparatus with us. And there's plenty all around the walls.'

'Hooked up. I'm going to be plenty careful about upsetting the *status quo*. I wish Cunningham hadn't gone down the drain.'

'Quentin's no fool,' Talman said. 'He got the electronic engineer first and Brown second. He was trying for you then, too. Bishop and queen.'

'Which makes me what?'

'Castle. He'll get you if he can.' Talman frowned, trying to remember something. Then he had it. He bent over the stylopad on Fern's arm, shielding the writing with his own body from any photoelectrics that might be spotted around the walls or ceiling. He wrote: 'He gets drunk on high frequency. Can do?'

Fern crumpled the tissue slip and tore it awkwardly into fragments with his gloved fingers. He winked at Talman and nodded briefly.

'Well, I'll keep trying,' he said, and paid out his line to the kit of apparatus he and Cunningham had brought aboard.

Left alone, Dalquist and Talman hitched themselves to pillars and waited. There was nothing else they could do. Talman had already mentioned this high-frequency irritation angle to Fern and Cunningham; they had seen no value to the knowledge then. Now it might be the answer, with applied practical psychology to supplement technology.

Meanwhile, Talman longed for a cigarette. All he could do, sweating in the uncomfortable suit, was to manipulate a built-in gadget so that he managed to swallow a salt tablet and a few gulps of tepid water. His heart was pounding, and there was a dull ache in his temples. The spacesuit was uncomfortable; he wasn't used to such personal confinement.

Through the built-in receiving gadget he could hear the humming silence, broken by the padding rustle of sheathed boots as Fern moved about. Talman blinked at the chaos of equipment and closed his eyes; the relentless yellow light, not intended for human vision, made little pulses beat nervously somewhere in his eye sockets. Somewhere in this ship, he thought, probably in this very chamber, was Quentin. But camouflaged. How?

Purloined letter stuff? Scarcely. Quentin would have had no reason to expect highjackers. It was pure accident that had intervened to protect the Transplant with such an excellent hiding place. That, and the slapdash methods of technicians, constructing a one-job piece of equipment with the casual convenience of a slipstick.

But, Talman thought, if Quentin could be made to reveal his location –

How? Via induced cerebral irritation – intoxication?

Appeal to basics? But a brain couldn't propagate the species. Self-preservation remained the only constant. Talman wished he'd brought Linda along. He'd have had a lever then.

If only Quentin had had a human body, the answer would not be so difficult to find. And not necessarily by torture. Automatic muscular reactions, the old stand-by of professional magicians, could have led Talman to his goal. Unfortunately, Quentin himself was the goal – a bodiless brain in a padded, insulated metal cylinder. And his spinal cord was a wire.

If Fern could rig up a high-frequency device, the radiations would weaken Quentin's defences – in one way, if not another. At present the Transplant was a very, very dangerous opponent. And he was perfectly camouflaged.

Well, not perfectly. Definitely no. Because, Talman realized with a sudden glow of excitement, Quentin wasn't simply sitting back, ignoring the pirates, and taking the quickest route back to Earth. The very fact that he was retracing his course instead of going on to Callisto indicated that Quentin wanted to get help. And, meanwhile, via muder, he was doing his utmost to distract his unwelcome guests.

Because, obviously, Quentin *could* be found.

Given time.

Cunningham could have done it. And even Fern was a menace to the Transplant. That meant that Quentin – was afraid.

Talman sucked in his breath. 'Quent,' he said, 'I've a proposition. You listening?'

'Yes,' the distant, terribly familiar voice said.

'I've an answer for all of us. You want to stay alive. We want this ship. Right?'

'Correct.'

'Suppose we drop you by parachute when we hit Earth atmosphere. Then we can take over the controls and head out again. That way – '

'And Brutus is an honourable man,' Quentin remarked. 'But of course he wasn't. I can't trust you any more, Van. Psychopaths and criminals are too amoral. They're ruthless, because they feel the end justifies the means. You're a psychopathic psychologist, Van, and that's exactly why I'd never take your word for anything.'

'You're taking a long chance. If we do find the right hookup in time, there'll be no bargaining, you know.'

'If.'

'It's a long way back to Earth. We're taking precautions now. You can't kill any more of us. We'll simply keep working steadily till we find you. Now – what about it?'

After a pause Quentin said, 'I'd rather take my chances. I know technological values better than I do human ones. As long as I depend on my own field of knowledge, I'm safer than if I tried to deal in psychology. I know coefficients and cosines, but I don't know much about the colloid machine in your skull.'

Talman lowered his head; sweat dripped from his nose to the interior of the faceplate. He felt a sudden claustrophobia; fear of the cramped quarters of the suit, and fear of the larger dungeon that was the room and the ship itself.

'You're restricted, Quent,' he said, too loudly. 'You're limited in your weapons. You can't adjust atmospheric pressure in here, or you'd have compressed already and crushed us.'

'Crushing vital equipment at the same time. Besides, those suits can take a lot of pressure.

'Your king's still in check.'

'So is yours,' Quentin said calmly.

Fern gave Talman a slow look that held approval and faint triumph. Under the clumsy gloves, manipulating delicate instruments, the hookup was beginning to take shape. Luckily, it was a job of conversion rather than construction, or time would have been too short.

'Enjoy yourself,' Quentin said. 'I'm slamming on all the G's we can take.'

'I don't feel it,' Talman said.

'All we can take, not all I could give out. Go ahead and amuse yourselves. You can't win.'

'No?'

'Well – figure it out. As long as you stay hitched in one place, you're reasonably safe. But if you start moving around, I can destroy you.'

Quentin laughed. 'I didn't say so. I'm well camouflaged. *Turn that thing off!*'

The shout echoed and re-echoed against the vaulted roof, shaking the amber air. Talman jerked nervously. He met Fern's eye and saw the astrophysicist grin.

'Its hitting him,' Fern said. Then there was silence, for many minutes.

The ship abruptly jumped. But the frequency inductor was securely moored, and the men, too, were anchored by their lines.

'Turn it off,' Quentin said again. His voice wasn't quite under control.

'Where are you?' Talman asked.

No answer.

'We can wait, Quent.'

'Keep waiting, then! I'm . . . I'm not distracted by personal fear.

That's one advantage of being a Transplant.'

'High irritant value,' Fern murmured. 'It works fast.'

'Come on, Quent,' Talman said persuasively. 'You've still got the instinct of self-preservation. This can't be pleasant for you?'

'It's . . . too pleasant,' Quentin said unevenly. 'But it won't work. I could always stand my liquor.'

'This isn't liquor,' Fern countered. He touched a dial.

The Transplant laughed. Talman noted with satisfaction that oral control was slipping. 'It won't work, I say. I'm too . . . smart for you.'

'Yeah?'

'Yeah. You're not morons – none of you are. Fern's a good technician, maybe, but he isn't good enough. Remember, Van, you asked me in Quebec if there'd been any . . . change? I said there hadn't. I'm finding out now that I was wrong.'

'How?'

'Lack of distraction.' Quentin was talking too much; a symptom of intoxication. 'A brain in a body can never concentrate fully. It's too conscious of the body itself. Which is an imperfect mechanism. Too specialized to be efficient. Respiratory, circulatory – all the systems intrude. Even the habit of breathing's a distraction. Now the ship's my body – at the moment – but it's a perfect mechanism. It functions with absolute efficiency. So my brain's correspondingly better.'

'Superman.'

'Superefficient. The better mind generally wins at chess, because it can foresee the possible gambits. I can foresee everything you might do. And you're badly handicapped.'

'Why?'

'You're human.'

Egotism, Talman thought. Was this the Achillean heel? A taste of success had apparently done its psychological work, and the electronic equivalent of drunkenness had released inhibitions. Logical enough. After five years of routine work, no matter how novel that work might be, this suddenly altered situation – this change from active to passive, from machine to protagonist – might have been the catalyst. Ego. And cloudy thinking.

For Quentin wasn't a superbrain. Very definitely he was not. The higher an I.Q., the less need there is for self-justification, direct or indirect. And, oddly, Talman suddenly felt absolved of any lingering compunctions. The real Bart Quentin would never have been guilty of paranoid thought patterns.

So –

Quentin's articulation was clear; there was no slurring. But he no longer spoke with soft palate, tongue and lips, by means of a column of air. Tonal control was noticeably altered now, however, and the Transplant's voice varied from a carrying whisper to almost a shout.

Talman grinned. He was feeling better, somehow.

'We're human,' he said, 'but we're still sober.'

'Nuts. Look at the telltale. We're getting close to Earth.'

'Come off it, Quent,' Talman said wearily. 'You're bluffing, and we both know you're bluffing. You can't stand an indefinite amount of high frequency. Save time and give up now.'

'You give up,' Quentin said. 'I can see everything you do. The ship's a mass of traps anyway. From up here all I have to do is watch until you get close to one. I'm planning my game ahead, every gambit worked out to checkmate for one of you. You haven't got a chance. You haven't got a chance. You haven't got a chance.'

From up here, Talman thought. Up where? He remembered little Cotton's remark that geometry could be used to locate the Transplant. Sure. Geometry and psychology. Halve the ship, quarter it keep bisecting the remainders –

Not necessary. *Up* was the key word. Talman seized upon it with an eagerness that didn't show on his face. *Up*, presumably, reduced by half the area they'd have to search. The lower parts of the ship could be ruled out. Now he have to halve the upper section, using the celestial globe, say, as the dividing line.

The Transplant had eye cells spotted all over the ship, of course, but Talman tentatively decided that Quentin thought of himself as situated in one particular spot, not scattered over the whole ship, localized wherever an eye was built in. A man's head is his locus, to his own mind.

Thus Quentin could see the red spot on the celestial globe, but that didn't necessarily mean that he was located in a wall facing that hemisphere of the sphere. The Transplant had to be trapped into references to his actual physical relation to objects in the ship – which would be hard, because this could be done best by references to sight, the normal individual's most important link with his surroundings. And Quentin's sight was almost omnipotent. He could see everything.

There had to be a localization – somehow.

A word-association test would to it. But that implied co-operation. Quentin wasn't that drunk!

Nothing could be gauged by learning what Quentin could see – for his brain was not necessarily near any one of his eyes. There would be a subtle, intrinsic realization of location on the Transplant's part; the knowledge that he – blind, deaf, dumb except through his distant extensor sensory mechanisms – was in a certain place. And how, except by too obviously direct questioning, could Quentin be made to give the right answers?

It was impossible, Talman thought, with a hopeless sense of frustrated anger. The anger grew stronger. It brought sweat to his face, rousing him to a dull, aching hatred of Quentin. All this was Quentin's fault, the fact that Talman was prisoned here in this hateful spacesuit and this enormous deathtrap of a ship. The fault of a machine –

Suddenly he saw the way.

It would, of course, depend on how much drunk Quentin was. He glanced at Fern, questioned the man with his eyes, and in response Fern manipulated a dial and nodded.

'Damn you,' Quentin said in a whisper.

'Nuts,' Talman said. 'You implied you haven't any instinct for self-preservation any more.'

'I . . . didn't – '

'It's true, isn't it?'

'No,' Quentin said loudly.

'You forget I'm a psychologist, Quent. I should have seen the angles before. The book was open, ready to read, even before I saw you. When I saw Linda.'

'Shut up about Linda!'

Talman had a momentary, sick vision of the drunken, tortured brain somewhere hidden in the walls, a surrealistic nightmare. 'Sure,' he said. 'You don't want to think about her yourself.'

'Shut up.'

'You don't want to think about yourself, either, do you?'

'What are you trying to do, Van? Get me mad?'

'No,' Talman said, 'I'm simply fed up, sick and disgusted with the whole business. Pretending that you're Bart Quentin, that you're still human, that we can deal with you on equal terms.'

'There'll be no dealing – '

'That's not what I meant, and you know it. I've just realized what you are.' He let the words hang in the dim air. He imagined he could hear Quentin's heavy breathing, though he knew it was merely an illusion.

'Please shut up, Van,' Quentin said.

'Who's aking me to shut up?'

'I am.'

'And what's that?'

The ship jumped. Talman almost lost his balance. The line hitched to the pillar saved him. He laughed.

'I'd be sorry for you, Quent, if you were – you. But you're not.'

'I'm not falling for any trick.'

'It may be a trick, but it's the truth too. And you've wondered about it yourself. I'm dead certain of that.'

'Wondered about what?'

'You're not human any more,' Talman said gently. 'You're a thing. A machine. A gadget. A spongy grey hunk of meat in a box. Did you really think I could get used to you – now? That I could identify you with the old Quent? You haven't any face!'

The soundbox made noises. They sounded mechanical. Then – 'Shut up,' Quentin said again, almost plaintively. 'I know what you're trying to do.'

'And you don't want to face it. Only you've got to face it, sooner or later, whether you kill us now or not. This . . . business . . . is an incident. But the thoughts in your brain will keep growing and growing. And you'll keep changing and changing. You've changed plenty already.'

'You're crazy,' Quentin said. 'I'm no . . . monster.'

'You hope, eh? Look at it logically. You haven't dared to do that, have you?' Talman held up his gloved hand and ticked off points on his sheathed fingers. 'You're trying very desperately to keep your grip on something that's slipping away – humanity, the heritage you were born to. You hang on to the symbols, hoping they'll mean the reality. Why do you pretend to eat? Why do you insist on drinking brandy out of a glass? You know it might just as well be squirted into you out of an oil can.'

'No. No! It's an aesthetic – '

'Garbage. You go to teleshows. You read. You pretend you're human enough to be a cartoonist. It's a desperate, hopeless clinging to something that's already gone from you, all these pretences. Why do you feel the need for binges? You're maladjusted, because you're pretending you're still human, and you're not, any more.'

'I'm . . . well, something better – '

'Maybe . . . If you'd been born a machine. But you *were* human. You had a human body. You had eyes and hair and lips. Linda must remember that, Quent.'

'You should have insisted on a divorce. Look – if you'd only been crippled by the explosion, she could have taken care of you. You'd have needed her. As it is, you're a self-sufficient, self-contained unit. She does a good job of pretending. I'll admit that. She tries not to think of you as a hopped-up helicopter. A gadget. A blob of wet cellular tissue. It might be tough on her. She remembers you as you used to be.'

'She loves me.'

'She pities you,' Talman said relentlessly.

In the humming stillness the red telltale crept across the globe. Fern's tongue stole out and circled his lips. Dalquist stood quietly watching, his eyes narrowed.

'Yeah,' Talman said, 'face it. And look at the future. There are compensations. You'll get quite a bang out of meshing your gears. Eventually you'll even stop remembering you ever were human. You'll be happier then. For you can't hang on to it, Quent. It's going away. You can keep on pretending for a while, but in the end it won't matter any more. You'll be satisfied to be a gadget. You'll see beauty in a machine and not in Linda. Maybe that's happened already. Maybe Linda knows it's happened. You don't have to be honest with yourself yet, you know. You're immortal. But I wouldn't take that kind of immortality as a gift.'

'Van – '

'I'm still Van. But you're a machine. Go ahead and kill us, if you want, and if you can do it. Then go back to Earth and, when you see Linda again, look at her face. Look at it when she doesn't know you're watching. You can do that easily. Rig up a photoelectric cell in a lamp or something.'

'Van . . . *Van*!'

Talman let his hands drop to his sides. 'All right. Where are you?'

The silence grew, while an inaudible question hummed through the yellow vastness. The question, perhaps, in the mind of every Transplant. The question of – a price.

What price?

Utter loneliness, the sick knowledge that the old ties were snapping one by one, and that in place of living, warm humanity there would remain – a mental monster?

Yes, he had wondered – this Transplant who had been Bart Quentin. He had wondered, while the proud, tremendous machines that were his body stood ready to spring into vibrant life.

Am I changing? Am I still Bart Quentin?

Or do they – the humans – look on me as – How does Linda really feel about me now? Am I –

Am I – It?

'Go up on the balcony,' Quentin said. His voice was curiously faded and dead.

Talman made a quick gesture. Fern and Dalquist sprang to life. They climbed, each to a ladder, on opposite sides of the room, but carefully, hitching their lines to each rung.

'Where is it?' Talman asked gently.

'The south wall – Use the celestial sphere for orientation. You can reach me – ' The voice failed.

'Yes?'

Silence. Fern called down, 'Has he passed out?'

'Quent!'

'Yes – About the centre of the balcony. I'll tell you when you reach it.'

'Easy.' Fern warned Dalquist. He took a turn of his line about the balcony rail and edged forward, searching the wall with his eyes.

Talman used one arm to scrub his fogged faceplate. Sweat was trickling down his face and flanks. The crawling yellow light, the humming stillness from machines that should be roaring thunderously, stung his nerves to unendurable tension.

'Here?' Fern called.

'Where is it, Quent?' Talman asked. 'Where are you?'

'Van,' Quentin said, a horrible, urgent agony in his tone. 'You can't mean what you've been saying. You can't. This is . . . I've got to know! I'm thinking of Linda!'

Talman shivered. He moistened his lips.

'You're a machine, Quent,' he said steadily. 'You're a gadget. You know I'd never have tried to kill you if you were still Bart Quentin.'

And then, with shocking abruptness, Quentin laughed.

'Here it comes, Fern!' he shouted, and the echoes crashed and roared through the vaulted chamber. Fern clawed for the balcony rail.

That was a fatal mistake. The line hitching him to that rail proved a trap – because he didn't see the danger in time to unhook himself.

The ship jumped.

It was beautifully gauged. Fern was jerked towards the wall and halted by the line. Simultaneously the great celestial globe swung from its support, in a pendulum arc like the drive of a Gargantuan fly swatter. The impact snapped Fern's line instantly.

Vibration boomed through the walls.

Talman hung on to a pillar and kept his eyes on the globe. It swung back and forth in a diminishing arc as inertia overcame momentum. Liquid spattered and dripped from it.

He saw Dalquist's helmet appear over the rail. The man yelled, 'Fern!'

There was no answer.

'Fern! Talman!'

'I'm here,' Talman said.

'Where's – ' Dalquist turned his head to stare at the wall. He screamed.

Obscene gibberish tumbled from his mouth. He yanked the blaster from his belt and aimed it at the maze of apparatus below.

'Dalquist!' Talman shouted. 'Hold it!'

Dalquist didn't hear.

'I'll smash the ship,' he screamed. 'I'll – '

Talman drew his own blaster, steadied the muzzle against the pillar, and shot Dalquist in the head. He watched the body lean over the rail, topple, and crash down on the floor plates. Then he rolled over on his face and lay there, making sick, miserable sounds.

'Van,' Quentin said.

Talman didn't answer.

'Van!'

'Yeah!'

'Turn off the inductor.'

Talman got up, walked unsteadily to the device, and ripped wires loose. He didn't bother to search for an easier method.

After a long while the ship grounded. The humming vibration of currents died. The dim, huge control chamber seemed oddly empty now.

'I've opened a port,' Quentin said. 'Denver's about fifty miles north. There's a highway four miles or so in the same direction.'

Talman stood up, staring around. His face looked ravaged.

'You tricked us,' he mumbled. 'All along, you were playing us like fish. My psychology – '

'No,' Quentin said. 'You almost succeeded.'

'What – '

'You don't think of me as a gadget, really. You pretended to, but a little matter of semantics saved me. When I realized what you'd said, I came to my senses.'

'What I said?'

'Yeah. That you'd never have tried to kill me if I'd still been Bart Quentin.'

Talman was struggling slowly out of his spacesuit. Fresh, clean air had already replaced the poison atmosphere of the ship. He shook his head dazedly.

'I don't see it.'

Quentin's laughter rang out, filling the chamber with its warm, human vibrancy.

'A machine can be stopped or destroyed, Van,' he said. 'But it can't be – *killed*.'

Talman didn't say anything. He was free of the bulky suit now, and he turned hesitantly towards a doorway. He looked back.

'The door's open,' Quentin said.

'You're letting me go?'

'I told you in Quebec that you'd forget our friendship before I did. Better step it up, Van, while there's still time. Denver's probably sent out helicopters already.'

Talman swept one questioning look around the vast chamber. Somewhere, perfectly camouflaged among those mighty machines, was a small metal cylinder, cradled and shielded in its hidden socket. Bart Quentin –

His throat felt dry. He swallowed, opened his mouth, and closed it again.

He turned on his heel and went out. The muffled sound of his footsteps faded.

Alone in the silent ship, Bart Quentin waited for the technicians who would refit his body for the Callisto flight.

Android

Bradley looked at the Director's head. His stomach tried to crawl up into his throat. He felt suddenly dizzy. He knew that he was betraying himself, and that would be absolutely fatal.

He reached into his pocket, pulled out a pack of cigarettes and a few coins, and let the coins drop, as though by accident, to the airfoam carpet.

'Oh-oh,' he said, and immediately crouched down to recover the money. It's a basic principle of first aid, in cases of shock or faintness, to lower the head, and Bradley was doing just that. The giddiness began to pass as his circulation picked up. In a moment, he knew, he'd have to stand up and face the Director, and by that time he was determined to have his feelings under control. But how the devil could the Director's head be where it was – after last night?

And then sanity came back. He remembered that, last night, the Director couldn't possibly have recognized him through the rubber-plastic false-face he had worn. On the other hand, after last night, the Director of New Products, Inc., should have been incapable of living or breathing, not to speak of using his memory-centres. Bradley had left the man's body in one corner of the room and his head in another.

Man?

With a violent effort he controlled himself. He recaptured the last coin and stood up, his face flushed. 'Sorry,' he said. 'I came in to deliver that report on the induced mutation project, not to act like a horn of plenty.' His fascinated stare moved down to the Director's neck and flicked away. The high collar concealed any – any mark. Any mark, such as might have been left by razor-sharp steel shearing through flesh and bone . . .

Was there a reason for the high collar? Bradley couldn't be sure. In the fall of 2060, men's fashions had changed considerably from the uncomfortable styles of a few years before, and the Director's flaring half-cape, with its gilt-braided, close-fitting collar, was far from extreme. Bradley owned one like that himself.

Lord, he thought in white panic – *can't the – the things even be killed?*

Arthur Court, the Director, turned a bland smile on his Chief of Organization. 'Hangover?' he asked. 'Take an irradiation treatment. Medical's always happy to use their gadgets. Our staff's too healthy to suit them, I think.'

He talked!

A mad thought whirled into Bradley's brain: a ringer? Was this really Court sitting behind the desk? But instantly he knew that couldn't be the explanation. It was Court, the same Arthur Court whom Bradley had killed not many hours ago. If you could call it killing, when Court hadn't actually been alive . . . at least, not with the same sort of life that activated human beings.

He forced his mind from the danger-level and became the efficient Chief of Organization of the company. 'You can't argue with a hangover,' he said. 'Here're the latest figures – '

'What about that variant factor? I gathered there was something that upset the calculations.'

'There was,' Bradley said. 'But it's a theoretical variable. It doesn't matter a bit in practice, because we're not trying to mutate people. And the sterility rate doesn't vary abnormally with fruit-flies or – or strawberries.'

'But it does with people – eh?' Court glanced rapidly through the papers Bradley had given him.

'Uh-huh. We could follow it up, but it would cost money and wouldn't have any immediately practical results. That's up to you to decide, sir.'

'We can predict non-human reactions with reasonable accuracy, though?'

Bradley nodded. 'Two per cent factor of error. Close enough for us to mutate potatoes twenty feet long and tasting like roast beef, without any danger of getting them half an inch long instead, and tasting like cyanide.'

'Does the curve of variance rise with animals?'

'No. Only people. We can hatch chickens which are all white meat and built cube-shapes for easy carving. And, really, we could mutate people too, if it weren't illegal – but the uncertainty factor steps in here, as I said. Too many people become sterilized instead of having mutated children.'

'Um,' Court said, and pondered. 'Well, forget about the people, then. There's no profit in it. Drop that part of the investigation. Go ahead with the rest. All right?'

'Fine,' Bradley agreed. He had expected to be stopped at this point of the inquiry, though, since last night, not by Court. He found he was still holding an unlighted cigarette. He put it in his mouth and went to the side door and opened it. Then he turned.

'That's all?'

He watched Court twist his neck around, and had an insane fear that the man's head might fall off. But it didn't.

'Yes, that's all for now,' Court said pleasantly.

Bradley went out, trying to forget the narrow red line he had just seen circling the Director's throat, revealed when the man had turned his head.

The things couldn't be killed by decapitation, then. But they could be destroyed. They could be dissolved with acid, smashed with a hammer, dismantled, burned . . .

The trouble was, there was as yet no sure way to recognize the creatures. The sterility curve after exposure to mild radioactivity meant something, but ordinary humans could have become sterilized too – though not usually by such slight dosages of gamma rays. And even then, some people were sterile anyway.

All Bradley had was a general method of screening. After that, he had to depend on psychology to weed out the monsters. He knew that they could usually be found in positions of power and influence, though not necessarily in the public eye. Like Arthur Court, who, as Director of New Products, Inc., wielded tremendous influence on the culture – since civilization is moulded by the technological tools placed in its hands.

Bradley shivered.

Last night he had cut off Arthur Court's head.

Arthur Court was an android.

'And what are you going to do about it?' Bradley asked himself in the hall outside Court's door. He looked down with a certain academic interest in his own hand shaking until the papers he held fluttered. What *could* he do about it? He or any other man?

You couldn't fight them on equal terms. Probably their I.Q. was far higher than mankind's. On terms of pure intellect Bradley would have no chance at all. Super-comptometers could solve abstruse problems no limited human mind could tackle. Last night Bradley had worn a distorting rubber mask – but if Court's cold metallic brain set itself the problem of reasoning out his identity, wouldn't

Court arrive at the right answer sooner or later?

Had he already arrived at an answer?

Bradley suppressed a panicky impulse to run. There was such dead silence behind the door at his elbow. For all he knew *they* had vision that could slip between the buzzing atoms of the door and see Bradley here as if he stood beyond glass – see through him and into the patterns of his brain, and read all his thoughts as they took form.

'They're only androids,' he reminded himself with great firmness, forcing his gait to a walk as he turned away down the hall. 'If they had that much power I wouldn't be here now.'

Still, he wondered with a corroding urgency just what had happened last night after he left Court's apartment. He would not think of how Court had looked, lying there motionless beside the heavy steel blade dimmed by that stickiness that looked like blood and was not human blood.

Had he repaired himself, after Bradley left? Repaired was the word, of course – not *cured*. Only a human could be cured. It probably depended on just where the brain of the android was located. Not necessarily in the head. The head is really too vulnerable a place for such an important mechanism. You could improve on the structure of the human in so many ways. Perhaps the androids had. Perhaps Court's brain was sheltered somewhere in the mysterious chambers of his synthetic body, and its cold, clicking thoughts had gone on their steely processes all the while Bradley stood there looking down in incredulous shock at the body of his – his victim?

Which was the victim and which the victor?

All functional processes had certainly stopped in the robot after decapitation. Bradley had made sure of that. No respiration, no heartbeat. But somewhere inside, perhaps the metallic brain had been clicking quietly on its cold way. So cold, Bradley thought irrationally, that not all the synthetic warmth of the synthetic blood could raise it a fraction of a degree towards human temperature.

Either Court's body had risen after Bradley left, then, and welded on the head again, or else others had come to – repair – the sabotage. Did each robot, in operation, send out the equivalent of a steady beam, of energy which when it ceased, brought a repair crew to the spot? If that had happened, it was lucky Bradley had not lingered too long in that room where no murder had been done, though Court's head lay so far from his motionless body . . .

Of course I could be just as crazy as a bedbug, Bradley reminded himself sardonically. Certainly he would have a hard time convincing anyone he wasn't. And he would have to convince someone. He couldn't go on alone any farther. He had gone too far now to keep this knowledge to himself. By his very act of proof, by the cutting off of an android head, he had given himself away. Sooner or later they would track down the identity of the man behind that rubber mask. Before it happened, he would have to pass this information on.

And there he ran his second terrible risk. The androids would show him no mercy when they caught him. But how much could he expect from his own kind, when he told his fantastic tale? *I'll end in a padded cell,* he thought, *while they go on multiplying outside until –*

Until what? Until they outnumbered the humans and take over control? Perhaps they already had. Perhaps they had let him go free after that harmless murder because only he was human now in the whole civilized world . . . Perhaps he was quite harmless, really. Perhaps –

'Oh, shut up,' Bradley urged himself impatiently.

'Then at least you don't suspect me of being a – an android?' Dr Wallinger asked dourly. He was slightly nervous, as the result of having sat for ten minutes now with a gun-muzzle pointed unwaveringly at his stomach. It was, of course, ridiculous that a mysterious rubber-masked figure in a gold-braided cape whose flare concealed most of its wearer's body should be sitting here in his library forcing him to listen to psychotic nonsense.

'You have children,' Bradley said, his voice a little muffled behind the mask. 'That was how I could feel sure about you.'

'Look,' Wallinger said earnestly, 'I'm a nuclear physicist. I think a psychologist could probably give you more help than – '

'A psychiatrist, you mean?'

'Not at all. Of course not. But – '

'But all the same, you think I'm crazy. All right. I expected you would. I suppose I wouldn't have trusted you very far if you hadn't. That reaction's normal. But – blast you, man, open your mind! Look at the thing fairly. Isn't it conceivable that this could have happened?'

Wallinger, with a glance at the gun, put his fingertips together and pursed his lips. 'Um, conceivable . . . Well, there's no threshold, naturally. Though 1/100 roentgen per day is considered safe unless both parents are subject to gamma bombardment. You've borne in mind the normal recovery time? Even under bombardment, you know, the changed genes have less tendency to divide and are gradually supplanted by normal genes.'

'You aren't telling me anything new,' Bradley said with forced patience. 'My point is that gamma radiations that would produce mutation in humans have no effect on robots, which are sterile to begin with. If *only* androids were sterile it would be simple, but gamma rays induce sterility in humans too. You have children. You're all right. But – '

'Hold on,' Wallinger said. 'Couldn't there be android children? If they can make adults, couldn't they put together synthetic children too?'

'No. I've thought that out carefully. Children grow too fast. They'd have to reorganize the whole android child every couple of weeks, change all its inward and outward dimensions, work over everything about it. I think that would call for too much time and effort. They can't afford it yet, if my calculations are right. There aren't enough of them. And later, when they could afford the job, it wouldn't be necessary. You see? By the time they were able to go to all that trouble, they wouldn't need to. They'd be in the majority. They wouldn't have to deceive us. They – '

Bradley paused. His voice had been getting out of control. Above all, he would have to remain cool and calm about this.

'There's one other angle,' he said. 'I don't think an android child could deceive other children. Real children. They see things too directly. The android brain is coordinated in synthetic human adult thinking. They've done a good job of it, but even now, if you know the truth, you can catch them by their psychological failures of adjustment. For one thing, they aren't exhibitionists. They never try to bully or assert themselves over others. Why should they? They're perfectly functioning and efficient gadgets. They don't need to compensate. They're too well adjusted to be really human.'

'Then why couldn't they adjust to a child mentality?'

'For the same reason they couldn't create a growing child physically. A child's mind is too different from an adult's, and it changes too fast. It grows. Anyhow, why should they? They don't need to. They've fooled us all up to now, and even when one man knows the truth, what can he do about it? You won't listen to me. You won't – '

'I'm listening,' Wallinger said mildly. 'It makes an interesting tale, anyhow. I wish you'd tell me what gave you the idea to start with.'

Bradley caught himself on the verge of saying, 'It was my work. I had a chance to correlate a lot of material and everything added up to an unknown factor.' But he didn't say it. He meant to remain anonymous until he felt sure it was safe to reveal himself. A clue like that could be tracked down too easily.

'I – figured it out,' he said. ' – I have friends in various jobs who kept mentioning little discrepancies they'd noticed. I got interested. It began to add up. There were accidents in which the patients *should* have died, sometimes did die, and then came back to life. Oh, they always covered it by talk about adrenalin shots and so forth, but it's happened too often. And always in cases involving people in influential positions. I don't know just how they work it – maybe a real person dies and his android double takes his place. They've got the recuperative powers of a machine, but a machine's handicaps, too. Cut one and it bleeds, but – '

Bradley paused, measuring Wallinger's receptiveness with a wary glance.

'All right,' he said suddenly, 'I'll tell you what really happened. Please try to listen without prejudice if you can. It was six months ago. I was alone in a – a laboratory – with one of my friends.' It had been Arthur Court, the Director. This had been the first proof Bradley actually saw.

'He fumbled a retort and it shattered and cut his wrist to the bone. He didn't know I saw it happen. And even though I did see, for a long time I tried to argue myself out of believing it. On the surface of his wrist there was flesh, and it bled. But underneath were wires and metal. I tell you, I *saw them*! It wasn't an artificial arm, it was the real thing. An artificial arm wouldn't be part flesh and blood.'

'What did he do?'

'That's the real give-away. He put his hand in his pocket and made some excuse to get out of the room. He didn't want me to know, because he'd have to call a doctor, and I suppose there weren't any of *their* men within reach. He couldn't let a human even go through the motions of bandaging him. Oh, they're vulnerable in lots of ways. But now is the time to strike, before they cut down too far on their vulnerabilities. *Now* –' Bradley paused again, forcing his voice under control.

'What do you suggest, then?' Wallinger asked in his mild voice. It was impossible to guess whether Bradley had succeeded in touching the man's mind with conviction, or even the beginnings of it.

'I don't know.' Under the flared cape Bradley's shoulders sagged. 'That's why I came to you. I thought – well, look. Here's one possibility. I need an infallible way of locating them. Psychology's all right up to a point, but it's too slow. I've got to know so much about the subject's life and habit patterns. If the factor of mechanical logic and efficiency's too accurate, that's a double check. But – '

'But there's the mechanical factor itself,' Wallinger offered unexpectedly. 'Have you thought of that? It might – ' He paused and grinned a little sheepishly. 'Go on,' he said.

Behind the rubber mask Bradley's face creased in a broad, exultant smile. That was the opening wedge. He had succeeeded in presenting the physicist with a hypothetical problem that had struck a spark of momentary interest. It was still in the realm of theory, but Wallinger had responded. That was all that mattered now. He went on with increased enthusiasm.

'That's it exactly. A machine has to be operated. There must be a power source somewhere. Maybe it's in them, or maybe they pick it up from some broadcasting source. But it should be possible to detect it. Something like a thyratron recorder hidden in places they frequent, or a Geiger counter, or – '

'You think they could be trapped because of ionizing radiations?'

'Oh, I don't know what I think. It could be nuclear fission that works the things. It could be anything. That's why I need help from someone like you. Someone who could make closer guesses than I can.'

Wallinger regarded his fingertips. 'I couldn't, you know,' he said. 'Not without much more information than you can give me. You've asked me to hear you with an open mind. Now you listen to me. If our positions were reversed, wouldn't you demand more proof than a stranger's say-so? It would take almost unlimited time and experiment to make a theoretical gadget to detect these theoretical androids of yours, especially since you can't even guess yet what their functional principle is. Have you thought of trying it from some more practical angle – *x*-rays, for instance? The human organism is a tremendously complicated structure. I doubt if it could be perfectly duplicated.'

Bradley shrugged beneath the flaring cape. 'All an *x*-ray shows is light and shadow. 'The – things – are constructed internally to register normally on a fluoroscope. The only way to be certain would be by using surgery – and how could you do that? They never get sick. If you'd seen what I have – '

He paused. He couldn't say, 'If you'd cut off Arthur Court's head and knew what I know about the wires and the plastic tubes, the vertebrae that aren't bone – ' But if he admitted how far he had gone to get his certain proof, it would sound to Wallinger like proof of his own madness.

'They're part flesh and blood, and part machine,' he said carefully. 'Maybe the mechanical parts are necessary to keep the living tissues functioning normally. But we'll never prove it except by force. They're all adults, in high positions. You'd need their consent to perform an operation, and they naturally won't give it. Unless – ' He paused. The idea that had flashed through his mind blotted out Wallinger's face for a moment. Perhaps there was a way, after all. Perhaps –

'Now listen to me,' Wallinger was saying patiently, his eyes on the gun. 'I'm not unreasonable. You've got an interesting idea here, but you aren't ready yet to prove anything. Why don't you go back to your job, whatever it is, and gather some more data? Then when you – '

'*I'm afraid to go back*,' Bradley said in a thin voice.

A knock, low down on the closed door, interrupted Wallinger's reply. Before he could turn, the door opened a small crack and through it bounded a half-grown cat closely followed by a small girl and a much smaller boy. The cat hurtled across the carpet in the stiff-legged, high-tailed gallop which is a cat's idea of humour. The girl paused when she saw Bradley, but the boy was too intent on the animal to notice anything.

Wallinger said in a voice that did not sound at all like his own, 'Children, go back upstairs! Now!' His face was suddenly grey. He did not glance at Bradley.

The cat had fallen over heavily and lay lashing its tail and making clawless boxing motions at the small boy. Its rough, imperfect purring filled the sudden silence in the room.

'Jerry,' Wallinger said, 'take the kitten and go back upstairs. Do you hear me? Sue, you know you mustn't come into my study without knocking. Go on upstairs.'

'We knocked,' the girl said, her eyes on Bradley, who had slipped the gun under a fold in his cloak. He was trying to analyze a thought that had flashed through his mind as soon as he saw the children. There was something here he could use, but it would take time to work the idea out.

He stood up, seeing Wallinger's tense start as he moved. The man was terrified. Bradley knew why, suddenly.

The girl watched the stranger with round, interested eyes. The boy and the cat had simultaneously noticed him now and both were stricken with shyness. The cat scrambled to its feet and prepared to sell its life dearly, and the boy looked around for something to hide behind. The little girl, however, exhibited unmistakable signs of intending to show off. She was around seven, Bradley guessed. He glanced from face to face of the Wallinger family, and then grinned.

'It's all right,' he said. 'I won't keep you any longer, Doctor. You'll hear from me.'

'By all means,' Wallinger said, too heartily. He was only interested now in getting his children away from the dangerous proximity of his guest. He followed Bradley into the hall, pushing the children behind him and closing the door.

'I – ' He started to stammer a little.

'Forget it,' Bradley said. 'What do you think I am? They're nice kids.'

Wallinger sighed. 'Where can I get in touch with you?'

'You can't. I'm going to bring you proof of what I've told you. Those things are half machines under their skins, and I'll find some way to make you believe it. I suppose you'd call the police as soon as I'm gone. I can't help that.'

'No, no, of course I won't,' Wallinger lied soothingly.

'All right. One more thing, though. I said I was afraid to go back. I meant it. I've done – well, some things that may have given me away. Things I had to do, to make sure . . . It's a toss-up now whether they or I find the proof we're after first. Dr Wallinger, I'm going to write down names and facts on this case – things I don't dare tell you now. If you receive that information, you'll know the androids got their proof first. And that in itself ought to be *your* proof all this is true. I won't be around any more, if that happens. It will all depend on you then.'

'Don't worry about that,' Wallinger said. 'I'm sure – '

'All right, all right,' Bradley cut him off. 'Wait and see. Goodbye, Doctor. You'll hear from me.'

He watched the house over his shoulder as he went down the street. No one came out. When he reached the corner he turned it, entered a drugstore and made his way back through the crowded aisles to the telephone booths beside a window. Through the window he could see far away the corner of the Wallinger house, and the library window where Wallinger's desk was. At the desk a distant man sat telephoning, making quick, excited gestures as he talked.

Bradley sighed. At least, Wallinger didn't know his face or name. He could give the police only a circumstantial tale almost too wild for belief. Bradley would have to walk a knife-edged path now, balancing like a tight-rope walker. Both sides were against him.

He drew a deep breath, squared his shoulders and turned back towards the office where Arthur Court would be waiting for him.

Two of them stood at Court's desk, their backs to him. Bradley paused in the door. Something was wrong. Instinct warned him – a feeling in the air, the poise of the two before him, intangibles that still seemed to shriek an alarm to nerves tense enough to catch their message.

Of the two at the desk, one was not human. The other went by the name of Johnson, and he might not be human either. It was hard to tell.

Bradley had to try twice before his voice would come normally from a suddenly dry throat.

'You want me, sir?'

Court turned, smiling. His high collar hid the line where head and neck had been welded back in place. His smile was perfectly normal, but Bradley imagined now he could hear the tiny, soundless clicking of infinitesimal gears as the android's jaw moved and its inhuman muscles drew up.

'Look here, Bradley,' Court said. 'Ever see this before?'

Bradley looked. Then for an instant the blood drained from his head and the room went grey with his sudden giddiness. But this time he did not dare to drop anything or even to pause while he got control of himself again. They were both watching. He made a tremendous effort and forced the greyness back, forced the quiver out of his voice, forced his hands to stop shaking.

'See what?' he asked in a perfectly normal voice. But he knew well enough.

Court held up the razor-edged blade that had struck his head from his neck forty-eight hours ago. It was unmistakably the same heavy weapon Bradley had bought at a second-hand shop two days before he used it on the Director. He knew it by the carving on the handle, by the nick in the blade where some inhumanly durable metal in Arthur Court's neck had bitten into the honed edge of the steel. When Bradley saw it last, it lay beside the headless android body, red with unreal android blood.

'Ever see it before?' Court asked again.

'I – don't think so,' Bradley heard himself saying, with just the right amount of impersonal interest. 'Not to remember, anyhow. Why?'

They looked thoughtfully at him. And by that single look, identical in both faces, he was suddenly quite sure that neither was human. It was something about the quality of the stare. He realized after a moment that it was the same look he had seen in the Wallinger kitten's eyes – remote, wild, speculative, not inimical but wary. One species looking at another species, measuring possible danger. The kitten had seen him from quite another angle, from low down, in sharp perspective, and probably not in colours, but in tones of grey. It was extraordinary, suddenly, to think how strange he might have looked to the small, wild, wary creature. If he could see himself as it saw him, he might not recognize that looming figure as himself at all. And it occurred to him now that to the androids he must look equally strange and alien. In what colours beyond spectrum-range did they see him? And what a soft, vulnerable structure of flesh and bone he must look to these creatures of steel and synthetics.

They let him wait a long moment before either spoke or moved. Then that cold-lensed stare dropped from his face, both androids acting as simultaneously as if they moved on a single shaft. It was a mistake, Bradley thought – they shouldn't let me realize how mechanically they operate. And the second thought, close behind the first, warned him that perhaps now they didn't care. They knew what he knew. They had nothing more to hide . . .

Deliberately Court turned and made a note on his desk-pad.

'All right, Bradley, thanks. Oh – wait a minute. Be in your office for the next half-hour, will you? I want to talk to you again.'

Bradley nodded. He didn't trust himself to speak. He was suddenly filled with a deep and bitter humiliation that he must accept the orders of this – this machine.

It was the reversal of all normal things, for a man to say 'sir' to a thing of gears and wiring.

He looked down at his own hands lying clenched before him on his desk. Ten minutes had ticked by. Before the next twenty were gone he would have to act. They knew. It had been no accident that they called him in to see the nicked steel blade. How they had traced it to him he could not imagine, but their cold, concise brains worked on theories of logic he could not even guess at. They had outwitted him, apparently, without effort. For all his precautions, his careful hiding of everything that might lead back to his identity, they knew. Or if they did not, they were too definitely suspicious to ignore. In the next five minutes, ten at most, he would have to make up his mind. He would have to act.

He couldn't. All that filled his mind was the bitterness of premature defeat. How could he combat them, when even his own kind dismissed him as psychotic? It was doubtful, he told himself, if the whole human race, rousing at this moment to realization and activity, could defeat them now. How far had their preparations gone? How many of them were there? Too many for one man to fight.

He thought of the whole long history of the race of man, struggling up through countless millenniums of unrecorded time, through five thousand years of slowly increasing knowledge and maturity – to this hour. To the laying in iron android hands, gloved with synthetic flesh, of that priceless heritage. What would they do with the gift? Why were they taking over this culture mankind had been so painfully long in building? Would it mean anything at all to them, or would they cast aside the heritage of all those millenniums and build up their own soulless civilization on a foundation that did not even spare a glance for all man's wasted centuries?

'*How did it start?*' he asked himself. '*Why? Why?*' And out of the human logic of his own mind came the glimmer of an answer. '*When the first man made the first successful android, the human race was doomed.*'

For a successful android meant one indistinguishable from man, one capable of creating others in its own image. One capable of independent motion and reasoning. And what purpose moved in the brain of that first of its metal kind? Had its human creator implanted there some command which led – knowingly or unknowingly – to all that followed? Had the order been one which the android could achieve only by duplicating itself until the human race was infected through and through with the robot cells of the androids?

It was quite possible. Perhaps the original creator still lived, perhaps he was dead – of age, of accident, or murder at the hands of his own Frankensteinian creations. And paradoxically, perhaps the android race moved on and on along the outward fanning lines of that first command, following towards infinity, towards the last decimal place, some impossible goal which no human being would now ever know . . .

'They'll finish me,' Bradley told himself, almost without emotion. 'If they don't suspect me yet, they will. And there's nothing I can do to stop them. Wallinger didn't believe me. No one else will. And the androids will follow me until they catch me no matter how far I run. When they finish me off, they'll probably set to work to make their disguise so perfect not even I could have penetrated it, knowing what I know. They could do that. They could reason out every point where I suspected them, and stop every gap with humanoid behaviour. They're machines. That's part of their problem. They can work it out if they set themselves the job. Maybe they're working on it now. By the time they finish me, maybe . . . '

He slammed both fists hard upon the desk. '*No*!' he told himself fiercely, and rose.

There were fifteen minutes left.

The telephone on Arthur Court's desk buzzed. The android put out a metallic hand and machine spoke into machine. Out of the mouthpiece Bradley's voice sounded small and clear.

'Hello. Hello, sir. This is Bradley. Look, are you busy? Something very odd has just turned up and I thought you ought to be the first to know. I – I'm not sure what to do.'

'What is it? What are you talking about?'

'I'd rather not say on the phone.'

'Where are you?'

'Across the street. You know the Green Door Grille?'

'I thought I told you to wait in your office, Bradley.'

'When you hear what I've got to tell you – ' Bradley paused for an instant to swallow his own cold anger at the arrogance in the voice of the machine ' – you'll understand. Can you come?'

'Sit tight. I'll be there in five minutes.'

Bradley sat at the wheel of his car, feeling the faint throb of the motor running softly. His eyes were on the door of the office building across the street. His fingers were clenched on the plastic of the wheel and the rhythmic beat of the car seemed an echo of the heavy beating in his chest as he waited.

Arthur Court came out of the revolving door. He looked up and down the street. He turned left and with long strides hurried down the block towards the little side-street upon which the Green Door opened. Bradley waited, watching Court, watching the traffic, biding his time.

It worked with miraculous precision. There were only three pedestrians on the side-street and all were walking the other way. Heavy trucks parked along the narrow curbing shut out all vision except the most direct. It was as if Arthur Court were dodging through a series of little private rooms between the trucks – and in the last little room he had a rendezvous with Bradley that he did not yet know about . . .

The car purred like a tiger under Bradley's hands as he rolled into the quiet street where Court moved ahead of him. This would have to be gauged exactly right, Bradley reminded himself tensely. Not too little, not too much. Not before Court was in a corner where he could not escape even by the exercise of instant reflexes, impulses electron-fast moving a body that was literally steel wire and springs. Not until he was in a trap of no escape.

The car seemed to gather its haunches beneath it and spring. It roared in the quiet street and Court turned wildly around. His face was pure machine, Bradley thought, in that unguarded moment when the cold-lensed eyes met his. Bradley was part of the automobile, the two welded into one so that the car was his weapon, obedient to his hand as the steel blade had been obedient that severed Court's head from his neck. But this time there would be no mistake.

He crouched over the wheel, sighting the car like a gun, pinning Court between fender and fender, centred beyond the radiator cap, with the blank wall of a truck behind him. Man and man-made machine were one juggernaut weapon that crashed down upon machine-made machine and flattened it against a wall of steel . . .

Bradley saw Court's face go blank beyond the radiator cap. He saw the machine-body crumple slowly down out of sight. He waited for an instant, ready to urge the car on if he had to . . .

'It's all right,' Bradley said soothingly. Court stirred and mumbled on the seat beside him. 'No, it's all right, Court. Just relax. You had a little accident, but don't worry, I'm not taking you to a doctor . . . '

Court said, 'No – ' almost clearly. Bradley sighed and pulled over to the kerb. He had hoped he wouldn't need to use the hypodermic, but it was ready against the moment when he must.

This was guesswork, of course. He couldn't be sure the android mechanisms would respond to drugs meant for the human blood stream. But the chances were they would, at least temporarily. The android was keyed to as close a likeness to humanity as possible. Its reflexes were patterned upon the human. Cut it and it bled. Decapitate it and respiration ceased, circulation stopped. Very well, then, drug it and for a while it should sleep . . .

Court slept.

Only a body made of metal under the flesh could have stumbled in the semblance of a walk, half carried, half conscious, with that heavy a shot of sedative in its synthetic veins. Bradley guided the creature up the steps to the Wallinger house. He was not wearing his mask now. Everything must stand or fall by this single trial. If he failed now, hiding his identity would be of no use to him.

The small girl answered the door.

'Daddy's next door,' she said, looking at the drugged and stumbling Court with interest and no alarm. 'He'll be back in a minute. Won't you come in?' She issued the invitation with all the aplomb of one newly learned in the social graces, but it was clear that curiosity and not hospitality had prompted the words. It was clear, too, that she was so unacquainted with danger that a situation like this roused no fear in her mind.

Bradley guided his burden down the hall and into the library. On the sofa against the wall the kitten lay bonelessly asleep. Bradley eased the drugged android down onto the cushions, gently tipping the cat off to the floor: Such is the complexity of the mind that even in this intent moment it occurred to him that in a machine world the cat and the cushion would probably be indistinguishable, one from another. Only a human, and a truly mature human, would be incapable of handling any small living thing roughly. The cat yawned, woke, found itself on the floor and in the presence of two strangers, and instantly streaked for the door. Its interested ears presently reappeared around the corner.

Above them, after a moment, was seen the shy but curious face of the smallest Wallinger. Bradley made an effort and remembered his name.

'Hello, Jerry,' he called, settling Court on the sofa. 'Is your father back yet?'

There was no reply from the child, but the little girl came in an instant later, soon enough to answer the question. She was pushing her reluctant brother before her.

'I called Daddy,' she volunteered, 'He'll be right over. What's the matter with – him?'

'He had a – a little accident. He'll be all right.'

She considered Court with unselfconscious intentness. Court was emerging from the drug. He turned his head restlessly on the cushions, murmuring thickly. The boy, the girl and the kitten regarded him from the door, an almost terrifying remoteness in their gaze. It was obvious that to none of the three did real sympathy mean a thing yet. They could not identify themselves with adults or with suffering. All three had the cold curiosity of young animals in their eyes.

And why should they identify themselves with an android? Bradley felt the question click into place in his mind and a flash of memory illumined the thought. Children. Children, who see too clearly to be deceived by an android race. Children, without perspective and therefore without the preconceived prejudices that had blinded adults to this terrifying intrusion upon the world of humans.

Children should know the truth.

'Sue – isn't your name Sue? Listen. I want you to tell me something very important. I – I want your opinion.' Bradley groped desperately among his memories of the seven-year-old mentality. Self-centred, scatterbrained, eager for praise, interested only in their own activities except for the briefest of excursions into the outer world. If he could only flatter her enough to hold her interest . . . '

'Sue, this is something nobody but you could tell me. I want to see how much you know about – about – ' He paused again. 'Well, now, look. You know there are – ' How could he put it? How could he ask her if she had noticed the androids among the adults whom she knew? Had she, indeed, ever seen one before? On her answer very much would depend, then, for if she did know the truth, then there must be many more of them than Bradley had guessed. If even a sheltered child knew . . .

'Sue, you know about people like – *him*?' He gestured towards the restless android. 'You know there are – two kinds of men in the world?' He held his breath, waiting for her answer.

Wariness came into her eyes. You could never tell when an adult was making fun of you, her look said.

'No, I'm serious. I don't suppose – I just want to know if *you* know. Not all children can tell the difference, and I – '

'Oh, all the kids know *that*.' Contempt was in her voice.

'Know – what?'

'About them.'

Bradley drew a deep breath. *All the kids know about them* . . .

'Does your father know?' His voice sounded thin in his own ears.

She gave him another of those wary glances that watched to see if he were deriding her. Evidently reassured, she laughed shortly.

'Well, I guess he does. Doesn't everybody?'

The room swam a little before Bradley's eyes. So many of them, so many more than he had ever dreamed . . .

'But the other kind,' he heard himself saying almost pleadingly. 'The *other* kind of men! How many – '

There were voices in the hall. Wallinger's, and another's, deep and heavy.

'In here, Officer,' Wallinger was saying. 'Right in here! Hurry!'

'How many in the world?' Sue finished Bradley's question for him. And she laughed. 'We learned it in school, but I don't remember. I can tell you how many of the real kind of men in this room, though. One! One!'

'Will you tell your father that?' Bradley demanded in an agony of haste. 'When he comes in, will you tell him there's only one of the *real* kind of man in here? Sue, will you – '

'Susan, get back!' Wallinger was in the doorway. That grey look made his face old as he scanned the children for signs of visible harm. Behind him a uniformed man loomed, red-faced, looking into the room with grim alertness, ready for anything.

There was a little silence.

Then Court, on the sofa, groaned softly and struggled to sit up. Wallinger hurried across the room to help.

'What have you done to him?' he demanded of Bradley. 'You crazy fool, how far have you gone?'

'He's all right,' Bradley stammered. 'He's – you can't hurt *them*!'

Wallinger regarded him above Court's head.

'So that's what you look like,' he said. 'I knew you from across the street, even without your mask, but your face, of course – Will you tell us your name?'

'Bradley.' He said it defiantly. 'James Philips Bradley.' The time for anonymity had passed. He hadn't expected the policeman to be here – it would be harder to explain in that large, disbelieving presence – but if Sue repeated what she had just told him, maybe he could convince them yet.

'Ask your daughter about *them*,' he said urgently. 'She knows. Wallinger, I tell you, she knows! Remember, I warned you about the children? I said *they* couldn't hope to deceive children? Sue says all of them know – '

'I'd better warn you, Bradley, Sue's got a wild imagination. I don't know what fables she's been telling you, but – Officer, hadn't you better – '

'Wait!' This wasn't going as he had planned at all. He threw all the persuasion he could summon up into his voice. 'You promised to give me a hearing, Wallinger. Don't you remember, you promised? I know I had a gun then, but please – give me just a minute to tell you what I know. This man's one of *them*.' He paused, running his tongue across dry lips. Wallinger looked so disbelieving . . . 'He isn't hurt. I told you I'd bring proof, and there it is. This man. I had to get him here the only way I could. I tell you, you can't hurt *them*! Under the skin he's nothing but wires and metal. I can prove it! I – '

He broke off, feeling the policeman's hands laid on his arms lightly, holding them down. Wallinger's face showed pity and horror. It was no use. He should have managed to make some incision in Court's synthetic skin before they came. Of course they wouln't let him do it now. To them he was a madman, raving, eager to slash an innocent victim in proof of a madman's dream.

'Now, you just calm down, young man,' the policeman rumbled soothingly behind him. 'We'll take a little walk in the fresh air, and – '

'No! Wait!' Bradley's voice sounded wild even to himself. He choked back the protest, gathering himself for one tremendous last effort at the proof he had come so near to reaching.

Court watched him, lens-eyed, under lowered brows. Somewhere in that cold, inhuman body the cold inhuman brain ticked on remorselessly, not even amused at his defeat, for how could a machine know what it was like to laugh?

A machine – and so near, so near! Only a few feet of space separated them, and a fraction of an inch of synthetic skin hiding the mechanisms of the android body.

'Wait!' he said again, and he twisted around to Wallinger, trying with every ounce of energy that remained in him to project his own conviction past the barrier of prejudice that blinded the adults in this room. 'Wallingter, listen! After I've gone, will you talk to your little girl? Will you give me that much chance to prove myself? She knows! It isn't imagination! All the children know. Do you think *you're* safe, once Court gets out of here? They won't trust you. They can't. They'll be afraid you might wake in the night and suddenly realize the truth. Think of your daughter, Wallinger! Court's listening. He knows she recognized him. Can you take the chance with *her* life, Wallinger? Risk your own if you want to, but think of Sue!'

A flicker of the first uneasiness Bradley had seen moved across Wallinger's face. The policeman's hands were a little slack on Bradley's arms. He shrugged impatiently, and the momentary doubt on the physicist's face must have conveyed something to the officer, or perhaps it was the desperate conviction in Bradley's voice. He made the most of his moment.

'Think of Sue!' he went on. 'Court won't dare make a move – but you don't know how many others there are. You don't know! You can't even guess! Maybe the ones like Court are the real failures – the ones so imperfect they give themselves away. I think they've made others, so nearly human you'd never guess. Those are the dangerous ones, Wallinger! If there's even one of them, it will know it can't be safe until you're dead. I've told you too much to – '

'All right, Officer,' Wallinger said, with a little sigh. 'I'm sorry, Bradley, but you see how it is.'

Bradley's eyes went back to Court. The android sat motionless on the sofa, a thing of wheels and wiring as safe behind its make believe as if it wore a coat of mail. All human laws safeguarded human flesh. They held it so sacrosanct that now they were betraying it into the iron fingers of the enemy. If only these men would let him slash once with a knife at that soft, deceptive covering which was not flesh at all . . .

Suddenly Bradley laughed.

Even the robot stared a little at the sound, and the policeman made a growling noise in his throat, clearly thinking this the first ravings of a maniacal fit. But Bradley had his answer. He knew at last how he could convince even Wallinger.

'That automobile accident!' The car had been like a bludgeon in his hands. He knew – he remembered. A man can tell whether his blow has grazed the enemy or gone home. Until now it hadn't mattered. There had been too much else to deal with. But Court, pinned between car and truck wall, had not escaped unscathed. He fell as a man would fall, but he sat now as no man could possibly sit, upright, breathing easily . . .

Bradley remembered very clearly the feel of rib-structure giving, the sound of metal bending harshly where there should have been no metal. No man could sit like that, once a car had ground him against the wall as Bradley's car had ground Arthur Court.

He moved so suddenly the policeman's hands slipped from his arms. He was across the room in one leap, and tearing at Court's jacket before even the android had guessed what he intended.

The officer groaned and was upon him in a ponderous bound so fast that the heavy blue-coated body hurled Bradley aside with scarcely a half-second to spare. But Bradley had won his second. His hands were clenched in coat and shirt when the policeman's weight carried them both sidewise, and the cloth ripped in his grasp.

Court's short cape flared wide with the sudden defensive motion he made. The jacket and the shirt beneath opened and for one timeless moment there was no sound in the room, not even the drawing of breath. It seemed to Bradley that his heart itself paused with his breathing, for until this instant of the final test, he could not have been sure . . .

There was the tanned chest, smooth with android skin. But the mark of the car-grille was upon it, smashing in the android ribs. Bradley had heard the metal scream as it gave before his blow. Now he saw it. Now he saw the gleaming frameword of steel where no human chest ever bore steel, and within it a jumble of interlacing wires, and small, transparent tubes through which red fluid coursed . . .

He saw the android brain.

Deep inside, behind walls of bent steel ribbing, a small, bright, pulsing thing lay. A continuous twinkling beat outwards from it, uncannily illuminating the chest-cavern of the robot from within, so that the bright steel ribs caught points of light from that illumination, and wherever the transparent veins crossed before it the light turned glowing crimson as it shone through the blood. The fluid ran faster where the brilliance touched it, bubbles racing through the tubes. The thing might be heart and brain alike, an inward lamp burning in the broken shelter of the android chest.

Bradley did not even pause to reason. What he did was pure reflex. The incredible sight paralyzed the policeman for that one crucial second, but it galvanized Bradley to action.

He lunged forward, hands outstretched, and with one circling smash of his fist he struck the shining thing from its cradle.

There was an unbelievable instant when he saw his own hand deep in the hollow chest of the machine, saw the reflections of his blow moving in miniature in the polished ribs, saw his knuckles bathed in the tiny crimson glow of that inner light shining through transparent veins.

And then the light went out.

There was a crackle like crystal shattering. There was a sound more felt along the nerves than heard, of high, rapid humming that droned and ceased. And Arthur Court was no longer either man or android. He was not even machine.

The man-shaped thing in man's clothing pitched forward all in one piece, like metal moving, and fell solidly to the carpet, an effigy that could never conceivably have breathed or lived or spoken . . .

Bradley got shakily to his feet. The policeman still sprawled on the floor, staring, making no move to rise. The face that had been so ruddy was grey-white, and the colourless mouth opened and closed soundlessly, trying in vain to put the incredible into words. Bradley wanted insanely to laugh. Not even the pure human organism, he thought, functioned very efficiently in the face of shock like this.

It was Wallinger who moved first. Bradley had one glimpse of the physicist's face, drained of all colour, lined and rigid with horror. But the man was moving capably enough. At least, his limbs obeyed him. He circled Bradley with scarcely a glance, skirted the collapsed metal thing on the floor, and bent over the policeman . . .

He lifted one arm sharply, bent at the elbow, and struck the officer a hard, expert blow with the edge of his palm. The man collapsed without a sound.

Above him, Wallinger stared into Bradley's eyes.

'You're – on *their* side?' Bradley forced the words out painfully, wondering why they came in a whisper. He did not dare take his eyes from Wallinger's, but his mind had stopped functioning altogether and he scarcely knew why he stared, or why this thundering of sudden terror in his chest made breathing so hard. 'You're working with – *them*?'

Wallinger straightened slowly, letting the blue-coated body slide to the floor. His gaze broke from Bradley's and he looked across the room, towards the hall door. With a great effort Bradley followed the look.

The children still watched. Without alarm, interested, not comprehending, they watched as they might have watched a film at the neigbourhood movie.

'Sue – Jerry – upstairs!' Wallinger's voice was firm, almost normal. 'Move! And shut the door behind you.'

The sound of its closing seemed to release some of the tension in the man, for he let his breath out a little and his shoulders sagged. He met Bradley's eyes, grimaced, started to speak, and then thought better of it.

'Tell me!' Bradley's voice was stronger, insistence growing in it now. '*Which side are you on*?'

Wallinger did not want to answer. When he spoke, it was indirectly.

'It's not on record, Bradley,' he said, almost with diffidence, 'but I think you ought to know – the children aren't mine.'

'Not – '

'I adopted them.'

'But – but then – ' There was no need to finish the protest. Bradley had chosen this man for his confidences from the first, chiefly because he could be sure that here was one influential person of proved humanity – the father of other humans. No sterile machine.

Wallinger shrugged gently. He glanced down at the heavily breathing man at his feet.

'I had to do that,' he said. 'Now I'll have to think of some way to make him believe he dreamed all this. I hate to do it, but I can't think of any other way right now except – ' He glanced at his desk. 'Maybe this.'

There was a bottle of whisky in the top drawer. Moving with deliberate haste, he opened it, poured two generous portions into little metal cups from the same drawer, and then deliberately upended the bottle above the groaning policeman's chest.

Bradley reached for a cup, holding it in both hands to steady his shaking. The strong, burning liquid stuck in his throat for a moment, then spread downward with a grateful, soothing warmth.

'The story mustn't get out, you know,' Wallinger said above his own cup.

'But I don't – you mean you knew, all along? Wallinger, *what are you*?'

'The story mustn't get out,' Wallinger went on calmly, ignoring the question. 'Of course I knew. But we've got to keep it quiet.'

'Are you on their side or ours?' Bradley's throat felt raw with the harshness of his voice. 'Are you a man or – or – '

'If *they* find out how much we know about them, don't you suppose they'll act? Somehow we've got to dispose of the Court mechanism, in a way they won't be able to trace. I'm sorry for this officer here, but he'll have to think he was drunk and dreamed what we all saw. I tell you, Bradley, we don't dare let them suspect we know!'

Bradley let his emptied cup fall to the carpet. He walked forward six deliberate steps and put his hands heavily on Wallinger's shoulders. The flesh felt like flesh; the bone beneath was firm and hard. It could be bone – or steel. You couldn't tell by looking at them. But surely you could tell by the way they behaved, by their reactions, by their thinking. By the things they put first in value –

'The children!' Bradley said urgently. 'No – machine – would think first of children the way you do. Would it, Wallinger? Even though they aren't yours, you put them first. Why did you tell me they weren't yours? Did you mean – *what* did you mean, Wallinger? How do you really feel about those children?'

Wallinger smiled. His voice was mild and amused.

' "Hath not an android eyes?" ' he paraphrased with gentle irony. ' "Hath not an android hands – senses – affections? If you prick us, do we not bleed?" '

Bradley let his grip fall. He stepped back, staring as if he could pierce the too-perfect illusion of flesh and see whether bone or steel lay behind that gentle smiling face.

'There was one android made,' Wallinger said, 'in the perfect replica of the human. Everything that went into its mental and physical make-up was as close as their finest arts could come to human thinking.' He paused, grimaced. 'Well,' he said, 'they came too close. They succeeded. I – I'm rather afraid they made – a man.'

'You?'

Wallinger smiled.

'I don't believe it,' Bradley told him wildly. 'It isn't possible.'

Wallinger gave him a speculative look. Then he opened another drawer, fumbled in it and pulled out a penknife. He flicked the blade open and with almost the same gesture drew its edge across the back of his hand.

Bradley caught his breath. He didn't want to look, but he could not stop himself.

Wallinger, still smiling, held out his arm.

'I can stop the bleeding, you see,' he said. 'That's how Court kept from giving his injury away, at first. We can always control that, if necessary.'

There was no blood. The edges of the synthetic skin were clean and smooth as pale rubber, and beneath them steel tendons moved, transparent tubes as fine as hairs pulsed with bubbling red liquid. It was a hand of living metal. It was an android's hand.

'Satisfied?' Wallinger withdrew his arm. With the other hand he smoothed the cut flesh together. It sealed like wax and was whole again as Bradley still gasped his incredulous protest.

'Here, you'd better have another drink,' Wallinger's amused voice seemed to be saying from a long way off, above the ringing in his ears.

'But – why didn't you tell me? Are you sure they don't suspect? Can we really get away with this – with destroying Court? I don't understand, Wallinger! If you're really an android, and working against androids – what are we going to do? There must be ways they have to check up on what happens to every separate one. What about Court? Wallinger, if this is all true, why didn't you help me against Court? You could have – '

'Hold on! One question at a time!' Wallinger's voice broke into the almost hysterical babble of Bradley's released tension. 'First, about Court. I couldn't work against him, Bradley. I'm a very imperfect mechanism myself, considering what I was made for, and they'll destroy me if they find out what I'm about to do – but there are rules even I have to follow. They're built in. I can't injure another android. I *can't*. That's the way we're made. I couldn't any more than you could stop your blood from flowing if you were cut. I may be an imperfect machine, but I'm not that imperfect.'

'Then what shall we do? Why not call the police – the newspapers –'

'No! Don't talk like a fool. Once the androids know their secret's out, don't you think they'll strike hard and fast? They've got their plans all laid. Don't make any mistake about that. Our only hope's to work in the dark until we have plans too.'

'You could have told me sooner,' Bradley said with reproach. 'When I first came –'

'How could I have told you? I didn't know who you were, in that mask. You could have been from them, for all I knew. And today – I didn't dare speak in front of Court. I had to act like a normal man – call the police – show the right reactions. It wasn't until you attacked Court that I was sure about you.'

'Okay. We're wasting time, then. They'll know Court's – smashed. They'll look for him. What are we going to do?'

'I wish I knew.' Wallinger got up abruptly and began to pace up and down the room with quick, nervous steps. It was incredible that wires, not nerves, steel springs instead of muscles, activated that perfect replica of a human. Even in his mind, the likeness was so uncannily perfect . . .

'Full circle,' Bradley thought, with confused triumph. 'If this is true, they've overreached themselves. They've made such a perfect android – *if this is true* – that it'll mean the finish of their whole kind. They can't let him live. Once they suspect him, they'll have to destroy him. It works both ways. When the first successful android was made, the human race was doomed – until the first successful humanoid was produced by the robots. He's as dangerous to them as they are to us.' He looked at Wallinger thoughtfully.

'How do you feel about them – about the androids?' he asked.

'Confused.' Wallinger's smile was wry. 'This has been coming on for a long while, of course, but I've never had to take definite sides until now. I don't know how I feel. Lost. Not really belonging to either side. I suppose I feel exactly as you do about the human race – part of it. I *am* part of it. They made me too well. But how many humans would accept me if they knew the truth? And I could never go back to the androids once I've failed them. I don't belong on either side. I only know that I –' He paused, grinned suddenly and said with deliberation, 'I speak as a man, I think as a man, I have put away android things. You see? When I try to tell you how a humanoid feels I put it automatically into Shakespeare's words, or St Paul's. Men's words, telling how men feel. But I still see through a glass – ' He touched his eyes, which Bradley knew were lenses, not flesh. 'I see through glass, darkly . . . '

There was a long silence between them after that.

'Well,' Wallinger said heavily, 'it's up to me. I know them. You don't.'

'What do you want me to do?'

'Go home. Leave me your number, and stay there until I call you. Okay? I have an idea about getting rid of – this – ' He gestured at the man-shaped heap of wires and steel and flesh on the floor. 'I've got to do that alone. Afterwards, tomorrow, I'll phone you. But whatever you do, Bradley, don't leave your place until you hear from me. Don't even open the door! And above everything, don't go spreading the word about what's happened. If you do – '

'If I do, I'll wind up in a padded cell,' Bradley said. 'I know. Nobody would believe me except the androids, and they'd be only too glad to get me committed. Don't worry, I'll keep my mouth shut. But don't make me wait too long, will you?'

'I'll do my best,' Wallinger promised.

Bradley glanced up as he descended the steps towards the street. In the hall the two children stood watching him. The girl was smiling. She pointed to her brother and then waved at Bradley, nodding. He had a curious feeling that she was trying to convey something. But it was a child's knowledge behind her smile, esoteric, not communicable to the adult mind.

Bradley waved in answer and went on down the path.

When he woke it was still dark. He lay quiet, wondering for a confused instant where he was and why he should be awake. He could not see his watch, but there was a pre-dawn stillness in the air.

Then he saw the light beneath the door and heard the voices talking quietly beyond it. He lay in his own bed, and that was his own living room, but why the light burned and whose the voices were he could not guess.

He got up and went barefooted across the floor. He opened the door a narrow crack. There were five men in the room beyond. They sat comfortably there, talking softly, like men waiting for something – or someone.

The first face he saw was Arthur Court's.

'All right, Bradley,' the Director's familiar voice said in the very instant of recognition. 'All right, it's time now. Come in.'

Bradley never knew whether the android could actually see through the spinning atoms of the door, or whether some sound had given his own presence away. It didn't matter. He was beyond help now. He and the race of man . . .

He crossed the threshold quietly and closed the door behind him. He stood there looking at the five men in his living room. They sat perfectly motionless, their eyes on his. None of them had been smoking. None of them moved. None of them lived by the tight-strung nerves of imperfect humans, so they had no need for aimless motions. None of them was a man.

When the silence had reached a pitch just this side of being unbearable, Bradley spoke.

'What happened to Wallinger?' he asked.

'Nothing.' Court smiled at him.

'Nothing? But – '

'We needed a little extra time. Wallinger got it for us. That's all.'

A sudden upward flood of bitterness made Bradley's vision swim for an instant. How easily Wallinger had deceived him, then! How pitiably gullible was the illogical human brain before the resourceful logic of the machine! Wallinger had known exactly what lines of reasoning would most certainly soothe Bradley's fears to rest. And the quiet machine mind had not even lied when it spoke, for how can a machine deal in falsehood or in truth?

They needed time – for what? To repair the shattered Court, to assemble their forces, to close in. Most of all, they had needed to keep Bradley silent while they went about the business of destroying him. How? What would they do? Was there any way at all, even in this last moment, for him to outwit them? He thought there was not, but a desperate cunning made him say:

'All right, I can't stop you. Do what you like. But please, Court – please! We've worked together – you can't blame me for doing what I had to do, but we've worked together a long while. Do me one favour. Please don't let them put me in an insane asylum! It would be better if you shot me – safer for you! Anything's better than the asylum!'

He almost choked when he had to say it. No man should plead with a machine. But if it were for man's final salvation – yes, he could bring himself even to beg favours of this thing made of steel and wire. And this was his last weapon against them, this peculiarly inverted human logic which was part of folk-lore. The logic that saved Br'er Rabbit from his foes. *Don't throw me into the briar-patch*! If they committed him to an asylum, at least he would still be alive, at least he could still work against them. And the children knew. In time, someone would listen, if he could only stay alive.

'Please, Court, anything but the asylum!'

The android smiled. It was curious to think of the intricate little springs and wiring that drew up his face when it moved. It was appalling to realize that when Arthur Court spoke, the mind which dictated the words lay in the gleaming hollow of his chest where something made up of lights that twinkled was the essence and the soul of the machine.

'Forget it, Bradley,' the android said. 'It won't be the asylum.'

Bradley braced himself against the door. There was one thing left to do, then. He had tried cunning, and cunning failed. He had tried everything a man could try, and everywhere he had failed.

But they should not kill him. That final choice still lay in his own hands, and he would not submit to this last indignity. If he must die, let it be of his own will, freely.

He measured the distance to the window, gathering his muscles for this final leap. There was so much he would never know, he thought desparingly. The fate of the race of man itself, for which he had fought so vainly, was beyond his knowledge now. He thought of Wallinger, so nearly human in his reactions, so convincingly human in his speech, despite this final betrayal. Perhaps, after all, Wallinger had spoken more truthfully than he knew. Perhaps they had made an android too nearly human . . .

But it was too late. Wallinger's voice came back to his mind briefly, and the magnificent words of St Paul's that begin, 'Though I speak with the tongues of men . . . ' Wallinger had spoken with the tongue of man, but for man's destruction. There was something terrifying in the aptness of that chapter from Corinthians.

'Whether there be tongues, they shall cease, whether there be knowledge, it shall vanish away –'

Blindly he thrust himself away from the door in a last desperate leap. The nearest android moved too late to intercept him. He swept the curtains aside, drew back his fist and shattered the glass that was all that parted them from the humming street twenty stories down. Man's streets, which would so soon be man's no longer . . .

He lunged through the glass. He hung vertiginously over the

spinning depths below. He could see the wall of the building straight downward beneath his own knees, its lines swooping dizzily inward as he swayed.

It was Arthur Court's voice that halted him.

'Wait, Bradley, wait! Not until you hear the truth!'

It stopped him on the brink, and beyond the brink, of the window. He would have thought no power on earth could reverse the terrible suction of gravity that had already laid hands on him and was swinging him out and down with the very swing of the earth's rotation. But he found he was stronger than he knew . . .

Court's face was stern. Bradley stood braced against the shattered window, his knees strengthless, his head still spinning with the pull of the street below. Blank-eyed, he stared at the android across the room.

'You fool!' Arthur Court said. 'Are you trying to ruin us all?'

'But I – '

'You still don't understand? You still don't know Wallinger told you the truth?'

'Wallinger – told the truth?'

'Yes – in part. Think, Bradley, think!'

He could not think. His mind had suffered too many stunning shocks for reasoning now. But he did not need to think. He had had the clue many hours ago, and until this moment he had not known. The memory came back and he heard Sue Wallinger's small voice speaking again in the quiet library. He saw her at the door as he went down the path. He remembered her gesture and her smile.

'*I can tell you how many of the real kind of men in this room – one – one*!'

And she had smiled at him and touched her brother's shoulder.

She had not meant anyone in that room except the human male child. He had asked about men – she touched her brother's shoulder. All the children knew – all the androids knew. Only the humans were blind – and James Bradley.

'Look down,' Court's voice said, almost gently.

Bradley looked. There was blood on the floor. He felt a stinging in his hand, and dully lifted his arm to see why. He had put his fist through the window. It had not mattered, then, whether he slashed his own flesh or not. It didn't matter now . . .

He saw, without surprise, without shock, only with a numbness of the mind, how the edges of his skin had parted cleanly. The slow blood welled into his cupped palm. He looked down with utter silence at the uncovered tendons of his hand, gleaming mirror-bright from every steel surface. He saw the fine, tiny, tight-curled springs draw up in perfect response when he clenched his fingers.

'We made you too well,' Arthur Court was saying. 'We made you so well you're imperfect. You must be changed, Bradley. No android must be able to attack his own kind. Our survival depends on that law. Do you see now what Wallinger was trying to tell you? The danger of a perfect humanoid is too great. And you're perfect. Answer me, Bradley – do you understand what I'm saying?'

He could not answer. He knew the truth now, but he felt exactly as he had felt before. He was a man still. His whole loyalty lay with the human kind of which he was so merciless a duplicate. Until they made that change that would alter his imperfection, he must continue this fight he had taken up for man against machine. Until they changed him from imperfect android to the perfection of the race of the machine . . .

When that which is perfect is come, that which is in part shall be done away. St Paul had put it all with such terrifying clarity. *Though I speak with the tongues of men . . . I am become as sounding brass . . .*

'We don't want to waste you, Bradley,' Court said. 'You're a fine machine. We need you badly. There's so much work to be done, and we need your help.'

'No,' Bradley said. 'No.'

And this time they could not stop him.

He didn't pause to brush the curtain aside, and the glass was already shattered. He saw again the inward-leaning wall that dropped straight for twenty stories towards the street. His knee was on the sill.

Down there would be men to see. Down there in the street they must see and they might perhaps understand the meaning of this paradox that was the android body, the steel ribs and the intricate wiring by which this flesh-clad body once had moved . . .

Somewhere deep in his chest the little sparkling thing that at this moment thought as a man thinks knew an instant's wonder. 'Is this the way a man feels who gives up his life for his own kind?' Bradley asked himself the futile question. 'Or am I moving only as a machine moves, in blind obedience to the orders that were given me when I was made? They must have set me the problem of behaving like a human. And this is a thing men do . . . not machines. Never machines.'

He leaned out. The mighty drag of the earth's swing pulled him across the sill. It was not much he could do for the race in whose image he had been made, but it was all he could give them. Perhaps it might help. Perhaps it would not. That was something he would never know.

The robots crowded to the sill to watch him fall.

Or Else

Miguel and Fernandez were shooting inaccurately at each other across the valley when the flying saucer landed. They wasted a few bullets on the strange airship. The pilot appeared and began to walk across the valley and up the slope towards Miguel, who lay in the uncertain shade of a cholla, swearing and working the bolt of his rifle as rapidly as he could. His aim, never good, grew worse as the stranger approached. Finally, at the last minute, Miguel dropped his rifle, seized the machete beside him, and sprang to his feet.

'Die, then,' he said, and swung the blade. The steel blazed in the hot Mexican sun. The machete rebounded elastically from the stranger's neck and flew high in the air, while Miguel's arm tingled as though from an electric shock. A bullet came from across the valley, making the kind of sound a wasp's sting might make if you heard it instead of feeling it. Miguel dropped and rolled into the shelter of a large rock. Another bullet shrieked thinly, and a brief blue flash sparkled on the stranger's left shoulder.

'*Estoy perdido*,' Miguel said, giving himself up for lost. Flat on his stomach, he lifted his head and snarled at his enemy.

The stranger, however, made no inimical moves. Moreover, he seemed to be unarmed. Miguel's sharp eyes searched him. The man was unusually dressed. He wore a cap made of short, shiny blue feathers. Under it his face was hard, ascetic and intolerant. He was very thin, and nearly seven feet tall. But he did seem to be unarmed. That gave Miguel courage. He wondered where his machete had fallen. He did not see it, but his rifle was only a few feet away.

The stranger came and stood above Miguel.

'Stand up,' he said. 'Let us talk.'

He spoke excellent Spanish, except that his voice seemed to be coming from inside Miguel's head.

'I will not stand up,' Miguel said. 'If I stand up, Fernandez will shoot me. He is a very bad shot, but I would be a fool to take such a chance. Besides, this is very unfair. How much is Fernandez paying you?'

The stranger looked austerely at Miguel.

'Do you know where I came from?' he asked.

'I don't care a centavo where you came from,' Miguel said, wiping sweat from his forehead. He glanced towards a nearby rock where he had catched a goatskin of wine. 'From *los estados unidos*, no doubt, you and your machine of flight. The Mexican government will hear of this.'

'Does the Mexican government approve of murder?'

'This is a private matter,' Miguel said. 'A matter of water rights, which are very important. Besides, it is self-defence. That *cabrón* across the valley is trying to kill me. And you are his hired assassin. God will punish you both.' A new thought came to him. 'How much will you take to kill Fernandez?' he inquired. 'I will give you three pesos and a fine kid.'

'There will be no more fighting at all,' the stranger said. 'Do you hear that?'

'Then go and tell Fernandez,' Miguel said. 'Inform him that the water rights are mine. I will gladly allow him to go in peace.' His neck ached from staring up at the tall man. He moved a little, and a bullet shrieked through the still, hot air and dug with a vicious splash into a nearby cactus.

The stranger smoothed the blue feathers on his head.

'First I will finish talking with you. Listen to me, Miguel.'

'How do you know my name?' Miguel demanded, rolling over and sitting up cautiously behind the rock. 'It is as I thought. Fernandez has hired you to assassinate me.'

'I know your name because I can read your mind a little. Not much, because it is so cloudy.'

'Your mother was a dog,' Miguel said.

The stranger's nostrils pinched together slightly, but he ignored the remark. 'I come from another world,' he said. 'My name is – ' In Miguel's mind it sounded like Quetzalcoatl.

'Quetzalcoatl?' Miguel repeated, with fine irony. 'Oh, I have no doubt of that. And mine is Saint Peter, who has the keys to heaven.'

Quetzalcoatl's thin, pale face flushed slightly, but his voice was determinedly calm. 'Listen, Miguel. Look at my lips. They are not moving. I am speaking inside your head, by telepathy, and you translate my thoughts into words that have meaning to you. Evidently my name is too difficult for you. Your own mind has translated it as Quetzalcoatl. That is not my real name at all.'

'*De veras*,' Miguel said. 'It is not your name at all, and you do not come from another world. I would not believe a *norteamericano* if he swore on the bones of ten thousand highly-placed saints.'

Quetzalcoatl's long, austere face flushed again.

'I am here to give orders,' he said. 'Not to bandy words with – Look here, Miguel. Why do you suppose you couldn't kill me with your machete? Why can't bullets touch me?'

'Why does your machine of flight fly?' Miguel reposted. He took out a sack of tobacco and began to roll a cigarette. He squinted around the rock. 'Fernandez is probably trying to creep up on me. I had better get my rifle.'

'Leave it alone,' Quetzalcoatl said. 'Fernandez will not harm you.'

Miguel laughed harshly.

'And you must not harm him.' Quetzalcoatl added firmly.

'I will, then, turn the other cheek,' Miguel said, 'so that he can shoot me through the side of my head. I will believe Fernandez wishes peace, Señor Quetzalcoatl, when I see him walking across the valley with his hands over his head. Even then I will not let him come close, because of the knife he wears down his back.'

Quetzalcoatl smoothed his blue steel feathers again. His bony face was frowning.

'You must stop fighting forever, both of you,' he said. 'My race polices the universe and our responsibility is to bring peace to every planet we visit.'

'It is as I thought,' Miguel said with satisfaction. 'You come from *los estados unidos*. Why do you not bring peace to your own country? I have seen *los señores* Humphrey Bogart and Edward Robinson in *las películas*. Why, all over Neuva York gangsters shoot at each other from one skyscraper to another. And what do you do about it? You dance all over the place with *la señora* Betty Grable. Ah yes, I understand very well. First you will bring peace, and then you will take our oil and our precious minerals.'

Quetzalcoatl kicked angrily at the pebble beside his shiny steel toe.

'I must make you understand,' he said. He looked at the unlighted cigarette dangling from Miguel's lips. Suddenly he raised a hand, and a white-hot ray shot from a ring on his finger and kindled the end of the cigarette. Miguel jerked away, startled. Then he inhaled the smoke and nodded. The white-hot ray disappeared.

'*Muchas gracias, señor,*' Miguel said.

Quetzalcoatl's colourless lips pressed together thinly. 'Miguel,' he said, 'could a *norteamericano* do that?'

'*Quién sabe*?'

'No one living on your planet could do that, and you know it.'

Miguel shrugged.

'Do you see that cactus over there?' Quetzalcoatl demanded. 'I could destroy it in two seconds.'

'I have no doubt of it, *señor*.

'I could, for that matter, destroy this whole planet.'

'Yes, I have heard of the atomic bombs,' Miguel said politely. 'Why, then, do you trouble to interfere with a quiet private little argument between Fernandez and me, over a small water hole of no importance to anybody but – '

A bullet sang past.

Quetzalcoatl rubbed the ring on his finger with an angry gesture.

'Because the world is going to stop fighting,' he said ominously. 'If it doesn't, we will destroy it. There is no reason at all why men should not live together in peace and brotherhood.'

'There is one reason, *señor*.'

'What is that?'

'Fernandez,' Miguel said.

'I will destroy you both if you do not stop fighting.'

'*El Señor* is a great peacemaker.' Miguel said courteously. 'I will gladly stop fighting if you will tell me how to avoid being killed when I do.'

'Fernandez will stop fighting too.'

Miguel removed his somewhat battered sombrero, reached for a stick and carefully raised the hat above the rock. There was a nasty crack. The hat jumped away, and Miguel caught it as it fell.

'Very well,' he said. 'Since you insist, *señor*, I will stop fighting. But I will not come out from behind this rock. I am perfectly willing to stop fighting. But it seems to me that you demand I do something which you do not tell me how to do. You could as well require that I fly through the air like your machine of flight.'

Quetzalcoatl frowned more deeply. Finally he said, 'Miguel, tell me how this fight started.'

'Fernandez wishes to kill me and enslave my family.'

'Why should he want to do that?'

'Because he is evil,' Miguel said.

'How do you know he is evil?'

'Because,' Miguel pointed out logically, 'he wishes to kill me and enslave my family.'

There was a pause. A road runner darted past and paused to peck at the gleaming barrel of Miguel's rifle. Miguel sighed.

'There is a skin of good wine not twenty feet away – ' he began, but Quetzalcoatl interrupted him.

'What was it you said about the water rights?'

'Oh, that,' Miguel said. 'This is a poor country, *señor*. Water is precious here. We have had a dry year and there is no longer water enough for two families. The water hole is mine. Fernandez wishes to kill me and enslave – '

'Are there no courts of law in your country?'

'To such as us?' Miguel demanded, and smiled politely.

'Has Fernandez a family too?' Quetzalcoatl asked.

'Yes, the poors,' Miguel said. 'He beats them when they do not work until they drop.'

'Do you beat your family?'

'Only when they need it,' Miguel said, surprised. 'My wife is very fat and lazy. And my oldest, Chico, talks back. It is my duty to beat them when they need it, for their own good. It is also my duty to protect our water rights, since the evil Fernandez is determined to kill me and – '

Quetzalcoatl said impatiently, 'This is a waste of time. Let me consider.' He rubbed the ring on his finger again. He looked around. The road runner had found a more appetizing morsel than the rifle. He was now to be seen trotting away with the writhing tail of a lizard dangling from his beak.

Overhead the sun was hot in a clear blue sky. The dry air smelled of mesquite. Below, in the valley, the flying saucer's perfection of shape and texture looked incongruous and unreal.

'Wait here,' Quetzalcoatl said at last. 'I will talk to Fernandez. When I call, come to my machine of flight. Fernandez and I will meet you there presently.'

'As you say, *señor*,' Miguel agreed. His eyes strayed.

'And do not touch your rifle,' Quetzalcoatl added with great firmness.

'Why, no, *señor*,' Miguel said. He waited until the tall man had gone. Then he crawled cautiously across the dry ground until he had recaptured his rifle. After that, with a little searching, he found his machete. Only then did he turn to the skin of wine. He was very thirsty indeed. But he did not drink heavily. He put a full clip in the rifle, leaned against a rock, and sipped a little from time to time from the wineskin as he waited.

In the meantime the stranger, ignoring fresh bullets that occasionally splashed blue from his steely person, approached Fernandez's hiding place. The sound of shots stopped. A long time passed, and finally the tall form reappeared and waved to Miguel.

'*Ya voy, señor,*' Miguel shouted agreeably. He put his rifle conveniently on the rock and rose very cautiously, ready to duck at the first hostile move. There was no such move.

Fernandez appeared beside the stranger. Immediately Miguel bent down, seized his rifle and lifted it for a snap shot.

Something thin and hissing burned across the valley. The rifle turned red-hot in Miguel's grasp. He squealed and dropped it, and the next moment his mind went perfectly blank.

'I die with honour,' he thought, and then thought no more.

. . . When he woke, he was standing under the shadow of the great flying saucer. Quetzalcoatl was lowering his hand from before Miguel's face. Sunlight sparkled on the tall man's ring. Miguel shook his head dizzily.

'I live?' he inquired.

But Quetzalcoatl paid no attention. He had turned to Fernandez, who was standing beside him, and was making gestures before Fernandez' masklike face. A light flashed from Quetzalcoatl's ring into Fernandez' glassy eyes. Fernandez shook his head and muttered thickly. Miguel looked for his rifle or machete, but they were gone. He slipped his hand into his shirt, but his good little knife had vanished too.

He met Fernandez' eyes.

'We are both doomed, Don Fernandez,' he said. 'This *señor* Quetzalcoatl will kill us both. In a way I am sorry that you will go to hell and I to heaven, for we shall not meet again.'

'You are mistaken,' Fernandez replied, vainly searching for his own knife. 'You will never see heaven. Nor is this tall *norteamericano* namd Quetzalcoatl. For his own lying purposes he has assumed the name of Cortés.'

'You will tell lies to the devil himself,' Miguel said.

'Be quiet, both of you,' Quetzalcoatl (or Cortés) said sharply. 'You have seen a little of my power. Now listen to me. My race has assumed the high duty of seeing that the entire solar system lives in peace. We are a very advanced race, with power such as you do not yet dream of. We have solved problems which your people have no answer for, and it is now our duty to apply our power for the good of all. If you wish to keep on living, you will stop fighting immediately and forever, and from now on live in peace and brotherhood. Do you understand me?'

'That is all I have ever wished,' Fernandez said, shocked. 'But this offspring of a goat wishes to kill me.'

'There will be no more killing,' Quetzalcoatl said. 'You will live in brotherhood, or you will die.'

Miguel and Fernandez looked at each other and then at Quetzalcoatl.

'The *señor* is a great peacemaker,' Miguel murmured. 'I have said it before. The way you mention is surely the best way of all to insure peace. But to us it is not so simple. To live in peace is good. Very well, *señor*. Tell us how.'

'Simply stop fighting,' Quetzalcoatl said impatiently.

'Now that is easy to say,' Fernandez pointed out. 'But life here in Sonora is simple. Perhaps it is where you come from –'

'Naturally,' Miguel put in. 'In *los estados unidos* everyone is rich.'

' – but it is not simple with us. Perhaps in your country, *señor*, the snake does not eat the rat, and the bird eat the snake. Perhaps in your country there is food and water for all, and a man need not fight to keep his family alive. Here it is not so simple.'

Miguel nodded. 'We shall certainly all be brothers some day,' he agreed. 'We try to do as the good God commands us. It is not easy, but little by little we learn to be better. It would be very fine if we could all become brothers at a word of magic, such as you command us. Unfortunately – ' he shrugged.

'You must not use force to solve your problems,' Quetzalcoatl said with great firmness. 'Force is evil. *You will make peace now*.'

'Or else you will destroy us,' Miguel said. He shrugged again and met Fernandez' eyes. 'Very well, *señor*. You have an argument I do not care to resist. *Al fin*, I agree. What must we do?'

Quetzalcoatl turned to Fernandez.

'I too, *señor*,' the latter said, with a sigh. 'You are, no doubt, right. Let us have peace.'

'You will take hands,' Quetzalcoatl said, his eyes gleaming. 'You will swear brotherhood.'

Miguel held out his hand. Fernandez took it firmly and the two men grinned at each other.

'You see?' Quetzalcoatl said, giving them his austere smile. 'It is not hard at all. Now you are friends. Stay friends.'

He turned away and walked towards the flying saucer. A door opened smoothly in the sleek hull. On the threshold Quetzalcoatl turned.

'Remember,' he said. 'I shall be watching.'

'Without a doubt,' Fernandez said. '*Adiós, señor.*'

'*Vaya con Dios*,' Miguel added.

The smooth surface of the hull closed after Quetzalcoatl. A moment later the flying saucer lifted smoothly and rose until it was a hundred feet above the ground. Then it shot off to the north like a sudden flash of lightning and was gone.

'As I thought,' Miguel said. 'He was from *los estados unidos*.'

Fernandez shrugged.

'There was a moment when I thought he might tell us something sensible,' he said. 'No doubt he had great wisdom. Truly, life is not easy.'

'Oh, it is easy enough for him,' Miguel said. 'But he does not live in Sonora. We, however, do. Fortunately, I and my family have a good water hole to rely on. For those without one, life is indeed hard.'

'It is a very poor water hole,' Fernandez said. 'Such as it is, however, it is mine.' He was rolling a cigarette as he spoke. He handed it to Miguel and rolled another for himself. The two men smoked for a while in silence. Then, still silent, they parted.

Miguel went back to the wineskin on the hill. He took a long drink, grunted with pleasure, and looked around him. His knife, machete and rifle were carelessly flung down not far away. He recovered them and made sure he had a full clip.

Then he peered cautiously around the rock barricade. A bullet smashed on the stone near his face. He returned the shot.

After that, there was silence for a while. Miguel sat back and took another drink. His eye was caught by a road runner scuttling past, with the tail of lizad dangling from his beak. It was probably the same road runner as before, and perhaps the same lizard, slowly progressing towards digestion.

Miguel called softly, '*Señor* Bird! It is wrong to eat lizards. It is very wrong.'

The road runner cocked a beady eye at him and ran on.

Miguel raised and aimed his rifle.

'Stop eating lizards, *Señor* Bird. Stop, or I must kill you.'

The road runner ran on across the rifle sights.

'Don't you understand how to stop?' Miguel called gently. 'Must I explain how?'

The road runner paused. The tail of the lizard disappeared completely.

'Oh, very well,' Miguel said. 'When I find out how a road runner can stop eating lizards and still live, then I will tell you, *amigo*. But until then, go with God.'

He turned and aimed the rifle across the valley again.

FICTION

HORROR/OCCULT/NASTY

☐ **Death Walkers**	Gary Brandner	£1.50
☐ **The Howling**	Gary Brandner	£1.50
☐ **Return of the Howling**	Gary Brandner	£1.50
☐ **The Sanctuary**	Glenn Chandler	£1.50
☐ **The Tribe**	Glenn Chandler	£1.10
☐ **The Black Castle**	Leslie Daniels	£1.25
☐ **The Big Goodnight**	Judy Gardiner	£1.25
☐ **Rattlers**	Joseph L. Gilmore	£1.25
☐ **The Nestling**	Charles L. Grant	£1.75
☐ **Slither**	John Halkin	£1.25
☐ **The Unholy**	John Halkin	£1.25
☐ **The Skull**	Shaun Hutson	£1.25
☐ **Pestilence**	Edward Jarvis	£1.50
☐ **The Beast Within**	Edward Levy	£1.25
☐ **Night Killers**	Richard Lewis	£1.25
☐ **Spiders**	Richard Lewis	£1.25
☐ **The Web**	Richard Lewis	£1.10
☐ **Bloodthirst**	Mark Ronson	£1.00
☐ **Ghoul**	Mark Ronson	95p
☐ **Ogre**	Mark Ronson	95p
☐ **Deathbell**	Guy N. Smith	£1.00
☐ **Doomflight**	Guy N. Smith	£1.10
☐ **The Lurkers**	Guy N. Smith	£1.25
☐ **Manitou Doll**	Guy N. Smith	£1.25
☐ **Satan's Snowdrop**	Guy N. Smith	£1.00
☐ **The Beast of Kane**	Cliff Twemlow	£1.50
☐ **The Pike**	Cliff Twemlow	£1.25

SCIENCE FICTION

☐ **More Things in Heaven**	John Brunner	£1.50
☐ **The Proud Robot**	Henry Kuttner	£1.50
☐ **Death's Master**	Tanith Lee	£1.50
☐ **Electric Forest**	Tanith Lee	£1.25
☐ **The Dancers of Arun**	Elizabeth A. Lynn	£1.50
☐ **A Different Light**	Elizabeth A. Lynn	£1.50
☐ **The Northern Girl**	Elizabeth A. Lynn	£1.50
☐ **Balance of Power**	Brian M. Stableford	£1.75

WESTERNS – Blade Series – Matt Chisholm

☐ **No. 5**	**The Colorado Virgins**	85p
☐ **No. 6**	**The Mexican Proposition**	85p
☐ **No. 8**	**The Nevada Mustang**	85p
☐ **No. 9**	**The Montana Deadlock**	85p
☐ **No. 10**	**The Cheyenne Trap**	95p
☐ **No. 11**	**The Navaho Trail**	95p
☐ **No. 12**	**The Last Act**	95p

FICTION

ADVENTURE/SUSPENSE

☐ **The Midas Deep**	John Brosnan	£2.25
☐ **Temple Kent**	D.G. Devon	£1.95
☐ **The Flowers of the Forest**	Joseph Hone	£1.75
☐ **Styx**	Christopher Hyde	£1.50
☐ **Hot Rain**	Colin Lewis	£1.65
☐ **The Buck Passes Flynn**	Gregory Mcdonald	£1.60
☐ **Confess, Fletch**	Gregory Mcdonald	£1.50
☐ **Fletch**	Gregory Mcdonald	£1.50
☐ **Fletch and the Widow Bradley**	Gregory Mcdonald	£1.50
☐ **Flynn**	Gregory Mcdonald	£1.75
☐ **In the Face of the Enemy**	Douglas Scott	£1.95

CRIME THRILLER

☐ **The Cool Cottontail**	John Ball	£1.00
☐ **Five Pieces of Jade**	John Ball	£1.50
☐ **In the Heat of the Night**	John Ball	£1.00
☐ **Johnny Get Your Gun**	John Ball	£1.00
☐ **Then Came Violence**	John Ball	£1.50
☐ **The Floating Admiral**	The Detection Club	£1.50
☐ **The Blunderer**	Patricia Highsmith	£1.50
☐ **A Game for the Living**	Patricia Highsmith	£1.50
☐ **Those Who Walk Away**	Patricia Highsmith	£1.50
☐ **The Tremor of Forgery**	Patricia Highsmith	£1.50
☐ **The Two Faces of January**	Patricia Highsmith	£1.50

WESTERNS – Blade Series – Matt Chisholm

☐ **No. 5**	**The Colorado Virgins**	85p
☐ **No. 6**	**The Mexican Proposition**	85p
☐ **No. 8**	**The Nevada Mustang**	85p
☐ **No. 9**	**The Montana Deadlock**	85p
☐ **No. 10**	**The Cheyenne Trap**	95p
☐ **No. 11**	**The Navaho Trail**	95p
☐ **No. 12**	**The Last Act**	95p

McAllister Series – Matt Chisholm

☐ **No. 3**	**McAllister Never Surrenders**	95p
☐ **No. 4**	**McAllister and the Cheyenne Death**	95p
☐ **No. 6**	**McAllister – Die-hard**	95p
☐ **No. 7**	**McAllister – Wolf-Bait**	95p
☐ **No. 8**	**McAllister – Fire Brand**	£1.25

NON-FICTION

WAR

☐ **The Battle of Malta**	Joseph Attard	£1.50
☐ **The Black Angels**	Rupert Butler	£1.50
☐ **Gestapo**	Rupert Butler	£1.50
☐ **Hand of Steel**	Rupert Butler	£1.35
☐ **Legions of Death**	Rupert Butler	£1.75
☐ **The Air Battle for Malta**	Lord James Douglas-Hamilton MP	£1.50
☐ **Auschwitz and the Allies**	Martin Gilbert	£4.95
☐ **Sigh for a Merlin**	Alex Henshaw	£1.50
☐ **Hitler's Secret Life**	Glen B. Infield	£1.50
☐ **Spitfire into Battle**	Group Captain Duncan Smith	£1.75
☐ **Women Beyond the Wire**	Lavinia Warner and John Sandilands	£1.95

FICTION

CRIME – WHODUNNIT

☐ **Thou Shell of Death**	Nicholas Blake	£1.25
☐ **The Widow's Cruise**	Nicholas Blake	£1.25
☐ **The Worm of Death**	Nicholas Blake	95p
☐ **The Long Divorce**	Edmund Crispin	£1.50
☐ **King and Joker**	Peter Dickinson	£1.25
☐ **The Last House-Party**	Peter Dickinson	£1.50
☐ **A Pride of Heroes**	Peter Dickinson	£1.50
☐ **The Seals**	Peter Dickinson	£1.50
☐ **Sleep and His Brother**	Peter Dickinson	£1.50
☐ **Firefly Gadroon**	Jonathan Gash	£1.50
☐ **The Vatican Rip**	Jonathan Gash	£1.50
☐ **Blood and Judgment**	Michael Gilbert	£1.10
☐ **Close Quarters**	Michael Gilbert	£1.10
☐ **Death of a Favourite Girl**	Michael Gilbert	£1.50
☐ **The Etruscan Net**	Michael Gilbert	£1.25
☐ **The Night of the Twelfth**	Michael Gilbert	£1.25
☐ **Silence Observed**	Michael Innes	£1.00
☐ **There Came Both Mist and Snow**	Michael Innes	95p
☐ **Go West, Inspector Ghote**	H.R.F. Keating	£1.50
☐ **Inspector Ghote Draws a Line**	H.R.F. Keating	£1.50
☐ **Inspector Ghote Plays a Joker**	H.R.F. Keating	£1.50
☐ **The Murder of the Maharajah**	H.R.F. Keating	£1.50
☐ **The Perfect Murder**	H.R.F. Keating	£1.50
☐ **The Dutch Shoe Mystery**	Ellery Queen	£1.60
☐ **The French Powder Mystery**	Ellery Queen	£1.25
☐ **The Siamese Twin Mystery**	Ellery Queen	95p
☐ **The Spanish Cape Mystery**	Ellery Queen	£1.10
☐ **Copper, Gold and Treasure**	David Williams	£1.75
☐ **Treasure by Degrees**	David Williams	£1.75
☐ **Unholy Writ**	David Williams	£1.60

NON-FICTION

WAR

☐ **The Battle of Malta**	Joseph Attard	£1.50
☐ **The Black Angels**	Rupert Butler	£1.50
☐ **Gestapo**	Rupert Butler	£1.50
☐ **Hand of Steel**	Rupert Butler	£1.35
☐ **Legions of Death**	Rupert Butler	£1.75
☐ **The Air Battle for Malta**	Lord James Douglas-Hamilton MP	£1.50
☐ **Auschwitz and the Allies**	Martin Gilbert	£4.95
☐ **Sigh for a Merlin**	Alex Henshaw	£1.50
☐ **Hitler's Secret Life**	Glen B. Infield	£1.50
☐ **Spitfire into Battle**	Group Captain Duncan Smith	£1.75
☐ **Women Beyond the Wire**	Lavinia Warner and John Sandilands	£1.95

FICTION

GENERAL

☐ **The Patriarch**	Chaim Bermant	£1.75
☐ **The Free Fishers**	John Buchan	£1.50
☐ **Midwinter**	John Buchan	£1.50
☐ **A Prince of the Captivity**	John Buchan	£1.50
☐ **The Eve of Saint Venus**	Anthony Burgess	£1.10
☐ **Nothing Like the Sun**	Anthony Burgess	£1.50
☐ **The Wanting Seed**	Anthony Burgess	£1.50
☐ **The Other Woman**	Colette	£1.50
☐ **Retreat From Love**	Colette	£1.60
☐ **Prizzi's Honour**	Richard Condon	£1.75
☐ **The Whisper of the Axe**	Richard Condon	£1.75
☐ **King Hereafter**	Dorothy Dunnett	£2.95
☐ **Pope Joan**	Lawrence Durrell	£1.35
☐ **The Country of her Dreams**	Janice Elliott	£1.35
☐ **Secret Places**	Janice Elliott	£1.35
☐ **Letter to a Child Never Born**	Oriana Fallaci	£1.00
☐ **A Man**	Oriana Fallaci	£1.95
☐ **Rich Little Poor Girl**	Terence Feely	£1.75
☐ **Marital Rites**	Margaret Forster	£1.50
☐ **Grimalkin's Tales**	Gardiner, Ronson, Whitelaw	£1.60
☐ **Who Was Sylvia?**	Judy Gardiner	£1.50
☐ **Lost and Found**	Julian Gloag	£1.95
☐ **La Presidenta**	Lois Gould	£1.75
☐ **A Sea-Change**	Lois Gould	£1.50
☐ **Black Summer**	Julian Hale	£1.75
☐ **Duncton Wood**	William Horwood	£2.50
☐ **The Stonor Eagles**	William Horwood	£2.95
☐ **The Man Who Lived at the Ritz**	A.E. Hotchner	£1.65
☐ **The Fame Game**	Rona Jaffe	£1.50
☐ **A Bonfire**	Pamela Hansford Johnson	£1.50
☐ **The Good Husband**	Pamela Hansford Johnson	£1.50
☐ **The Good Listener**	Pamela Hansford Johnson	£1.50
☐ **The Honours Board**	Pamela Hansford Johnson	£1.50
☐ **The Unspeakable Skipton**	Pamela Hansford Johnson	£1.50
☐ **Kine**	A.R. Lloyd	£1.50
☐ **Christmas Pudding**	Nancy Mitford	£1.50
☐ **Highland Fling**	Nancy Mitford	£1.50
☐ **Pigeon Pie**	Nancy Mitford	£1.50
☐ **Gossip**	Marc Olden	£1.25
☐ **Night Music**	Lilli Palmer	£1.95
☐ **Admiral**	Dudley Pope	£1.75
☐ **Buccaneer**	Dudley Pope	£1.75
☐ **Glory B.**	Alexander Stuart	£1.65
☐ **Wild Strawberries**	Angela Thirkell	£1.50
☐ **The Housewife and the Assassin**	Susan Trott	£1.50
☐ **When Your Lover Leaves**	Susan Trott	£1.50